TO SQUEEZE

A PRAIRIE DOG

An American Novel by **SCOTT SEMEGRAN**

MUTT PRESS

Austin, Texas

Mutt Press
Austin, Texas
https://www.muttpress.com
info@muttpress.com

ISBN 978-0-9997173-8-7

Edited by Brandon R. Wood & Lori Hoadley
Proofreading by David Aretha at Yellow Bird Editors
Cover Illustration by Andrew Leeper
Cover Layout by Scott Semegran & Andrew Leeper
Photo of Scott Semegran by Lori Hoadley

Books by Scott Semegran:
To Squeeze a Prairie Dog
Sammie & Budgie
Boys
The Spectacular Simon Burchwood
The Meteoric Rise of Simon Burchwood
Modicum
Mr. Grieves

Find Scott Semegran Online:
https://www.scottsemegran.com
https://www.goodreads.com/scottsemegran
https://www.twitter.com/scottsemegran
https://www.facebook.com/scottsemegran.writer/
https://www.instagram.com/scott_semegran
https://www.amazon.com/author/scottsemegran
https://www.smashwords.com/profile/view/scottsemegran

"An amusing yet heartwarming romp... *To Squeeze a Prairie Dog* is an entertaining slice-of-life story that's humorous yet uplifting at the same time. By the novel's last page, readers will be longing for more."

— *BlueInk Review* (Starred Review)

"A comic sendup of state government that remains lighthearted, deadpan, and full of affection for both urban and rural Texas."

— *Kirkus Reviews*

"*To Squeeze a Prairie Dog* paints a rollicking story that careens through the office structure to delve into the motivations, lives, and connections between ordinary individuals... an uplifting, fun story."

— *Midwest Book Review*

"An accomplished tale... a recommended read for fans of humor, drama, and office politics."

— *Readers' Favorite Book Reviews*. 5 stars.

"Fascinating and heartfelt."

— *IndieReader*

For Margaret Downs-Gamble

And, as always, for my wonderful wife, Lori Hoadley

Table of Contents

PART III.

"If any animal has a system of laws regulating the body politic, it is certainly the prairie dog."
—George Wilkins Kendall, *Texan Santa Fe Expedition*

"I don't think human beings learn anything without desperation. Desperation is a necessary ingredient to learning anything, or creating anything."
—Jim Carrey, *60 Minutes*

"It is the purpose of government to see that not only the legitimate interests of the few are protected but that the welfare and rights of the many are conserved."
—Franklin D. Roosevelt, *Looking Forward*

"I think it is not wise for an emperor, or a king, or a president, to come down into the boxing ring, so to speak, and lower the dignity of his office by meddling in the small affairs of private citizens."
—Mark Twain, *Mark Twain in Eruption*

PART I.

PART I

1.

When J. D. Wiswall arrived outside the building of the Texas Department of Unemployment and Benefits in downtown Austin, Texas, he already needed to go to the bathroom, his bladder full from drinking thirty-two ounces of soda during lunch—something that sounded good at the time but had become an unfortunate inconvenience. He was excited to start his first day of work but his excitement had gotten the best of him. He simply ate and drank too much, something he was prone to do all too often.

Dang it! he thought. Even when he cussed in his mind, his cussing was toned down as if someone might hear him.

He ascended the granite steps to the building entrance with trepidation, his left hand over his gut, his right hand clinching his lunch box full of afternoon snacks: roasted pecans, pecan rolls, and pecan pralines. He loved pecans; they fondly reminded him of his rural hometown: Brady, Texas. Inside the great, granite building, the mustiness of decades of public service molested his nostrils, but he was determined to relieve his bladder before starting his new job. He approached the only person he thought could help him: a security guard. The black fellow in uniform manned a desk—holding a telephone receiver to the side of his weary head with one hand and supporting his body with the other hand planted on the desktop—and spotted J. D. as he frantically approached him. The security guard's name was Emmitt, as stated on a name tag pinned to his starched white shirt. Emmitt raised a patient index finger to J. D., indicating silently to wait for him to get off the phone. J. D. danced impatiently. Soon, Emmitt hung up.

"Can I help you?" he said, flashing a pleasant, toothy smile.

"Is there a restroom I can use?" J. D. said, still dancing a urination two-step.

"Well, that depends if you have business here today."

"Excuse me?" J. D. said, his face flushed.

"Do you have *business* here today at the Texas Department of Unemployment and Benefits?"

"I start my new job today."

"Well, well! A new face for a new day! That's wonderful. Who is supposed to come down and get you?" he said, lifting a guest log from a drawer in the desk. He waited with a shiny grin for J. D. to answer.

"Mr. Baker," he said, tiptoeing in place. "Can I use the restroom now? I really have to go."

"I'll call him while you use the restroom," he said, pointing over J. D.'s shoulder. "It's right over there, down yonder."

"Thank you!" J. D. said, running down the hallway in the direction Emmitt pointed, except when he got to the restroom, a sign perched on the door declared it closed for repairs. A similar sign was taped to the ladies' room as well.

Dang it! J. D. thought. He couldn't wait another minute. He speed-walked back to where Emmitt guarded the entrance.

"Mr. Baker isn't answering his phone," the guard said. But J. D. didn't respond. He quickly turned and left the building. "Where are you going?!"

Outside, the warm afternoon sun hung high over the great Capitol lawn, an expansive garden of grass, oak and pecan trees, statuary and monuments, and shrubbery that separated the Texas Department of Unemployment and Benefits building and the Capitol Building of Texas. J. D. hoped to find a building to run into so he could relieve himself but, being from a small town in the country like Brady, Texas, he also wasn't opposed to peeing in the out of doors if the need arose—emergency situation, accident, or otherwise. He preferred avoiding humiliation almost above all else, though, particularly on his first day at work. *Why is this happening to me?* he thought, as he scrambled to find a business or building.

Seeing a nondescript building just beyond the Vietnam Veterans Memorial, he ran in that direction, pressing his palm against his belly. The St. Augustine grass was thick and lush, and treading across it was akin to running in wet sand. The pressure in his bladder increased to emergency level. But as he rounded the monument, something caught his eye that stopped him in his tracks, something very strange to see laying in the grass jutting out from behind a granite bench: a foot. The pressure in his gut dissipated as he stared at the well-worn, leather, men's dress shoe.

What the heck?! he thought, looking around to see if anyone else had seen what he'd seen, but no one was around except an uninterested squirrel a few feet away in the grass, juggling a pecan in its paws.

He slowly stepped toward the foot, thankful that it was still attached to a leg, which belonged to a man, laying on his back in the grass, a stranger sight J. D. had not seen in years— maybe even stranger than seeing one of his pet dogs trying to mate with a goat a while back at his parents' home. He knelt next to the middle-aged, white man to see if he was alive, and it seemed to J. D. that he might be sleeping, except for the weird angle his head rested, twisted and bent at the end of his neck as if he had been sucker-punched by Mike Tyson and left for dead. His chest slowly raised and descended with his breathing but he didn't look good. J. D. looked around again for someone to call to, someone to help him, but only the squirrel was close by and it was more interested in cracking his pecan nut than helping this poor guy in the grass. J. D. wished at that moment that he was somewhere else—far away—ripping open the packaging of his own pecan snacks.

Also, J. D. knew deep down that he had to do something, *anything* to help. So, being the good young man he was, he ran back to the building of the Texas Department of Unemployment and Benefits to tell the security guard about who he had found outside in the grass and hoped—by God, he hoped—that the restroom was finally available for him to relieve himself before he started his new job.

2.

Emmitt the security guard couldn't believe what J. D. was telling him. It just seemed too strange to be true. As he listened to J. D., his thin arms gesticulating and flapping like that of a baby bird, Emmitt thought, *This white boy is crazy!* He looked the short, thin young man up and down, examining him from his short-sleeve, red and green, plaid shirt down to his pressed khaki pants and worn canvas shoes, then back up to his mane of auburn hair with a cowlick at the back like a stalk of wheat dancing in the breeze. It certainly seemed *what* J. D. was saying was too strange to be true except that he was sincere in his pleading, so sincere that Emmitt second-guessed his own judgmental prognostication.

"Well, come on, then," Emmitt said, sarcastically. "Show me this *man* in the grass."

J. D. led the security guard across the great lawn, toward the Vietnam Veterans Memorial, where he had left the stranger in the grass. The squirrel was still juggling a pecan nut but in a new, safer location further from the trouble. As the two men approached where J. D. had witnessed the unconscious man on the ground, the foot was not where he had left it.

"I'm certain he's back here," J. D. said, skepticism in his voice.

"Mmm-hmm," the security guard said. "I'm not supposed to leave my post, you know."

"He has to be back here."

They rounded the back of the monument and to J. D.'s relief—the unconscious man was still there, except this time, not unconscious at all. He sat in the grass, rubbing his noggin with blades of grass sticking out from his hair like thorns of a cactus. He didn't seem to know what planet he was on and he looked around in a confused state, but, once Emmitt the security guard recognized him, he looked relieved that he was being rescued.

"Sir, sir!" Emmitt said, rushing to the ground to assist him. "Are you OK, sir?"

"Yes, yes. I must have blacked out."

"Oh no, not *again*!" Emmitt said, offering support.

"I'm afraid so," the man said. "Again."

"Let me help you up," Emmitt said, assisting him to his feet, dusting blades of grass from his back and shoulders. "Luckily, this young man found you and asked me for help." They both looked at J. D., who stood sheepishly a few feet away. He waved a limp acknowledgment.

"I'm fine. Really. I'm good," the man said, dusting off the front of his gray slacks. As he straightened his posture, he appeared to J. D. to be rather lanky and tall, his business attire starched yet worn at the ends of the sleeves and collar of his light blue shirt, the cuffs of his starched, grey pants lightly frayed at the ends. The only thing he found unusual about the befuddled man were the bright tattoos around both of his wrists: one of a green lizard and the other of an orange fish. "Will you accompany me back to our building?" he said, putting his arm around Emmitt's shoulders for support.

"Of course, Mr. Baker. Of course!"

The security guard escorted him back to the building of the Texas Department of Unemployment and Benefits as J. D. followed behind them, relieved that the man he had discovered in the grass on his back was not actually dead, just temporarily unconscious. He worried that this was a bad omen for his first day at work, a stranger thing he couldn't imagine happening.

Back inside the lobby, Emmitt manned his desk again while Mr. Baker straightened his shirt and lifted his pants in place. Then unceremoniously he said, "Thanks again, Emmitt," and began to walk away.

"Wait, sir!" Emmitt said, waving his arms. Mr. Baker stopped and turned around. "I believe *this* man is here to see you." Emmitt extended his arms toward J. D. to accentuate his presence.

"See *me*?" he said, confused. He looked at J. D., examining his manner of dress from head to toe. "Why would he want to see me?"

The uncomfortable pressure in J. D.'s bladder had returned and he danced a little two-step again. He was embarrassed at his predicament.

"Today is my first day of employment," J. D. said. "And I'm sorry to say, I really have to go to the restroom."

Mr. Baker looked at the security guard, who confirmed what J. D. had said, then added, "He does need to *tinkle*."

"Yes, yes!" Mr. Baker said, approaching J. D. and then patting him on the back. "You must be the new guy in our unit. And your name is?"

"J. D. My name is J. D. Wiswall."

"Yes, that's it! J. D. Wiswall. The coolest name I've heard in a while. Want to use the facilities before I take you to Unit 3?"

"I would love to," J. D. said. "But the restroom is *closed*."

"There's more than one restroom in this building, my man. There are many modern amenities here. It's 2005. Follow me." Mr. Baker offered a fist bump, to Emmitt, who enthusiastically bumped his fist in return and then followed it with a routine too elaborate for Mr. Baker to follow. He then led J. D. to the elevators. After pushing the up button, the elevator door opened and the two got inside.

"Excited for your first day?" Mr. Baker said, pushing the button labeled "3." The elevator herky-jerkied up.

"Oh, yes," J. D. said. "Very excited!"

"Are you from Austin?"

"No, I'm from Brady, Texas," J. D. said, his hand over his bladder.

"Brady, huh?" he said, noticing J. D.'s discomfort. The elevator bell dinged and the door slid open. "I'll ask you more about Brady after you take a leak. Come on!" Mr. Baker led him to the restroom nearby. "Here you go."

"Thanks, Mr. Baker," J. D. said.

"Call me Brent."

"OK. Thanks Brent," J. D. said, then he entered the restroom.

As J. D. placed his lunch box on the plumbing pipes above the urinal and relieved himself—a finer feeling he hadn't experienced in quite some time—Brent appeared next to him, out of thin air, continuing their conversation as he peed into the other urinal.

"Is Brady near Dallas?" Brent said, examining the sheer amount of urine he was releasing. "Too much beer!" he said, chuckling.

"No, Brady isn't near Dallas. It's kind of in the middle of nowhere. I guess you could say it is *literally* in the middle of Texas."

"I see," Brent said, zipping up his pants before leaving the restroom without washing his hands. J. D. quickly splashed his hands with cold water and followed him.

"Sir?" he said, catching up to Brent. "Why were you laying in the grass?"

"Epilepsy," Brent said.

"Epilepsy?" J. D. said.

"Yep."

"And it's happened *before*? You passing out?"

"Hundreds of times."

"Hundreds?"

"Yep, hundreds, maybe thousands. It's not a big deal, really."

"*Thousands?*"

"Never mind that. This here building is the Main Building of the Texas Department of Unemployment and Benefits. But this isn't where our unit resides. Unit 3 is in the Annex Building, just across the skywalk, up there."

As they crossed the skywalk, J. D. stopped and gandered out the window, down at the pedestrians below, other government workers hurrying to their jobs, no doubt. *Dang,* he thought. *It's a long way down from here.*

"Pretty cool, huh?" Brent said, not stopping to look. "Let's go! No time to waste."

J. D. followed Brent into the Annex Building, which he noticed smelled mustier and danker than the Main Building, the scents of mold, mildew, and dust mingled like an offensive potpourri. The walls and floor tiles were beige, as well as the ceiling tiles, although it was clear they were once white, maybe a long, long time ago. Brent briskly entered the first door to the left, the entrance to J. D.'s new workplace: Unit 3. J. D. followed him inside.

The clickity-clack of the computer keyboards of the three workers typing in the back of the small office space was like the cacophony of a chorus of cicadas while they performed their data entry duties. J. D. was surprised at just how small the office was, seeming almost too small for five people to work in comfortably and humanely, the aisle between the four desks of the data entry clerks barely wide enough for someone to walk through sideways. The three workers didn't seem to mind the close proximity of their desks and they happily typed away, their synchronized tapping accompanied by the whirring and buzzing of dot-matrix printers lined up on a table against a wall in front of them to the left. Nearest the doorway was Brent's desk, which he stood behind, checking something on his computer. As J. D. stood there in the doorway—looking around like a child in a strange, new world—he noticed the three workers who would inhabit his new work life in the coming months: Rita Jackson, Deborah Martinez, and Conchino Gonzalez. As well as Brent Baker, the manager of Unit 3, all of them occupied this tiny space called an office. J. D. had seen pigpens in Brady, Texas, bigger than the office of Unit 3. The three soon stopped typing and J. D. cautiously raised his hand to greet them.

"Everyone, listen up! This here is J. D. Wiswall, originally from Brady, Texas, now your new coworker here in Unit 3. He will be sitting at Melvin's old desk." Melvin Tell retired a few weeks before, after working for the State of Texas for thirty-three years and developing a horrendous case of carpal tunnel syndrome so severe that it rendered his hands into useless claws. He was glad to retire although he knew he would miss the camaraderie of his coworkers. "J. D. is full-time, not a contractor."

"G' day," Rita said, waving at J. D. She sat at the desk directly behind Melvin's—J. D.'s desk now—nestled in front of windows on the wall facing the outside world. She was a black woman of portly proportions and a grandmotherly demeanor, her black and white hair neatly done in a shiny coif that resembled a small helmet of some sort. Her smile was bright and infectious while her clothes revealed that she was a lot older than J. D., the clothing's style looking well-suited for the late 1970s or early 1980s, around the time J. D. was born.

"Howdy!" said Deborah, a white woman of similar age and size to Rita, yet with a more boisterous hairdo of auburn and brown, lifting from her scalp with stiff peaks like a pile of meringue on a lemon pie. Her desk was also in front of the windows and to the left of Rita's. One of the panes was cracked open, allowing the outside breeze and an occasional leaf to come drifting into the office. "Glad to meet ya. And this is Conchino," she said, raising her hand to the young man sitting at the desk in front of her. "He doesn't talk much."

Conchino appeared to be about J. D.'s age, young and in his twenties. He stood up with his hands at his side, like Frankenstein's monster—tall and doughy and thick around the neck and arms—wearing a San Antonio Spurs T-shirt, baggy jeans, a burly, black leather belt, and high-top sneakers, like the uniform of a street thug, his hair shorn close to his scalp, and a spider web tattooed on the side his neck. He was of Japanese and Mexican descent and almost tall enough for his head to scrape the ceiling. He tilted his head back to greet J. D., as if to say, "I see you." Then he sat back down behind his desk and continued to enter data on his computer.

"See?" Deborah said. "He doesn't talk much."

"He barely says a damn word," Rita said, snickering. "But don't let that fool ya. He's a good boy."

"All right, all right," Brent said. "Enough about Conchino and his lack of communication skills." The attention from the others pleased Conchino and he smiled slyly as he continued to type. "Does anyone need anything before I go?"

"Where are you going *now*?" Rita said, adjusting the papers on her desk.

"I have to go talk to the Big Boss," he said.

"What about J. D.?" Deborah said.

"What about him?"

"Who is going to show him what to do?"

"Thanks for volunteering, Deborah," Brent said, opening the door to the small office. "I'm sure *you* will do a great job training J. D." He quickly left before she could protest, the heavy wood door slowly closing by the spring-tension closer mounted at the top, then slamming at the last second, as it always did.

"That son of a gun!" Deborah said, adjusting her chair so she could continue working. "J. D., sweetheart, why don't you sit at your desk and make yourself at home. There's not much to show you now. We're almost done with our day's workload anyway."

"OK," J. D. said as he set his lunch box of afternoon snacks on his new desk and then sat down. His office chair was set too low for him to sit comfortably at his desk so he tried adjusting the seat with the levers underneath the cushion, but to no avail. The metal levers clicked and clacked, causing the seat to descend lower than it already was.

"That seat never worked right for Melvin," Rita said, typing again. "If you're lucky, Mr. Baker will get you a new one. But I doubt it."

All three were entering data again, like they were when J. D. had first arrived. The sound of their keyboards clickity-clacking, the cadence of the keys, made a plastic *thwack* that was hypnotizing.

J. D. examined his ancient wood desk, opening empty drawers on the left and right sides and then closing them—an errant paper clip or ballpoint pen here and there—then felt the cold, wood desktop with the palms of his hands. The last drawer he opened was the middle drawer, one for pens and pencils and papers. Inside, it was empty except for a line of sugar ants marching the width of the drawer, emerging from a tiny hole in the crease at the right of the drawer and then disappearing into thin air on the opposite side. He slowly closed the middle drawer, not disturbing the ants. On the desktop sat a sleeping computer, a metal document holder (for holding papers upright to be read), and a telephone. One of the bottom drawers was deep enough for his lunch box so he sat it in there. He looked around the office as the other three worked.

"You can look around if you'd like," Deborah said.

"Feast your eyes about, my boy!" Rita said, then cackled.

J. D. stood from his low-riding office chair, then walked over to the table where the dot-matrix printers belched paper into neat piles, the result of the data being entered by his three coworkers. Each printer sat behind a deep, metal basket where the paper piled inside, the ribbon housed within the yellowed plastic printers zipping left and right as the data seared onto the striped paper. The printers squawked a terrible racket, accompanying the clickity-clack of the keyboards in the office buzz. At the left end of the table, a blue-tinted, clear glass cookie jar sat, halfway filled with cookies. Conchino lurched to the table as J. D. examined it, quickly procuring a cookie from the antique jar and then sitting back down, eating the cookie while typing—both of his hands on the keyboard as he chewed the cookie with his gash of a mouth.

J. D. noticed a bulletin board above the printers. It was covered with an assortment of fliers, brochures, and notices, many of which advertised nearby restaurants and cafes and pubs, their menus catering to the measly budgets of the thousands of underpaid state employees in the surrounding blocks.

"The burger place is pretty good," Deborah said, not looking away from her computer screen as she typed. "If that's your kind of thing. Do you like to eat out or bring your lunch?"

"I like to bring my lunch," J. D. said.

"You must like to watch your weight then. That's why you're so *skinny.*"

"We bring our lunch, too," Rita said. "Why we not skinny?" She cackled again.

"Good question!" Deborah blurted.

One notice on the bulletin board caught J. D.'s eye, printed in glossy color on speckled paper with a blue award ribbon attached to the bottom right. It read with gold embossed letters at the top:

STATE EMPLOYEES COST-SAVINGS SUGGESTION
PROGRAM
$10,000 REWARD
For the best suggestion that saves the State of Texas
money and time.
Do YOU have any ideas?

J. D. unpinned the notice and read the rest of it.

"We been trying to come up with ideas for years," Rita said. "We wants to win that money!"

"We have a pact," Deborah said. "If any of us comes up with a cost-savings idea and wins that money, then we *all* will share it. Maybe you will come up with our winning idea."

"I don't know," J. D. said, pinning the notice back on the bulletin board. "I just started working here. I have no idea what I'm doing."

"Who does?!" Rita said, then cackled.

Rita always cracked herself up. It was her way of lightening the mood. She wanted to lighten the mood for everyone. No one ever seemed to mind since no one complained about her cracks, so she continued to make light of things.

"Besides, if we don't win that prize, maybe we'll win the lottery. You gonna contribute to our office pool?" She stopped typing and pulled a Ziplock sandwich bag from the middle drawer of her desk. It was filled with dollar bills and coins and lottery tickets. "The jackpot is $7 million this week. That's crazy money!"

"How much do I contribute?" J. D. said, patting his pockets. "I don't have much money on me." He pulled a ragged, cloth wallet from his back pocket. He separated the velcro holding the wallet together, dust spewing from it. There was one wrinkled, sad dollar bill inside among folded pieces of paper, business cards, and movie theater tickets. He pulled the limp bill out and offered it to Rita.

"That'll do. Anything helps," she said, putting the sad bill in the Ziplock bag. "All for one and one for all, I always say. Ain't that right, Conchino?"

He nodded silently.

"We have a lottery jackpot pact, too. Whatever money we win, we share. We won $72 once!"

"That's great," J. D. said, sitting back down at his desk. He surveyed the small office, pleased with what he saw, feeling the camaraderie from his coworkers. "I hope we win, then."

"Me too!" Deborah said, typing again, smiling. "Me too."

Most people would have felt disillusioned and saddened sitting in that cramped office engulfed in noise with those lowly state employees, but not J. D. For the first time in his young life, he felt he was on his way to fulfilling his dream, branching out from his small-town family and their struggling small business, becoming a man in the big city all on his own. He was on his way to bigger and better things and this was the first step. He knew he was where he was supposed to be. To celebrate, he ate a pecan log from his stash of snacks in his lunch box as his coworkers furiously entered the last of the applications for unemployment so they could wrap up for the day, then go home.

3.

J. D.'s landlord initially assumed he was a college student when he applied to rent the miniscule, one-bedroom, cinder block house in the backyard behind her house because he looked so young and owned a bicycle. She was surprised to learn that he was a salaried employee of the State of Texas. The neighbors in Hyde Park called the tiny, backyard shack with gray walls and a metal roof the "slave quarters," although in reality it was built in the 1960s for the immigrant housekeeper—a wispy brunette from Spain with dreams of earning a bachelor's degree from the University of Texas but never did—who died a few months before J. D. leased it. He wanted to live there because of its close proximity to his work, allowing him to ride his bicycle since he didn't own a car. His landlord advised him against riding his bike to work.

"You'll get run over," she told him flatly.

"I'll make sure to wear my helmet," he said.

She shook her head as he signed the lease agreement. She also told him to take care of the place since it reminded her of her beloved housekeeper. She was still quite sad that "her friend" was gone. He assured her he would take care of it the best he could.

After J. D.'s first day of work at the Texas Department of Unemployment and Benefits, he rode his bike the twenty blocks from downtown to his home in Hyde Park—a neighborhood whose houses were originally built in the 1920s and '30s (mostly of pier and beam construction in an arts and crafts style) and were very desirable to students and employees of the University of Texas, its campus straddling the southern boundary of the neighborhood—with cars and busses and trucks angrily honking their horns at him the entire way. Miraculously making it home without getting run over, he navigated up the gravel driveway of his landlord's house to his cinder block shack around back. After locking up his bicycle with a bike chain—using an elaborate braid of twists and loops through both spoked wheels as well as the body frame and around the handlebars, secured to a large ceramic pot filled with succulent plants that must have weighed two hundred pounds—J. D. noticed a package emblazoned with UPS stickers and labels sitting on his front porch. A feeling of joy consumed him.

"Yes!" he said to himself as he picked up the package, unlocked his door, then went inside.

The front door led into the kitchen and dining area, a space barely large enough for two people to stand side by side. J. D. set the package on his dining table and then hung his bike helmet on a hook on the wall. The kitchen was hardly equipped enough to be called such, being that it contained the minimum required appliances: an electric hot plate, a two-slice toaster, a microwave the size of a shoebox, a sink without a garbage disposal, and a compact refrigerator barely large enough to hold a gallon of milk and a package of bologna. All of these things were lucky to occupy counter space. He had to make do without a dishwasher or conventional oven or regular-sized refrigerator, basic modern conveniences most people had in their homes or apartments. Even so, J. D. was content in his miniscule abode—it was exactly where he wanted to live in the city—and he examined the package as he sat at his tiny dining table. The package was addressed to him from his mother—her delicate, cursive handwriting neatly inscribed on the shipping label. He had high hopes for what the package contained, and, as he ripped it open, his hopes were fulfilled.

"Yes!" he said, again to himself.

Inside the box was an assortment of pecan snacks and a letter from his loving parents. He set the letter on the table as he inventoried the snacks: pecan logs (his current favorite), pecan pralines, pecan cookies, pouches of roasted pecans, coffee cake with crumbled cinnamon and pecans on top, and more. It was the ultimate care package for him, a thoughtful reminder of what he loved most about his hometown of Brady, Texas. He debated about which snack to eat for dinner—especially since his refrigerator only contained a can of soda, a package of hot dogs, and a jar of mayonnaise—then grabbed the letter from his parents, and a pecan log, and retired to his bedroom for the night.

Half of his house consisted of his bedroom and a bath area, separated by a curtain. The bedroom was large enough for a twin bed, a squat night stand, and a small dresser. The bath area had a small porcelain sink with a beveled mirror attached to the wall, a round galvanized steel washtub on the floor with a chrome showerhead suspended from the ceiling, and a composting toilet. Hot water was supposed to come in the shower from a water tank on the roof of the house—theoretically heated by the afternoon sun—but sprinkled lukewarm water recently because of the unseasonably mild weather. The composting toilet scared off all potential tenants who wanted to rent the tiny house except for J. D., who had spent plenty of time in cow pastures around a variety of manure piles, cow chips, and poop pucks. He wasn't scared of composting his own turds; neither was the housekeeper who had lived there before him for over forty years. That made him the ideal tenant.

He laid on his bed, eating his pecan log, and reminisced about his hometown. When he thought of home, he usually thought of the same good things: tipping cows at night with his high school friends, riding his bike by himself down the gravel roads outside of town, and buying treats at the drugstore on the weekends. His favorite treats were from the pecan farmer (of course), just like the one he was eating in bed. As he devoured it—plucking stray, sugary crumbs off his shirt and licking them from his fingertips—he opened the letter and read it. The sight of his mother's handwriting brought an unexpected feeling of comfort and joy, wringing a small amount of salty water from his tear ducts. This is what the letter said:

> My Dearest J. D. –
> Oh, how we miss you, your father and I. We hope your new life in Austin, Texas is as grand as you'd hoped. Your Aunt Ethel complains that Austin is infested with hippies and fears that you will be corrupted by their marijuana-smoking ways. I keep insisting that you would never befriend hippies or smoke marijuana, but she is inconsolable. She is difficult to reason with when she's crying but you know that. Your father insisted I tell you that he wishes you well, although I can sense that his feelings are still hurt from the argument you two had before you moved away. Your father wants everyone to think he's tough as nails but, really, he's an old softie. I'm certain he will forgive you one day. He always does, whether you know that or not. He does love you very much! Your father and I are also dealing with the loss of the new girl, Joan, who worked the front desk. Remember her? We hired her just a few months ago to greet customers and answer phones but she up and vanished yesterday, not coming to work or returning our calls. Hopefully, we will find someone soon to

replace her. It is difficult wearing all the hats we business owners have to wear— your father and I. Sometimes, it just gets to be too much to bear. We hope deep down in our hearts that you will one day return to Brady and help us run the family business. That is what we truly feel is your destiny. One day, it could be <u>all</u> <u>yours</u>. But, until then, please take care and enjoy your favorite snacks we sent you. We bought them just for you. And we hope this letter finds you well.
Sincerely, Your Loving Parents, Mom and Dad
P.S. I refuse to send you emails as they are not very personal. More letters to come.

J. D. felt pangs of guilt in his heart as he finished reading the letter. He felt so bad that he didn't even want to eat another pecan treat. The one he just finished upset his stomach, so he sat up and wiped the tears from his face. He wasn't sure he'd ever return to his hometown of Brady, Texas. It just wasn't in his plans.

As he sat in bed, the sound of amplified angelic crooning and guitar strumming could be heard in the distance, so J. D. cracked open his bedroom window and listened. His landlord had warned him about the nearby neighborhood bars and cafes, all of which hosted live music at night on their patios, which she complained about constantly and reported to the police, citing noise ordinance violations at night. It bothered his landlord to no end but J. D. actually enjoyed hearing the music. It pleased him to hear the folk music seep into his tiny house along with the scent of the blooming wisteria flowers that grew on the fence behind his house. It was an intoxicating combination for him and, rather than change into his night clothes and then brush his teeth, he simply laid down in his bed and allowed the folk singer to serenade him to sleep.

4.

When J. D. entered Unit 3 around 8 a.m., the small office was already abuzz. Deborah and Conchino were busy at their desks entering data while Rita stood at the printer table, uncovering a clear, glass dish filled with homemade brownies. The printers belched paper into their paper baskets. Brent was nowhere to be found, his desk abandoned.

"G' morning!" Rita said to J. D., folding the aluminum foil used to cover the dish of baked goods so she could reuse it later. "I brought some goodies for us to share. I baked brownies for my grandkids but we need these treats more than they do. We *work* for a living!" she said, then cackled. "They tell me school is hard but nuttin's harder than workin' every day and supportin' your family. Go on and take one. They good for your soul." J. D. took a brownie and bit into the delicious treat. She returned to her desk, sat down, placed the aluminum foil in her purse, then began typing.

J. D. set his lunch box on his desk and then sat down. He opened the right, bottom drawer so he could set his lunch box in there but he discovered a platoon of sugar ants marching single-file across the bottom of the drawer.

Deborah noticed J. D. staring into his desk drawer and said, "Our office is infested with sugar ants. We've tried everything to get rid of them but they won't go away."

"They now our suite mates!" Rita said. Both women giggled. "They don't bite, though. They not fire ants."

J. D. closed the drawer—not disturbing or killing the sugar ants—and kept his lunch box where he sat it on the desktop. He tapped a few random keys on his keyboard, which awoke the computer sleeping on his desk. On the screen was an image of the state of Texas—drawn in green ASCII characters on a field of pitch black—which looked like this:

J. D. stared at the image of Texas, mesmerized by its simple yet accurate depiction. *How long did it take to do* that? he thought to himself. *Will I be drawing pictures on the computer, too?*

"Make yourself at home," Deborah said while typing. "I'll sit next to you in a bit and train you as soon as I get done with this batch of apps."

"OK," J. D. said, continuing to examine the ASCII image of Texas on his computer screen.

"The café downstairs sells coffee," Deborah continued. "You can go down and grab some, if you'd like."

"That's OK," J. D. said, eating his brownie, crumbs falling into the folds of his shirt and pants, as he inventoried the various punctuation marks and characters of the border of Texas on the screen. "I don't drink coffee."

"You don't drink *coffee*?!" Rita blurted. Her exclamation interrupted Conchino's trance—the same hypnotic trance J. D. would learn to succumb to as he typed and entered data all day long at his new job—and he stared at J. D., shaking his head in disbelief. Rita continued, "How you goin' to get through your day without *coffee*? And nuttin' goes better with homemade brownies than coffee."

"So true," Deborah said. Conchino agreed with an emphatic nod. "Nothing gets you through the boring routine of entering these unemployment applications than a good cup of *coffee*."

"I can't agree more!" Brent Baker said, the door to Unit 3 flying open and then smashing against the wall. He tossed his shoulder bag behind his desk, plopped in his chair, and slammed his head on the desktop. "Coffee sounds really good right now."

"What's wrong? You hung over?" Rita said, sarcastically.

"I wish," Brent said, covering his head with his arms, as if shielding himself from his obligations and duties. "You guys entering apps?"

"Of course we are," Deborah said. "You could be helping us, you know. We're swamped."

"I will, I will," he said, sitting up and then pushing his hair back into its usual style: controlled shagginess. "But first things *first*. COFFEE! Anybody else want some?" he said, standing up, his hands plundering his pockets for money, then looking around the room for takers.

A collective groan came from the old crew. J. D. smiled at Brent, then said, "No thank you."

"You bring lunch today?" Brent said to J. D. while opening the door to Unit 3.

"Yes, I did."

"Don't bring tomorrow. I'll take you to lunch. How's that?" he said, punctuating the order with a thumbs-up.

"Sounds great," J. D. said, flattered.

"I'll be back in a jiffy." Then he vanished from Unit 3, the door slamming closed behind him.

Deborah pushed her chair from behind her desk, parked it next to J. D., then plopped down—setting a manila folder filled with papers on her lap.

"Get used to it. He's *always* gone," she said, adjusting her sitting position in her chair, scooching close to J. D.'s desk. "Ready to learn how to enter apps into the system?"

"Sure," he said.

"OK. Well, before we start, let me tell you a little about our computer system."

She went on to tell him about the Texas Application Processing Entry System, or TAPES as most in the agency liked to call it since it was an easy-to-remember acronym. TAPES was a mainframe data entry application that had been around since the 1970s, used to enter unemployment applications from the citizens of Texas applying for unemployment benefits through a "green screen" terminal. In the 1990s, personal computers eventually replaced mainframe "green screens" but the TAPES interface was converted into a terminal emulation, allowing agency employees to still enter data into TAPES via their personal computers. J. D. was surprised at the specificity of Deborah's knowledge of TAPES, definitions of processes and steps of procedures rolling off her tongue like a comic book enthusiast rattling off the super powers and backstories of all the heroes in the Marvel Universe, except she wasn't a computer genius; she was a low-level, state government data entry clerk who looked like she was about to be a grandmother. She went on dryly for a good fifteen to twenty minutes about the history of TAPES. J. D. struggled to focus but at least absorbed some of what she had to say.

"And that's everything you'll ever need to know about TAPES. Got any questions?"

"Well...," he said, pausing for a breath or two. "Does Mr. Baker's epilepsy cause him a lot of—"

"Epilepsy? Mr. Baker?!" she said, cackling. "Boy, he doesn't have *epilepsy*. That's funny. Any other questions?"

"No."

"Good. So, what you do first is, set a paper application on your paper holder, like so." She took the first application from the manila folder on her lap and clipped it on the metal paper holder on his desk, then turned it to face J. D. "Then enter all the filled-in places on the app to the data fields on the screen."

J. D. attempted to read the chicken-scratch handwriting on the application. The citizen's handwriting was barely legible, awful to the point of indecipherable, but—to J. D.'s amazement—Deborah was able to read it.

"I'll read it out loud and you enter. Got it?"

"OK."

Deborah rattled off all the information: First Name, Last Name, Address, so on and so forth. With two fingers, J. D. pecked at the keyboard like a farm hen gingerly searching for grubs on the ground. Deborah chuckled.

"Boy! Where did you learn to type like *that*?"

"I did take a keyboard class in high school."

"*Keyboard* class? I've never heard of such a thing."

"I really don't know how to type, if that's what you're gettin' at."

"Well, I can *see* that. Don't worry about it. You'll be a pro before you know it. You'll just catch on."

"Thank you," he said, grateful that she didn't tease him more about his abysmal typing skills.

"You remind me of my son. You two are about the same age, too. Getting yourself in things when you don't know how to do things." J. D. turned to see Deborah smiling at him. "You're much nicer than my son, though. He's mean to me."

"Why is he mean to you?"

"Beats me. Spoiled, I guess. Anyways, let's keep going. The social security number is 459-55—," she continued.

J. D. typed as fast as his two fingers allowed him. Conchino examined the two, first J. D. and then nodding at Deborah. She nodded back, then smiled. She continued to feed

J. D. information from the application until she reached the end. He looked up at the computer screen. A prompt hung on the screen. He read it out loud. It said: "Submit data or save and print?"

"Which do I do?" J. D. said, looking for guidance.

"Hit Ctrl Shift P on the keyboard to save and print."

"OK," he said.

"See? It's printing. Then you move on to the next application. Any questions?"

"Hmmm," J. D. said, thinking. "Why not just submit the application?"

"*Submit?* What do you mean?"

"Well, the screen says, 'Submit data or save and print?' Why don't I just *submit* the application?"

"Good question. We've *always* just saved and printed. I don't even know how to submit. Rita?" she barked, over the typing of the other two.

"Yeah?!"

"Why don't we submit instead of save and print?"

"'Cause there is no *submit*! Must be a typo or somethin' on the screen."

"Typo?" Deborah said, confused.

"Yeah, a typo. You know? A *misspelling.*"

"I know what a typo is, my dear."

"Then why did you ax me?" Rita said, halting her data entry, peering at Deborah.

"Don't get your panties in a wad," Deborah said, rolling her eyes.

"My panties are just fine," Rita said, typing again. "Pristine, even."

"It's a typo," Deborah said to J. D. "Just save and print."

"OK."

"And that's it. Want to try yourself?"

"Sure," J. D. said. He grabbed the next application, set it on the paper holder, and began to enter the data on his own. Deborah was pleased.

"Just to let everyone know," Rita called out, while typing. "We weren't jackpot winners last night but we did win $6!"

Deborah and Conchino clapped softly, like the gallery of a golf tournament. Rita pulled the Ziplock bag from her middle desk drawer and opened it.

"Everyone, pitch in for the next one," she said, handing the bag to Deborah. "One of these days, we're goin' to hit it big. I can feel it!"

"Hallelujah!" Deborah said.

But in the meantime, they were just ordinary folks doing ordinary things at just another ordinary place of employment.

5.

The next day—as soon as he stepped into Unit 3—Brent informed J. D. that he would be taking him out to lunch, as he promised. Brent tore through the door like a tornado mowing through the plains of Oklahoma and accosted J. D. at his desk.

"Remember, we're going out for lunch today. Right?"

Dang it! J. D. thought. The sleepy country boy was what many liked to call a "creature of habit," being that he made his lunch every work morning like clockwork—peanut butter and jelly sandwich on white bread, plain potato chips, a soda, some variety of pecan snack from Brady, Texas, and so forth. J. D. was a little embarrassed that his efficient morning routine might have just ruined his first week on the job.

"Sorry, Mr. Baker. I forgot about our lunch plans. I brought my lunch today, as usual."

"That's OK. Save it for tomorrow. And call me Brent. Mr. Baker is how people used to address my father. I'm just good ol' Brent."

"All right," J. D. said, meekly.

"But before we leave for lunch, I'll give you a little tour of the building. You know? Show you around. You down?"

"How can I say no?"

"Great!" Brent said, careening around his desk and then plopping in his office chair, tossing a messenger bag from around his neck to the floor. He surveyed the pile of papers on his desk—monuments reminding him of the high unemployment of the State of Texas as well as the endless amount of applications that poured in daily—and he sighed deeply. "This shit never ends, does it?"

"Never does!" Rita squawked while she typed.

J. D. turned to look at Rita and marveled that two of his new coworkers—Rita and Deborah (not Conchino because he hadn't spoken a single word to anyone since J. D. started work)—not only could talk but seemed to be able to have full conversations while entering data. In a way, their ability to do two things skillfully at once reminded him of the acrobats and clowns from the circus who visited Brady, Texas, last summer, the way they could ride unicycles and juggle tennis balls at the same time or traipse across high wires in ballet shoes while spinning colorful hula hoops on their hips. It was miraculous to watch: the circus. J. D. wondered if he would graduate from two-fingered pecking with deep concentration to ten-fingered typing while idly chatting. It seemed like a pipe dream, too good to be true. He also wondered if Conchino might actually be mute since he hadn't spoken a word. *Dang,* he thought. *He's quieter than a horny toad running for cover.*

"Well, get on it then. No time to waste," Brent said, then he laid his head on his desk as if ready to take a nap.

"What time do you want to leave for lunch?" J. D. said to him.

"11:30 sharp," Brent said, his head on his desk hidden behind stacks of papers.

"OK."

J. D. placed an application on the paper holder and then began to peck slowly at his keyboard, entering the information on the app into TAPES as Deborah trained him to do the day before. As he worked, Deborah and Rita struck up a breezy conversation, one where they compared the good and bad about their children and—in Rita's case—her grandchildren as well. Turns out, Deborah's son—who was close to J. D.'s age as she had mentioned before—enjoyed making extra money by selling questionable items in various ways, whether it was on the internet or through acquaintances. Some of the items he sold were run-of-the-mill household appliances or electronics. But some of the other things he sold placed him precariously close to being categorized as a criminal, something which irked Deborah to no end.

"He's just like his father," Deborah lamented. "That no-good son of a bitch. And yes, my *former* mother-in-law is a bitch. I said it!"

"Oh, my Reggie's mother was a saint, rest her blessed soul," Rita said. "And Reggie, too. Lord, I miss his sweet face." Rita blew a kiss to the heavens, the place she felt her late husband and his late mother resided, where they were sitting together and waiting patiently for her. As it also turned out, Rita was widowed not long ago—her poor husband Reggie dying from heart disease and diabetes, both so malicious to his health that the doctors couldn't decide which actually caused his early demise—and she was left to live her elderly days as the matriarch of her large brood of five adult children and thirteen grandchildren. The adjective she used most to describe her five children was *worthless*. The adjective she used most to describe her grandchildren was *mischievous*. But that didn't stop her from doing her best to be the greatest mother and grandmother to them all. "I just wish Reggie was still here to help me. I told him to eat better!"

"Amen, sister," Deborah said.

J. D. learned a lot about Deborah and Rita just from listening to their idle chats. Conchino, on the other hand, was still a mystery and would be for quite some time. He never said a word, except for occasional guttural grunts or conspicuous nods or headshakes when spoken to. Unlike Deborah and Rita—whose desks were covered with photos of their children and, in Rita's case, grandchildren—Conchino did not decorate his work area with family memorabilia. What Conchino loved most was his car (he was obsessed with street racing), and his work area reflected that. His desk was covered with car parts, car audio equipment, and tools. When he had a break from work, he piddled around with the car parts and accessories at his desk, screwing and unscrewing things, snipping and then clamping other things. J. D. knew nothing about cars, so watching Conchino silently mess around with these parts was mysterious and fascinating to him.

What kind of car does he drive? J. D. thought. *I bet it's fast.*

The four coworkers entered applications all morning, the printers belching endless reams of serrated paper into metal baskets. Once 11:30 approached, a man entered Unit 3— a pale man with a balding pate, short-sleeved button-down shirt containing a bulbous stomach, thin and hairy arms, and legs as slender and frail as dried twigs. He slowly pushed a metal cart, which he parked next to the printer table, then watched the paper spill from the printers into their baskets. He waited patiently, his hands resting on his boney hips.

When Rita noticed the odd-looking man, she said, "It's Ken. Almost lunchtime!" She stopped typing and then the others—including J. D.—eventually followed suit.

The printers soon stopped printing, then the man named Ken ripped each paper pile from their respective printers and stacked them on his cart. Once done gathering the printed applications, he slowly pushed the cart back to the door of Unit 3.

"Have a great day, Ken!" Deborah said. He raised his hand above his head, as if attempting to wave but not moving his hand, then closed the door behind him. The sound of the door slamming awoke Brent Baker, who had been snoozing on his desk.

"Is it lunchtime?" he said, rubbing his crusty eyes and wiping drool from his mouth.

"Sure is, Rumpelstiltskin," Deborah said, cackling.

"Great!" he said. "Ready to go, J. D.?"

J. D. looked around at the other three, all pulling their homemade lunches from the drawers of their desks. For a moment, J. D. regretted agreeing to go to lunch with his new boss, not because he didn't want to eat lunch with him, but because he had been looking forward to the lunch he had lovingly made for himself. But he also knew he could just eat his lunch for dinner, which eased his regret.

"Yes," he said to his boss, standing up.

"Then let's go!"

J. D. followed Brent out of the office and down the hall toward the skywalk. As they crossed over to the Main Building, J. D. could briefly see the pedestrians scurrying outside, walking around, appearing like ants on the ground.

"Where are we going for lunch?" J. D. said.

"There's a pub I like to go to," Brent said, walking briskly. "Want to see what one of the other data entry units looks like?"

"Sure, I guess," J. D. said, struggling to keep up.

"Up here."

Brent reached for the doorknob of the first door in the Main Building. He opened the door for J. D. to look in, the inside of the small office like an alternate universe of Unit 3. There was a similar configuration of desks for four employees and one supervisor, just like Unit 3, except with different office furniture and different faces manning their desks, of course. They were still entering data with a similar clickity-clackity buzz to Unit 3, their printers spitting out reams of paper, too. They must not have known it was lunchtime. Ken, who had just been in Unit 3 collecting printed paper, pushed his cart out of the small office. Brent acknowledged Ken with a nod.

"This is Unit 9. They enter unemployment apps, just like we do," Brent said, then pointed at the supervisor at the front of the office. "And that's Mr. Beard, their supervisor."

Mr. Beard saluted J. D., who meekly waved in return.

"Beard and I are in a fantasy football league. You should join," he said, abruptly walking away.

J. D. glanced into the busy space of Unit 9 as much as he could before the door shut, then chased after Brent, who was following Ken the paper collector. Ken slowly pushed his squeaky cart down the hall, then stopped at the next door so he could open it.

When J. D. caught up to Brent, he told him, "Now, I'll show you where all the unemployment apps go. Follow me."

Brent helped Ken open the door, then held it open so Ken could push his cart inside. Once J. D. was inside the door, he discovered a vast sea of cubicles, dozens upon dozens, manned by employees shuffling papers. Brent smiled as J. D. gawked at the immense office space.

"And this is Validations. They check all the printed applications for accuracy."

"For accuracy?" J. D. said, confused.

"Yep, make sure we dotted the Is and crossed all the Ts when we entered the data. You know? For typos."

"Typos?"

"Yeah, typing mistakes."

"Oh!" J. D. said. He marveled at the sheer number of validators in an office larger than a basketball court, which seemed to go on forever, then around a corner in the distance. "How many people work in Validations?"

"How many? Shit. Hundreds. Maybe a thousand."

"A thousand *people*?!"

"At least. You hungry?" J. D. looked at Brent and then nodded. "Let's go eat!"

Outside, they walked a few blocks to a pub called O'Sullivan's, a shabby hole in the wall nestled in between a liquor store and a boot repair shop. Brent flung the door to the pub open wide and entered the black hole. J. D. reluctantly followed. It took a moment for his eyes to adjust to the dark, cavernous pub from the bright outdoors. But once his eyes adjusted, he saw his boss sitting on a stool at the bar. J. D. then sat next to him. He noticed that they were the only patrons inside.

"I got your lunch," Brent said, raising his hand to the bartender, who briskly approached them. Punk rock played from a jukebox in the distance.

"My man!" the bartender said, initiating a handshake ritual with Brent too complex for J. D. to follow. "Glad to see you make lunch after such a crazy night last night! Right?!"

"Yeah, it was pretty crazy," Brent said. He tilted his head to J. D. "This is my new employee. I got his lunch."

The bartender extended his hand—leathery and massive like an old, weathered baseball glove—to J. D. "Call me P. Nice to meet you."

"*Pee*?" J. D. said, confused, thinking of himself urinating in a toilet, a thought that made him shudder.

"P, like the letter in the alphabet. People are always mispronouncing my name, so I just go by P."

J. D. extended his little hand for a shake. P's large hand enveloped his, crushing it.

"Can you bring us two club sandwiches and two drafts?" Brent said.

"You got it! You playing next week?" P said, entering their order into a computer.

"What night?" Brent said.

"Thursday."

"You got it."

P poured two draft beers and then set them on the bar for Brent and J. D.

"Your boss is a rock star. You know that?"

J. D. shook his head while P washed dirty pint glasses, left out from the night before, in a sink filled with gray, soapy water underneath the bar. J. D. stared in disbelief at the beers on the bar. He really couldn't believe that his boss ordered beer during lunch and wondered how much trouble they would be in if someone from the Texas Department of Unemployment and Benefits spotted them. Brent noticed his apprehension and chuckled.

"It's not against the rules to drink alcohol during lunch. It's cool."

J. D. still didn't believe him. It seemed too good to be true. He wasn't much of a beer drinker, anyway. In almost every instance, J. D. preferred soda to beer. Even with his boss's approval, he was reluctant to drink the draft beer. He would have preferred a root beer, if Brent had just asked him.

"You're in a rock band?" J. D. said.

This question was always music to Brent's ears. He loved to hear people ask him that. The attention stroked his ego in a way that nothing else did.

"Yeah, living the dream," he cooed.

"That's cool."

"I started the band to meet chicks but now it's so much more than that. It's rock 'n' roll, man. It's a way of life."

P dried his hands with a towel, then said, "I'll go check on those sandwiches. Be back." He tossed the towel on the bar, then disappeared into the kitchen.

"Working in Austin is my dream," J. D. told him. Brent patted him on the back.

"That's cool, too," he said, then lifted the pint of beer and drained it in four gulps. He slammed the empty glass on the bar, wiping the beer foam from his lips with his forearm. "Being a state employee is a good gig. Good hours. Good retirement. What more could you want?"

"Exactly."

P returned with two plates of club sandwiches and French fries, setting them on the bar in front of Brent and J. D. P continued to wash pint glasses in the sink.

"You gonna pay your tab from last night?" he said to Brent.

"What tab? And can I have another beer?"

P reluctantly shook his wet hands and then poured Brent another beer, placing it in front of him on the bar. Brent chugged the second beer.

"The tab from last night?"

"How much?" Brent said, wiping more beer foam from his mouth, then biting into his club sandwich.

"$113 plus tip," P said, putting his hands back in the dirty dish water. J. D. nibbled his sandwich as the two bickered. He hadn't witnessed such excitement since he moved to Austin.

"$113?! What the hell? I thought the band got *free* beer?"

"The band got drink tickets for free beer but your lady friend ordered drinks on *your* tab. She said, 'Put them on Brent's tab.' So I did."

"She did?!" Brent said, exasperated. P nodded. "That skeezer."

P laughed a deep, guttural laugh—placing his sudsy, wet hands on his stomach—like it was the funniest thing in the world. He took a deep breath when he was done laughing and then continued washing glasses. Brent chewed his sandwich, annoyed.

"Did you at least get some after the show?" P said.

"No!"

P laughed some more. J. D. giggled as well, annoying Brent, who then smiled. He liked seeing J. D. enjoy himself, even if it was at his expense.

"Whatever," Brent said, devouring his sandwich. He looked at J. D.'s full beer glass sweating on the bar. "Are you gonna drink that?"

J. D. examined the beer, then picked it up with two hands—the sweaty glass suspended by the tips of his fingers—like a child lifting a sippy cup. He daintily slurped the beer foam.

"I'll have another beer, P. And I'll pay my tab next week. Cool?"

"It's cool. I was just giving you shit, my man."

"I know. Always giving me *shit*."

"Always," P said, pouring Brent a third beer, then setting it on the bar.

"When do we have to be back to the office?" J. D. said, his mouth full of food.

"Whenever," Brent said.

"But won't the others wonder where we are?"

"Nah. It's all good."

Brent chugged his third beer while J. D. finished his sandwich and P finished washing the dirty pint glasses.

6.

Rita sat in a rocking chair on the front porch of her ramshackle house, watching some of her grandchildren play and run around her fenced front yard, some of them spilling out the front gate to the surrounding sidewalk on their scooters or bicycles. This was her typical after-work routine, waiting for her grown children to drop off their kids for Rita to watch while they worked evening shifts—some in retail, some in service, all struggling with low-paying jobs. Rita was the most successful of them all—living in the home she had grown up in and then inherited from her parents as well as being employed as a longtime state employee—and she enjoyed watching the grandkids to help out. It was one of her joys in life. She loved being the matriarch of her family. She also loved scratching lottery tickets as she watched the kids on the front porch, the dream of hitting a big payday for her, her family, and her coworkers always in the back of her mind. She scratched them enthusiastically, looking up when she heard a child yelp or squeal—sometimes scolding Malik or Zion or Kiara.

"Malik!" she commanded. "No roughhousing!"

The little boy froze and then turned to his grandmother, realizing his clinched fist aimed at his cousin betrayed him.

"I'm Jordan, Granny! Don't you know my name?!" he said, hiding his clenched fist behind his back.

"I know *who* you are. Don't get sassy with me. And quit roughhousin'!"

"Yes, Granny!" Jordan said, continuing to play, monitoring his grandmother from the corner of his eye.

After scratching off all the silver, opaque layer that covered the numbers of the lottery ticket, Rita discovered that she had won $20, a result that never ceased to bring her joy and excitement—no matter the prize amount. She raised the ticket closer to her face—examining the winning numbers again, then rereading the game instructions—to make sure she had really won, which she did.

"Oh, thank you, Lord!" she said.

She kissed the ticket and then raised it above her head, as if offering it to her Savior as evidence of his love for her. She shimmied in her seat then grabbed a small, metal, recipe card box from the rusty, metal side table, opened it, then sorted through the various cards and placards in it—some were labeled for recipes, others were labeled for lottery tickets. She shuffled to a section labeled "Winners!"—past sections labeled "To Check" and "Unit 3 Lottery"—and placed the winning scratch ticket in the back. She had other winning tickets to claim, too, and would do that the next time she was at the grocery store. She had plenty of losing tickets as well, but those could be entered into secondhand drawings through the mail for special prizes. She kept those in a section labeled "Second Chance." Some of her friends had hobbies like sewing or singing in the church choir or baking cakes for bake sales. Rita's hobby was playing the lottery.

After placing the recipe card box back on the side table next to a framed photo of her late husband, Reggie Jackson Sr., one of the grandchildren appeared next to her, startling Rita. A squeal escaped unexpectedly from her mouth. She was in her dream world; she didn't expect a kid to appear so suddenly.

"Oh, child! Do you want to give your grandmother a heart attack?!" she said, her hand covering her heaving breast.

"No, Granny. Why would I want *that*?" she said. Her name was Jada and her hair was meticulously made up in a swirl of braids on the top of her head, fastened with hairpins and barrettes.

"'Cause I feel like I'm having a heart attack, my child."

"When is dinner?" she said, excited—hopping up and down.

"There's a pot roast in the kitchen," Rita said, thinking of the crockpot she had set to keep warm on the kitchen counter. She loved making dinner for the grandchildren with the crockpot. It was easy to use, convenient, and usually made a great dinner for a lot of people with very little effort on her part. "You know Granny always has dinner ready."

"Can I go eat some?"

"Of course! Go help yo'self," she said, patting the girl on her arm. Jada ran inside, slamming the screen door behind her. "And quit slamming my door!" she barked.

"You see, Reggie," Rita said out loud to herself, picking up the photo of her late husband, lovingly gazing at him. "You should be *here* helping me. Why did you have to leave this world so soon?"

As she gazed at the photo of her loving husband, a car parked in the street in front of her house. The black American-made sedan with gold rims wheezed as the engine died. Two more grandchildren hopped out—the real Malik and his sister Makayla—followed by their father, Michael. His arrival always brought a smile to Rita's face. He was the baby of the family and the one with the most striking resemblance to his father and her beloved husband Reggie—both father and son as handsome as can be with bright, alluring smiles and broad, sturdy shoulders. He sauntered across the lawn, winking at his nieces and nephews, enjoying their adulation. Rita stood to greet her youngest son with her arms wide.

"My baby!" she said, reaching out for a hug. "Come give yo' mama a hug."

He ascended the front steps and obliged his mother, hugging her tightly. She leaned back and examined his face, both her hands on his cheeks.

"Can I sit with you, Mama?" he said, smiling.

"Of course, my boy. You hungry? There's a roast in the kitchen."

"I'm good, Mama," he said, waiting for his mother to sit before he took a seat next to her. Once she sat, he did the same.

"How you been?" he said. "You doin' all right?"

She gazed out at all the children playing in front of her house. It pleased her to see them buzzing around, like excited bees bumbling in a field of wildflowers. As she watched, Michael reached over and placed his hand in hers, squeezing it gently.

"I'm just fine, my boy. Just fine! How they treatin' you at the warehouse?"

"All good," he said.

Michael worked the night shift at a distribution warehouse for a high-end grocery store chain that specialized in selling organic foods and specialty food items like micro-brewed beers and locally sourced vegetables. He liked his coworkers very much even though he felt that management was slightly racist. He always wondered why the brown and black boys mostly worked the night shift while the white boys mostly worked the day shift. His questions about scheduling always seemed to fall on deaf ears. But he enjoyed the steady, manual labor even though it only paid $10 per hour. It was difficult supporting a family on $10 per hour. But, despite the meager wages, driving a forklift was enjoyable and a couple of the dudes he regularly worked with made him laugh a lot. That meant something to Michael.

"You ever hear back from yo' supervisor about working the day shift?"

"Not yet, Mama."

"I bet you will soon," she said, patting his hand gently. "You're a good man."

The compliment made him smile and a little ashamed. He had an ulterior motive for his visit.

"Thanks, Mama. Can I ax you for a favor?"

"Of course, my boy," she said, patting his hand some more and watching the kids play in the yard.

"Can I borrow a couple hundred dollars? The rent's due and I don't get paid till next week. I'll pay you back when I get paid."

Her head sagged down, as if the weight of his request was difficult to bear. She sighed, then reached for her recipe box, flipping the lid open after resting it on her lap.

"Yo' wife found a job yet?"

"Not yet. She still looking, though."

Rita flipped through the cards until she reached the section labeled "Winners." She pulled the first card out and quickly handed it to her son, as if she didn't want the grandchildren to see what she was giving him. An astonished look appeared on his face, with a smile bright and white like the glow from a lightning bug.

"Go to the store down the street and cash it. Worth five hundred, I think."

"Thanks, Mama!" he said, leaning over and hugging her.

"And tell yo' wife that the State is hiring. They always hiring."

"Yes, Mama," he said, jumping up and slipping the winning lottery ticket in his shirt pocket. "I'll remind her again when I get home."

"You do that," she said, slowly standing up and closing the recipe box, then cradling it in the nook of her arm. "Send her my warmest regards as well."

"I will. Bye, Mama!" he said. He ran to his car and then called out to her before getting in, "I love you!"

She waved to him as he drove away. It warmed her heart to help him even though it uneased her mind. *When will he be a man and stop asking me for money?* she thought. But she didn't worry about that too much. It was getting dark and it was time for the grandchildren to eat dinner.

"Time for dinner! Come inside!" she called out.

They came up to the porch from the yard and sidewalk. As they filed inside, another car parked on the street in front of her house—a maroon, Japanese-made sedan that was lowered to the ground with dark, tinted windows. Two more grandchildren jumped out: Aliyah and Destiny. Their mother, Janice, followed them and then corralled the girls to the front door. She smiled at Rita, who returned a concerned look. She could see that Janice appeared flustered and it worried her.

"You all right, child?"

"Yes, Mama," Janice said. "Are the girls late for dinner?"

"It's never too late for dinner at my house."

"Great!" Janice said, giving her girls quick hugs and then pushing them through the front door. Once the girls were inside, she turned to her mother and said, "Do you have a minute to talk?"

"I always have a minute for my babies. Is everything OK?"

"Well, I need to ax you a favor?"

"Are you hungry?" she said, placing her hand on her daughter's shoulder.

"Smells like roast. Can I have some?"

"Of course, my dear." She smiled and patted her daughter on the back.

Janice stepped inside. Rita stood there for a moment, holding the door open. She looked around the yard to make sure there weren't any more young stragglers left playing outside. Also, she opened the recipe box and sorted through the winning lottery tickets, pulled one out, and closed the box. Once satisfied that there were no more grandchildren outside—and ready to give some charity to her daughter, if she needed it—she went inside to serve herself some roast and eat dinner with her family.

7.

J. D. opened the bottom drawer to his desk as soon as he sat down. After a long, stressful bike ride to work, he was glad to be sitting still without aggressive drivers honking and yelling at him. *Why are they so angry?* he thought, while he casually rode his bike. *It's such a beautiful morning.* But when he looked in the bottom desk drawer so he could place his lunch box in there, he noticed two lines of ants this time, marching parallel but in opposite directions. The fluid motion of their marching mesmerized him and he sat there spellbound, his lunch box sitting on his lap. Rita noticed that he was hypnotized by something unusual and deduced what caused him trepidation.

"If you gots ants in your desk, then get used to it," she said, typing as she spoke to him. "They been here since the day I started, *decades* ago."

"We all have ants in our desks," Deborah said.

"You do?" J. D. said, surprised. He looked over to Conchino, who nodded as he typed on his computer while eating a piece of coffee cake.

"We just put an offering in our desks, something for the ants to have as their own. Like a crumb of bread or a sugar cube. Don't worry. They'll leave you alone if you give them something. Here...," Rita said, handing J. D. a sugar cube from the coffee supplies she kept stashed in her desk. "Set this in the back of your drawer, then put your lunch box at the front. They won't bother your lunch. I promise. You'll see."

J. D. did as Rita instructed and was shocked to see the ants immediately make a beeline to the sugar cube at the back of the drawer. With a little faith now, he slowly closed the drawer, hoping deep down that what Rita told him to do would keep his precious lunch safe from the pesky ants.

"Thanks, Ms. Rita," he said, adjusting his seat to begin work.

"Of course, child. I'm here to help. And if you hungry, I brought a homemade coffee cake. It's over there on the printer table."

J. D. couldn't imagine starting work without partaking in a bit of homemade coffee cake, something that Conchino seemed to be enjoying immensely already. He devoured his piece of cake baked by Ms. Rita with one hand while entering unemployment applications with his other hand, two tasks that didn't seem possible to do together efficiently. But there was Conchino, whaling away at his keyboard with one hand with the same speed and dexterity as an expert typist who used both of their hands.

Dang! How does he do that? J. D. thought, as he made his way to the printer table, cutting himself a large piece of coffee cake, noticing large pieces of toasted pecans baked into the cake. It pleased him to see his favorite snack nut baked into Rita's coffee cake. And just as Rita had suggested, a small hunk of cake sat at the back of the printer table—adjacent to one of the printers and near the edge of the table—with a platoon of ants mounting it. He fought his urge to smoosh the ants and then went back to his desk, placing the piece of cake on the desktop next to the pile of unemployment applications that would take up the next couple of hours of his morning. As he began his work (taking bites of coffee cake as often as he could), Deborah watched him as he entered data, giving helpful suggestions, when she noticed his typing slow down or stop completely, the green cursor insistently flashing on the screen.

She knew every data entry field and all the keystrokes to the point that she rarely even had to look at her screen while she worked. This made it easy for her to watch over J. D.'s shoulder and offer assistance when he needed it, which was often.

When she stopped hearing the clickity-clack of his keyboard, she would often peer over and chime in something like, "Hit Tab, then Enter" or "Tab twice, then F3."

J. D. found that her advice or direction was always correct, in which case he soon regarded her as the Oracle of Unit 3, something that the others would agree with whenever J. D. broached the subject. One time, he asked Conchino if he thought Deborah knew what she was talking about when it came to TAPES in hopes of confirming his suspicion that she was an actual oracle (but also to see if he could get Conchino to utter the confirmation since he hadn't heard him speak at all). Of course, Conchino simply nodded without saying a word.

On another occasion, he found himself walking down the hall with Rita toward the restroom and, out of extreme curiosity, asked her if Deborah knew everything there was to know about TAPES.

"Oh, my dear Lord, YES!" she said, looking to the ceiling as if witnessing greatness. "Deborah knows TAPES like she knows her own child. Maybe even better than her own child. Her son is a selfish bastard. You know that?"

"She said he wasn't nice to her," J. D. said.

"Not nice is putting it gently. He ruthless!" she said, shaking her head. "But if you have a question about TAPES, then Deborah is the one to ask. She know it all."

"OK," J. D. said, then sprinted to the restroom. He was always sprinting to the restroom to pee, the unfortunate result from drinking too much soda.

J. D. was then curious about Brent's knowledge of Deborah's expertise. So, the next time Brent asked him to lunch (which became somewhat routine), J. D. asked in return, "Is Deborah the TAPES expert of Unit 3?"

"Oh yes, very much so. She trained us all how to use TAPES. She's been here longer than all of us in Unit 3. She's the veteran by a mile. How about pizza and beer for lunch?"

"Pizza *and* beer?"

"Did I stutter?" Brent said, cackling.

J. D. didn't find this to be as amusing as Brent did. Brent mostly just confused J. D. In fact, if J. D. found Deborah to be the Oracle of Unit 3, then Rita certainly was the Den Mother—always bringing snacks and baked goods and coffee and leftovers from the meals she had made for her children and grandchildren to share with her coworkers. And if Rita was the Den Mother, then Conchino was without a doubt the Silent yet Dependable One; he always seemed to be working silently, keystrokes smashing endlessly like waves in the background. This left Brent, who, for all intents and purposes, was just a mystery to J. D. It seemed to J. D. that the only thing he was really enthusiastic about was making lunch plans or regaling his band's shenanigans after a gig the night before. The last thing he seemed smitten with were his duties pertaining to Unit 3. To J. D., he rarely seemed to work at all except to give minor direction here and there, and even then, his directions were shoddy at best.

One morning—after a few mornings of peaceful routine and camaraderie between J. D., Rita, Deborah, and Conchino—Brent barnstormed the office space of Unit 3 and declared that he would be observing J. D.'s progress to see if he was up to speed on the ins and outs of entering data into TAPES. Deborah was quite offended about his misgivings.

"What do you mean, 'Up to speed?'" she said, annoyed.

"Well, maybe 'Up to speed' was a poor choice of words. Everyone knows you're the TAPES expert," Brent said sarcastically, parking his desk chair next to J. D.'s desk, then plopping in it.

J. D. became instantly flustered, looking to Deborah for reassurance. She simply rolled her eyes at Brent's irascible skepticism. She flashed J. D. a confident thumbs-up, easing his anxiety, and encouraged him to continue. He placed an unemployment application on his paper holder and began entering data into his computer. But before he could get too far, Brent halted his progress.

"You should Shift, Tab, R there," he commanded J. D., pointing at the green screen.

"No!" Deborah insisted. "Shift, Tab, Z is the correct keystroke combination, Mr. Baker."

"Mmm-hmm," Rita agreed.

J. D. wasn't sure he wanted to get in between his supervisor and coworker's dispute, but more than anything, he had grown to trust Deborah's knowledge. He patiently pecked the keystroke combination that Deborah called out—despite his supervisor's insistence—and it worked. Brent demurred.

"Well, you can enter *that* combination as well. Whatever works," Brent said, folding his arms across his chest. "You should listen to Deborah. She knows what she's talking about."

"I will, Mr. Baker," J. D. said.

"And call me Brent, please."

"OK."

J. D. continued to enter the application into TAPES and Brent didn't say a word, except for an occasional "Mmm-hmm" or "That's correct." When J. D. was done entering all the data, a prompt came on the screen. He read it out loud. It said: "Submit data or save and print?"

"Save and print at this point," Brent said.

"I know," J. D. said.

The printer across the room belched out the printed application into its basket. Brent was pleased.

"Did you know we receive over thirty thousand applications a month for unemployment benefits here at the Texas Department of Unemployment and Benefits, or T-DUB as I like to call it."

"*T-DUB?*" J. D. said.

"That's right. Our agency is so large, we have our own zip code! Can you believe it?"

"No, I can't believe it, sir," J. D. said, baffled. He pondered the enormity of the Texas Department of Unemployment and Benefits, or T-DUB, which he contrasted to some of the cattle ranches back home in Brady, Texas, some of which were thousands of acres in size but did not have their own zip codes. How could a seven thousand-acre cattle ranch *not* have its own zip code? *Dang,* he thought.

"We have over ten thousand employees. We're the largest state agency in Texas."

"That's incredible," J. D. said.

"Keep it up, J. D. You're doing just fine," Brent said, standing up and then pushing his office chair back to his desk. "Lunch tomorrow?"

"Sure."

"Great! Pizza and beer!" he said, then immediately recognized his mistake. "Root beer! I meant *root* beer."

Conchino snickered, then shook his head at his supervisor's *faux pas*. The amused reaction startled J. D. That was the first sound of any kind at all he had heard come out of Conchino's mouth since he had begun working at T-DUB and, hopefully, it wouldn't be the last.

J. D. placed the next application on the paper holder and continued to work.

8.

The next morning, J. D. personally struggled to *not* make his lunch, a routine he enjoyed doing every morning before work. He knew he was going to lunch with his supervisor, Brent, that day. But for some reason, he felt uneasy about going with him, mainly because he had witnessed him drink beer while lunching. Also, Conchino had snickered at the slight mention of beer the day before. The thought of the consumption of alcohol during a work lunch gnawed at J. D.'s soul. He didn't know why, for certain—it just did. He felt bad for judging his supervisor, too, so he tried not to do that. J. D. hated the thought of anybody judging him for any reason. But the more he thought about the beer drinking, the more the pangs of guilt wore him down. Just thinking about it exhausted him. So, rather than ruin his morning thinking too much about it, he decided to put on his helmet and enjoy his bike ride to work.

The commute to work was calmer than normal. The cacophony of car horns and brake squeals and screaming commuters was almost nonexistent and the roadway clear of aggressive drivers. It made for a peaceful bike ride for J. D., allowing him to gander at the neighborhood homes and apartment buildings of his neighborhood: Hyde Park. He became so enthralled with the old homes and buildings—most he had never noticed before because of the horrible traffic— that he came within inches of sideswiping the one car that drove a tad too close to him. The driver honked the horn and then swerved away, avoiding a collision. J. D. stopped as fast as he could and watched the car retreat, a woman who looked remarkably like his coworker Rita in the backseat peering out the back window.

Dang it! he thought. *I almost got smooshed.* That would have ruined his morning, for sure.

When he finally got to work and entered Unit 3—setting his helmet and lunch box on his desk—Rita confirmed her worst fear.

"We almost killed you on the way to work!" she said. "Forgive us! Conchino swears he did his best to avoid hitting you."

"It *was* you," J. D. said, sitting in his chair and wiping his brow. "It's all good. I forgive you."

He looked at Conchino, who was sitting at his desk, fumbling with a carburetor or alternator or something (J. D. didn't know for sure). When Conchino realized he was being watched, he set the car engine contraption on his desk, put his hands together as in prayer, and bowed his head. J. D. mimicked the gesture in return.

"You should join our carpool. We have a spare seat in Conchino's car," Rita said, setting a plate of cookies on the printer table.

"Carpool?" J. D. said.

"Yes, he gives Deborah and me lifts most days. We carpool to save money. Cookie?" she said, offering one to J. D. He gladly accepted it.

"It's better than getting killed on a bicycle," Deborah said.

"Maybe," J. D. said, placing his helmet and lunch box in his desk, careful not to crush the ants in the drawer. "I really like riding my bike."

Soon after, he began working, as did all the others. Their choir of keyboards clicked and sang.

Before they knew it—as it happened some mornings as the time flew by from busy work—Ken the paper collector arrived, pushing his squeaky cart into Unit 3 to collect the reams of paper containing all the personal information of dozens of unemployment applicants from across the great State of Texas. As Ken tore the serrated edges of the reams of paper from their printers, the Unit 3 team ceased typing and prepared for lunch.

Brent noticed their preparations (having sat in a hypnotized state) and then remarked to J. D., "Ready to go to lunch?"

"Yes, I think so."

"Meet me outside. I have something to do real quick."

"OK."

Brent jumped up to hold the door open for Ken the paper collector, then followed him quickly out the door. Conchino ate the last of the cookies while Rita and Deborah gathered their things. It appeared they were going on a picnic, their lunches contained in two large wicker baskets.

"Can I accompany you ladies outside?" J. D. said to them.

"Of course," Deborah said. "You can sit with us while you wait for Mr. Baker."

"He likes to be called Brent," J. D. said.

"I know," she said, slyly.

Outside the building on the great lawn behind the Texas Department of Unemployment and Benefits—or T-DUB as Brent claimed *everyone* called it—Rita and Deborah made their way to the Vietnam Veterans Memorial, a tranquil place with surrounding shade trees and benches to sit on, as well as the site where J. D. discovered Brent on his back in the grass the afternoon of his first day at work. As time went on, J. D. believed less that epilepsy was the cause of Brent's supine state, and pondered if beer was the culprit, although he didn't know for sure and didn't know Brent well enough to doubt him for certain. Rita and Deborah settled on a shaded bench and sat down. J. D. stood next to them, admiring their great picnic lunch. They opened their baskets to reveal plenty of food.

"Those are nice lunches," he said. "I love bringing my lunch to work, too."

"Then why are you going to lunch with Mr. Baker?" Rita said, unwrapping foil from a smoked turkey leg.

"I guess 'cause he asked me."

"You can say no, you know," Deborah said, uncovering a tub of potato salad. "No one is forcing you to eat with the boss."

"I know. I don't mind sometimes," he said, licking his lips. Their lunch looked appetizing. "Do you ever eat lunch with Brent?"

"Lord no!" Rita said, biting the turkey leg and then continuing with food in her mouth. "We like peaceful lunches. That's why we bring our own lunch and sit outside, here in the shade. Isn't it wonderful?"

J. D. gazed around the great lawn. Besides a few pedestrians and squirrels, they were the only ones out on the lawn. It was peaceful and quiet. J. D. wondered what Rita was eluding to by contrasting their peaceful lunch to his suggestion she eat with their boss but didn't pursue the topic further.

"It is wonderful out here."

"Right?" Deborah said, chewing potato salad. "Do you have any questions about work so far?"

J. D. pondered her question for a moment, but the only thing he could think of to ask was about his other quiet coworker.

"Is Conchino one of those people that doesn't talk?"

"Like a *mute*?!" Rita said, cackling. She thought that was the funniest thing she had heard all day. "Oh, that boy talks, all right. Just not out loud very often. Do you like to sing in front of other people?"

"Not really," he said.

"Well, Conchino prefers not talking in front of most people. Don't ask me why."

"He prefers to text message," Deborah said. "He sends us little messages about rides or work or whatever. All the time."

An electronic sound dinged from inside Deborah's basket. She reached in and pulled out a cell phone, flipping it open. She read something on the screen, chuckled, then showed J. D.

"See? He messaged me asking the time to leave work today. I'll probably get a dozen more messages from him before the day is over."

"Me too," Rita said.

"Really? What else does he message about?" J. D. said.

Deborah pondered his question and then said, "Advice about girls."

"*Girls*?" he said.

"And he asks me about recipes," Rita said.

"*Recipes*?!" he said, then noticed Brent coming out of T-DUB and jogging across the great lawn toward them. J. D. waved at him to come over, which he soon did.

"Good afternoon, ladies," Brent said to them. "Enjoying your lunch?"

"Yes, sir," Rita said. "Immensely."

Brent turned to J. D. and then said, "Ready?"

"See you after lunch," J. D. said to Rita and Deborah.

"Be good," Deborah said to J. D.

"I will."

J. D. followed Brent across the lawn and the two old friends watched them disappear around the building.

"Looks like trouble," Deborah said.

"Mmm-hmm," Rita said, taking another bite from the turkey leg.

9.

As the sun set, Deborah stood in her front yard—a water hose in one hand and a glass of cheap red wine in the other hand—watering her grass. It was one of her greatest pleasures in life: taking care of her lawn. Ever since she moved into the small, two-bedroom, two-bath home thirty-three years ago— the property boundary barely extended a few feet past the exterior of the house—watering the lawn while drinking wine was something she did most evenings after washing the dinner dishes. She enjoyed the peace and quiet of standing in the wet grass; she also watched the neighbors come home from work and mill about in their yards, too, just like she did.

Her son, Ricky, was a newborn baby when she bought the home (the down payment reluctantly supplied by her parents). Before Ricky could stand up on his own, she would set him in a baby hammock on the driveway so he could watch her water the grass. He loved that and would coo and giggle, especially when she lightly sprayed him with cold water. As the years passed and Ricky grew, he spent less and less time in the front yard with his mother, although he never left their home. He still lived there as an adult, occupying the same room he did when she first set up his crib in there, soon after she divorced his father. His room didn't look much different from when he was in high school. His walls were decorated with the ephemera of his senior year: posters of rock bands and NBA basketball players, photos of various female classmates long since gone, dusty sports medals and ribbons, handwritten notes of self-motivational quotes, and the like. It was as if these youthful remnants calcified onto the drywall, becoming permanent fixtures of his bedroom. And just like when he was a teenager, he rarely picked up after himself or cleaned his room. Deborah wasn't going to clean the pig sty for him, either. She had too much on her plate anyway as a single mother.

So rather than do extra chores in the house—like washing the dirty laundry or unclogging her toilet or caulking the back-patio sliding door—she poured herself a large glass of wine instead and wandered out to the front lawn, watering the grass with her hose and dousing her soul with the red wine as the setting sun bathed her property in gauzy shades of pink, orange, and yellow, enveloping her baby-blue 1983 Bronco II until it almost seemed to turn lavender in color. She sneered at her pastel jalopy. Just the sight of it made her angrier than a trapped, scared raccoon.

Piece of shit! she thought. *Why can't I catch a break?!*

The Bronco's tires were deflated from sitting in place for over four months and the windshield was splatter-painted with bird shit. It needed a new alternator and a new battery to bring it back to life but, since she still owed $947 for the title loan she received the week before it died, the alternator and battery were out of the question. Her and Ricky still had to eat and, besides, Conchino graciously gave her rides to and from work. She enjoyed riding to work with Conchino and Rita. She only had to contribute what she could for gas, which wasn't very much.

Oh well. It'll get fixed one of these days, she thought while watering a brown patch at the corner of her yard.

As darkness consumed her neighborhood street, the wooden garage door to her house screeched as it ascended the rusty rails, pulled by a tired, cobweb-covered garage door opener. Ricky's shiny sports car roared to life, then slowly backed out of the garage, stopping next to Deborah's jalopy. Just the sight of Ricky's operational vehicle made her madder than hell.

Where does he get the money for that?! she thought.

She wasn't aware that her son was leaving for the evening so she dropped the hose in the grass, tiptoed to his sports car, and rapped her knuckles on the passenger-side window. The power window slid down inside the door. Deborah leaned closer to the car as its engine gurgled.

"Where you going?" she barked.

"Out!" he said, pulling the visor down and then fixing his hair.

"When will you be home?" she said.

"I don't know," he said, putting the car in reverse and backing out of the driveway.

Deborah stepped back into the grass, picked up her hose, and watched Ricky drive away, leaving a skid mark as he floored the gas pedal.

That son of a—, she thought, stopping short of saying it because it hurt too much to curse at her son like that. She loved him dearly even though he caused her so much pain and stress. Without cursing, she continued to chide him. *He's just like his father! That no good—*

Once the roar of Rick's sports car engine dissipated into the night air, Deborah heard footsteps behind her. She turned to see one of her neighbors standing on the sidewalk. His name was Steve and he was a man close to Ricky's age: mid-thirties. Steve, his wife, and two young children lived a couple of houses down from Deborah and Ricky. Steve was somewhat successful with a full-time job doing something Deborah didn't understand, something with computer programming (C Sharp or C+ Flat or something). Steve's wife, Melissa, was a real estate agent. Their children were as cute as buttons. Steve stood on the sidewalk with his hands on his sides, his frame slender and fit as a responsible husband's should be, his pitch black hair still sculpted as it was when he first left for work that morning.

"You all right, Deborah?" he said. He sounded concerned and that pleased her.

"Yeah, doing great! How about you?"

"Oh, fine. Just fine. The kids are fine. The wife's fine. We're all good."

"Good, good," she said, sprinkling the grass some more, sipping her wine. She was used to its vinegary aftertaste, which she believed gave the wine character. "Your kids are getting sooo big."

"Yes, YES! They are getting big. Time flies, right?"

"Yes, it does," she said, chuckling, images from over the past thirty years flipping through her mind, her son growing from a cute toddler to an even cuter teenager. She turned to face him, watering the grass at her feet.

"Well, I just wanted to check on you," he said.

She knew what Steve was insinuating even though he didn't actually say it, about that time a few nights before when she and Ricky had a shouting match in the front yard. Ricky cursed her and she cursed him. It even appeared to Steve from the vantage point of his driveway that Ricky might slug her, although in reality Deborah knew that Ricky would *never* do that. It was an ugly scene and Deborah was mortified. But what could she do? She knew Ricky was rebelling like a teenager, even though he was technically an adult (at least in age but not mentality). The thought that Ricky didn't need her anymore tore a fissure through her heart, one almost too wide to mend.

"Thanks, Steve. You're a good neighbor," she said.

"If you ever need anything, don't be afraid to ask. See ya later," he said, then walked back to his house.

Deborah sighed and then turned off the water, wrapped the hose into a tight coil, hung it on the side of the house, and went inside to drink more wine by herself, closing the garage door behind her.

Why can't Ricky be more like Steve? she thought.

On the couch, she sprawled out with the bottle of red wine in one hand and her wine glass in the other. She was too tired to turn on the TV so she just laid there on her back, staring at the ceiling. Her troubles consumed her, and as she debated about which piece of lawn equipment to pawn to cover the car title loan payment due in a few days, she soon fell asleep. The bottle of red wine fell on the carpet and stained it. The wine glass rested on her lap.

After a few hours of very deep, inebriated sleep, her phone rang, scaring her. She quickly picked up the receiver to answer the call.

"Hello?!" she said.

The line crackled for a few seconds, then her son answered. "Ma, it's Rick."

"Ricky?! Are you all right, dear? It's late."

"Ma, I only got one phone call so... Can you come bail me out of jail?"

"*What?!*" she said, resting her face in her free hand.

"I don't have time to explain. Just, can you come get me out?"

"Sure, dear," she said.

The line went dead. She sat on the couch for a few tense minutes, debating if she should try to bounce a check to get him out of jail or show the bail clerk some cleavage. She decided she had a little bit of dignity left and opted for the bounced check.

As she washed her faced and then brushed her hair, she thought, *Ricky* still *needs me.*

She grabbed her purse and worthless checkbook before locking up the house, then walked over to her neighbor Steve's house in the dark to kindly ask him for a ride downtown to the police station.

10.

When the members of Unit 3 settled into their morning routines, they all discovered that their workload was larger than usual. The piles of unemployment applications on their desks were thicker than any of them expected and it stressed them all out. The banter between Rita and Deborah was less jolly, which in turn radiated a sense of urgency and uneasiness to the other three in the office. Even Brent felt the stress of the unexpected situation and offered to enter applications into TAPES to assist his team.

"It's been a while since I entered apps into TAPES!" he said, shoving stacks of paper around his desk, looking for his paper holder to prop up his work. Once he found it, he placed his stack of applications on the paper holder and began entering data, just like the rest of his team. "I hope I can remember how to do it."

"Like riding a bike," Rita said, smirking as she typed.

Deborah typed furiously as well, peeking occasionally over at J. D., like a mother watching her nervous child ascend the ladder of a searing hot slide on a treacherous playscape.

"You doing OK, J. D.?" she said.

"Yes, ma'am. Thanks to your excellent training!"

His compliment warmed her heart, especially after what had happened to her son, Ricky, the night before. It had been a late night, one that she would love to forget. Her son failed to thank her after bailing him out, an unsettling lack of decorum she was still very upset about. She didn't even make her son breakfast that morning, she was *that* mad. *If only Ricky could be more like J. D.,* she thought, then blushed. *Such a nice young man. And hardworking!*

Even Conchino's stoicism was more cryptic than usual, his hulking frame hunched over his empty desktop, his occasional smirks and grimaces replaced with consternation and stress. That hectic morning, there was no time for tinkering with car parts and components or even text messaging Rita or Deborah. It made for a somber morning.

But before too long, Rita remembered that she had brought a treat for her coworkers and hoped that telling them so would lift their spirits.

"I forgot to say," she said, pulling a wad of aluminum foil from her purse, unwrapping it to reveal a dozen oatmeal and raisin cookies. She set the cookies at the end of her desk. "I made extra for everybody. My gran'kids don't get to eat all the cookies!" she said, snickering.

"Yes!" Brent said, the first to her desk for a cookie. His presence was an invitation to the rest to pause their heavy workload and appreciate Rita's kind gesture. Before long, the entirety of Unit 3 was standing around Rita's desk, enjoying her homemade cookies.

"I wish there was something more I could do to bring joy to all of us besides cookin'," she said. Seeing smiles on her coworkers' faces did bring her immense joy.

"Cookies are all I need," Brent said, devouring his snack.

"Me too," J. D. said.

"What more would you like to do?" Deborah said, curious.

Immediately, Rita pointed to the other side of the office and said, "I want us to win that $10,000! All we gots to do is come up with the winning suggestion." She grabbed a cookie from the foil and chewed on it. "If cookies could win, then I'd already be a winner."

Conchino nodded while eating his cookie, confirming Rita's statement. He loved her cooking and didn't miss an opportunity to partake in the treats she brought to the office.

"Good luck coming up with a winner," Brent said, conspicuously reaching in the foil for another cookie. "I've never heard of anybody winning that prize."

"Well, I have," Rita said, and just the mention of knowing about a winner pricked the ears of all her coworkers. "I knew someone at the Department of Mental Health who had a coworker that submitted a winning suggestion. She won the $10,000! And you know what she did? She bought herself a *Cadillac*. Can you believe it?!"

The idea of buying a car sounded pretty nice to Deborah, who just earlier that morning was glaring at the useless jalopy in her driveway while waiting for Conchino to give her a ride to work. She knew that the $2,000 she'd receive—if one of her coworkers won the prize—could help her pay off her title loan, then she could use the rest for a down payment for a new car, at least one that was new to her. She could even come out ahead in the deal if she could sell the clunker to someone else, maybe someone who liked working on beat-up cars. She knew that Unit 3 had a sincere pact to share the prize but also felt—deep down inside—that the likelihood of any of them winning it was close to zilch. But that didn't stop her from feeling excited, nonetheless. It was very exciting to talk about what-ifs that involved buying herself nicer things.

"What would you buy if we won that prize, Rita?" Deborah said.

A serene smile slid across her face as she contemplated the fortune of $2,000 dropping in her lap. "There's so much I'd do," she said. "Sooo much."

"I'd buy a new amp for my guitar!" Brent blurted. He had been using a small amp he had bought cheap at a pawn shop, but it was underpowered and amateurish compared to the gear his bandmates had. It made him self-conscious and feel he wasn't good enough to be in the band, let alone the front man. A vintage tube amp would fix that dilemma, he suggested.

While Brent went on and on about tube amps, Conchino made his way to his desk, quietly sat down, then picked up his cell phone. He pecked a sentence into his messaging app, then sent it to Deborah. He leaned back in his chair and fell into a trance. Deborah's phone dinged a notification and the group went silent. She pulled her phone from her purse and read the message, one that everyone assumed was from Conchino since he never spoke out loud. She read his message to the group.

"I'd buy a performance chip and air intake system for my car," she said. The group oohed and aahed, confirming their knowledge about his passion for cars and street racing. "Makes sense." She put her phone back in her purse.

Rita noticed that no one had asked J. D. what he would buy so she asked him, "What about you? What would you buy yourself?"

J. D. had been contemplating this question since the group began their fantasy session. The idea of $2,000 dropping in his lap seemed unfathomable, which made it even harder to daydream about what he would do with that amount of money. He stammered.

"Oh, I don't know," he said, putting his hands in his pockets, wanting nothing more than to deflect the attention from his coworkers, and maybe eat another cookie.

"You don't have *any* idea?" Brent said, a little shocked. "I could think of a dozen things off the top of my head."

"Then I guess I'd give the $2,000 to you."

This shocked Brent even more, rendering him speechless. Rita laughed a deep belly laugh.

"You could do a lot better than giving your money to Mr. Baker with all the poor kids in this world!"

"Thanks, Rita," Brent said sarcastically, his pride crushed.

"I'm just saying. But what about this?" she said, pausing to add emphasis to her new question. Her coworkers were intrigued. "What if we won that *lottery* prize? What if we won the *jackpot*? What would you do then?!"

The group collectively gasped. Even Conchino vocally acknowledged just how exciting that prospect would be. How could they all not be excited about that idea? It was potentially a lot of money, more than any of them would ever have, even to the point of being ludicrous. Rita was beside herself.

"I mean, sometimes that jackpot gets to $25 million, $26 million. Can you imagine it?" she said. Certainly, she could imagine it. Joyous thoughts of grand prize excursions and purchases danced through her head. "I'd buy an apartment building and put all my children and gran' babies in it. I'd name it Rita's Retreat! Or somethin' like that."

"Your family would love that!" Deborah said.

"What would you do?" Rita replied, smiling. "I know you would buy yourself a new car, wouldn't you?"

"Yes, I would. And probably pay off my mortgage and then put the rest away."

"What about your son?" Rita said.

"What about *him*?!" Deborah said, perturbed. "He already has a new car and he's grown. He needs to take care of himself."

Rita laughed, then turned to Brent and said, "What about you?"

Brent pondered her question while walking back to his desk. He sat in his chair and threw his legs on his desk, leaning back to narrate his daydream.

"You know, I know exactly what I'd do. I'd buy some old BBQ joint, build a big stage, install a killer sound system, and my band would be the house band. We'd play every Friday night! I can just see it now," he said, his face all aglow. It was clear to the others that he had thought about this before. He was awestruck within his daydream.

"Sounds good," Rita said, then turned to Conchino. "What about you?"

Conchino picked up his phone and pecked a reply for Rita. Once she was notified, she picked up her phone and read it for the group.

"He says, 'I would pay for my grandfather to come to the U.S. from Japan so he could live with my parents. He's old and is having a hard time taking care of himself.'"

"Ah, jeez," Deborah gushed. "I wish you were *my* son."

Everyone in Unit 3 laughed at Deborah's comment and misfortune of having an insensitive son. Conchino blushed.

The only one left not to tell their lottery jackpot fantasy was J. D. He quietly sat at his desk listening to the others while eating another cookie. Rita noticed his coy reticence and wasn't going to let him off the hook from their game.

"What about you, J. D.? What will you do if we win the jackpot?"

J. D. sat silently for a minute, the others watching him. It seemed he was in a trance, thinking about what he'd do, pulling his cookie apart, looking at the crumbs like a fortune teller examines tea leaves. Then he knew what to say.

"My parents have a family business in Brady. I guess I would help them. They've been struggling and want me to go home. But I like it here in Austin. I like living here and working here with all of you. But I know money would help them out so I guess that's what I'd do. Help my parents."

The group acknowledged his wish and he felt good getting that off his chest, except he had one more thing to share.

"And I'd buy all the pecan snacks in Brady. In the world, even. Pecan rolls for all!"

Everyone laughed. It was a funny comment but one that also rang true to J. D. and who he was as a person. Everyone in Unit 3 wanted to help their families or friends and it warmed J. D.'s heart knowing that he worked with such kind and thoughtful people, even though he knew that they weren't going to win the lottery. *No one wins the lottery,* he thought. *Especially not me. I'm the unluckiest person I know.*

After the laughing stopped and the cookies were all gone, Brent sat up and declared, "All right. Break time is over. Back to work. We have a lot of apps to get in TAPES."

A collective groan bellowed from the group but they complied. Soon, the orchestra of keyboards were clickity-clacking their song, serenading the dejected in the great State of Texas with hopes and dreams of a better future.

11.

As the workdays went on, Brent decided that he really liked J. D., but not for the same reasons the others in Unit 3 liked him. Deborah and Rita discovered J. D. to be a hard worker and appreciated that he deferred to them for their knowledge and experience with TAPES as well as departmental procedures. He was also very generous, not only with his time but with the pecan snacks his family from Brady, Texas, frequently shipped to him, often placing them on the printing table alongside the homemade treats Rita brought from home. Everyone in Unit 3 soon developed cravings for the sumptuous pecan rolls, just like J. D. had since he was a little boy. Deborah and Rita assumed Conchino liked J. D. as well, since he ceased driving too close to him on his bicycle as they passed him in Conchino's car on the way to work every morning, a level of kindness he didn't extend to other commuting bicycle riders that clogged the city streets. As for Brent, he discovered he liked J. D. not for his generosity or his kindness or his assiduousness—none of these traits appealed to him that much. What appealed to him about J. D. was his unerring willingness to go along with whatever whim Brent desired, particularly if it meant avoiding work. In J. D., Brent found a willing accomplice to his secret agenda: having fun.

At every opportunity, Brent avoided work and sought amusing diversions like roaming the halls of T-DUB, enjoying long lunches that included drinking beer or whiskey, or smoking cigarettes wherever he could find a hiding place in or around the building. Of course, he told the others in Unit 3 that he had important matters to attend to. As their supervisor, they had no reason to doubt him. Whenever he asked J. D. to accompany him, J. D. never declined. And whenever J. D. witnessed Brent's willingness to pursue diversion, he never complained. Brent couldn't tell if J. D. really enjoyed tagging along with him or not but, without fail, whenever he asked J. D. to accompany him, there he was—along for the ride.

So, when Brent decided out of the blue one morning that he wanted a wingman to tag along while he ducked out of Unit 3 and ditched work, he knew J. D. wouldn't refuse. He would have bet money on it, if he was a betting man (which he was).

"J. D.?" he said while pretending to fill out paperwork. He was diligently writing on sheets of paper, but what the others couldn't see was that he was drawing doodles of cartoon ducks, not writing anything of importance.

"Yes?" J. D. said. He was busy entering a pile of unemployment applications, as he was supposed to do.

"Want a tour of Validations? I need to talk to one of the managers. I can show you around."

J. D. was puzzled. He had already seen Validations and didn't want to trouble his boss with a second, unnecessary visit. He preferred completing his work over a tour of another department, although he would go if Brent insisted.

"Well, we *already* went to Validations a while back. Are you sure you want me to go with you again?"

"I'm sure," Brent said. "I can show you the mailroom, too."

"Well... OK."

J. D. wrapped up entering the application he was working on and then saved and printed it. Deborah noticed it was an hour before lunch and protested.

"Mr. Baker? We are all behind and the apps are piling up. Maybe J. D. should stay and help us get through them."

"No worries, Deborah. I'll help enter apps when we get back," Brent said. "OK?"

This annoyed Deborah because she was skeptical of his offer to help them. Brent could see her face scrunch with displeasure but he commanded J. D. to follow him anyway.

"Let's go, J. D.!" he said, and the two quickly left the office.

Conchino turned to Deborah and Rita, quietly shaking his head. His two coworkers agreed with him.

"I smell trouble," Deborah said.

"Mmm-hmm," Rita agreed. "That's some stinky shit right there."

Out in the hall, Brent speed-walked like he was on an important mission. J. D. didn't realize quite yet that this was a simple ruse. He really thought Brent wanted to take him on a tour of Validations. He didn't even second-guess it.

"Is something the matter?" J. D. called out, trying to catch up to Brent, who was a few paces ahead of him. He didn't slow down when he heard J. D.

"Keep up, my man!" he said.

As they approached the door that J. D. remembered was the entrance to the Validations Department, Brent pointed at the door and then said, "And there's Validations!"

But he kept on walking past the door. J. D. peered at the door for Validations with confusion. *Where is he going?* he thought. *He just passed the door!*

At the end of the hallway was a door labeled "Stairs" and Brent crashed through the door, shoulder first. J. D. followed him down three flights of stairs, Brent skipping steps and sliding down handrails. When they reached the bottom of the staircase, they burst through a door that led them into the underground parking garage. Brent didn't relent his pace, pulling a pack of cigarettes from one of his pant pockets. With a Zippo lighter from his other pocket, he lit his smoke as they careened through the garage.

"Where are we *going*?" J. D. said.

"Somewhere to take a break," Brent said, hurtling to a picnic table with an ashtray next to it in a corner of the underground garage. Next to the table was a metal bicycle rack, the very one where J. D. parked and locked his own bicycle every morning. It pleased him to see it at this time of day.

"That's my bike!" J. D. said, pointing to it.

"That's nice, kid," Brent said, sitting on the table top with his feet on one of the table benches. "I don't know how you ride your bike to work without getting killed." Smoke from the cigarette poured out of his nostrils like a dragon releasing steam from its sinus cavity.

"I'm a careful bicycle rider," J. D. said. "It's fun."

"What other things do you do for fun?" Brent said, sucking on his cigarette.

"Oh, I don't know. Listen to the singer at the café near my house."

"You go see live music?"

"Oh no!" J. D. said, snickering. "I can hear her sing in my room when I open the window."

Brent sucked on his cigarette some more, looking at J. D. with an inquisitive eye. "That's a little weird, J. D."

"I know but I like it. What about you? What do you like to do for fun?"

Brent absorbed his question and then finished his cigarette. He flicked the extinguished cigarette butt into the metal ashtray next to the table and said, "I try to have fun whenever I can. I even try to have fun at work. Life is too short to be working all the time. Don't you think?"

"Life is short," J. D. said. He briefly remembered being at the funeral of a high school classmate who had died while riding a bucking bronco at the county fair. He remembered he thought the exact same thing back then. *Life is short!* J. D.'s eyes glazed over as he remembered his poor classmate who died too young.

"I know the others in Unit 3 probably tell you that I skip out all the time but... that's only partly true."

This startled J. D. out of his trance. He blinked and said, "Well, they've never said that to me."

"I'm sure they think it even though they don't tell you. I try to be a good boss. I'm always approving their leave requests and sick days and whatever—without question. I just wish it was more fun. I can't help it if this place can be super *boring*."

"I like it here," J. D. said. "I'm glad to work here."

"I'm glad you work here too, buddy. Want to grab some lunch?"

J. D. felt guilty for not returning to Unit 3 to complete his workload. He knew Deborah would still be mad, or at least displeased. He didn't like to annoy her; he preferred pleasing her. It made for a nicer work environment when his coworkers were happy.

"Shouldn't we get back to the office so I can finish my work?"

A sly smile slid across Brent's face, then he said, "Nah. I'll help you when we get back. Come on!" he insisted. "There's a great beer garden a couple blocks down. Are you in?"

Since his boss insisted, J. D. just simply couldn't refuse.

"OK," he said.

"Great! Come on."

J. D. followed Brent out of the underground garage and down the street, huffing the two blocks in the sun to Schertz Beer Garten, a food and beer hall that was established in the 1860s and was renowned as the oldest operating business in Texas. It could be a raucous place at times, depending on the disposition of the bartenders and the generosity of their pouring hands.

Inside, J. D. quickly discovered a large dining area filled with rows of picnic-style tables covered with red and white gingham tablecloths, all the tables packed with patrons. The ceiling was high like the interior of a barn with speakers mounted up in the rafters, perched like barn owls. Country music played while the patrons drank beer and devoured sausages or tacos: the preferred alcoholic accompaniments. Brent was already at the bar—nestled in a nook at the right of the dining room—ordering beer and food for the two of them. He waved at J. D. to find a place to sit, which he did at the end of one of the rows, a spot barely large enough for the two coworkers. He sat on one side of the table, sliding a napkin holder across to the other side as if reserving the place for his supervisor. Next to J. D. on the bench sat a burly man—dense and round like a granite boulder and almost as old—who was enjoying his lunch with a massive stein of beer while joking with his equally large friend sitting across from him. His sharp elbow jabbed J. D. a couple of times, although not maliciously. He apologized as soon as he realized J. D. was there.

"My apologies," the burly man said, his fermented breath hot and rancid. "Didn't see ya."

"No worries," J. D. said, rubbing his assaulted bicep. "Sorry to bother you."

"You didn't bother me. Like I said, didn't know you were there."

"OK," J. D. said. He certainly didn't want to antagonize the giant, being that he must have been three or four times his size and two hundred pounds heavier. J. D. favored nonconfrontational ways whenever possible. Once, in high school, he was pounded by a senior football player, simply because he looked in his general direction. J. D.'s face was puffy and bruised for weeks. He didn't want something like that to happen to him again.

Unbeknownst to J. D., Brent observed the minor confrontation from the bar while chugging a beer and waiting for the bartender to ring up the rest of his lunch order. From that distance—fifty or sixty feet away—their conversation seemed much more tense and confrontational than it actually was, the curdled face of the burly man tweaking Brent's disposition. He worried that the giant was causing trouble, as some of the patrons were known to do if drunk, and he made his way to the table as soon as he could with two mugs of beer and a small sign with their order number for tacos on it.

"You doing OK?" Brent said, sliding a beer to J. D. and then sitting down. J. D. slurped the foam like a child enjoying a frothy ice cream float. Brent gave the burly man the stink eye, which didn't help matters.

"Yeah, I'm OK," J. D. chirped. "No problems."

This tweet caught the ear of the burly man, who turned to look at J. D. and then at Brent, who seemed to appear out of thin air. Brent's stinky stare irritated the burly man, who was simply trying to enjoy the company of his friend.

"He said he was OK, ya turkey!" the burly man barked. "Listen to your friend or else."

This irked Brent. He wasn't quite sure why this giant was causing problems, but the twenty-two ounces of beer he chugged a couple of minutes before gave him the confidence and gumption to find out.

"Or else *what*?!" Brent said, peering at the burly man.

Irritated to the point of no return, like a lion pestered relentlessly by a cub, he decided a display of dominance was best. The burly man stood up—towering over Brent and J. D. at almost seven feet in height—and clenched his fists. It was a sign to J. D. that lunch was most likely ruined.

"Why don't you come closer and I'll show you?!" the giant proclaimed.

And that was the last coherent sentence J. D. remembered anyone saying. The rest of his memory of that lunch was a vision of blurred fists and angry faces and bodies dropping on the ground. His memory had a distinct smell of stale beer and body odor and fried foods. Yelling and the sounds of broken glass and moving furniture were the soundtrack. He somehow ended up on the ground under the table, watching a frenzy of legs dance a bizarre jitterbug behind a curtain of red and white gingham. He certainly hadn't foreseen his day turning out like that. In fact, that morning he felt his day would go smoothly and without distraction. But, as he later learned, spending time with Brent meant knowing that there was a level of uncertainty and a possibility for chaos that came along with his company, and this lunch at Schertz Beer Garten was the genesis of that precious nugget of knowledge.

Deborah is going to be really mad..., he thought as he sat under the table, his knees held tightly to his chest, *...if we don't get back soon and enter apps into TAPES.*

12.

Conchino parked in front of Rita's house, hopped out of his car, and ran around to open the door for her. As he extended his hand to help her, she placed a few dollars in his hand.

"For gas," she said, smiling.

Conchino shook his head and refused her money. As she stood on the sidewalk—clenching the bills in her hand and looking around to see if any of her grandkids were home yet—he leaned into the car to retrieve her lunch bag, which she left on the back seat. She reached up and patted his shoulder when he gave it to her, his tall frame hulking over her.

"If you won't take my money for gas, then I'll put it in the lottery pool," she said, looking up to him. "See you in the morning."

She turned around and shuffled to her house, through the metal gate and up the steps to her front porch. Conchino jumped back in his car and sped off. With his car empty of passengers, he was free to drive the way he preferred—fast and aggressively.

He pushed and pulled on the gear shifter as if trying to snap it from the console, stomping the clutch pedal when ready to shift gears. He loved to drive his car more than anything and maneuvered fiercely north on the interstate highway. When the power of the car's engine vibrated through the floor into his feet, he felt free. He watched the other commuters on the highway in his rearview mirror fade away as he listened to the original gangsta rapper, Ice-T, boom from the speakers. By the time he arrived home and parked in the driveway, the evening setting sun bathed the house he shared with his parents in warm pastels. He opened the garage door with a remote clipped to his sun visor.

Inside the garage, the walls were lined with tool chests (some red and some black), wooden chests of drawers (all from the secondhand store just outside the neighborhood), and a refrigerator that had seen better days (its scaly exterior infected with rust and mold). Conchino peeled his work shirt off his back as he stepped in the garage, replacing it with a black T-shirt he had left in there the night before. The front of the T-shirt said "HATE" and the back said "LOVE." He grabbed a can of Mexican beer from the fridge and sipped it while turning on a lamp that illuminated his evening's task: a new alternator and cables laying on the workbench like a beached squid. He pressed play on a boom box, also on the workbench, playing the original song that Ice-T sampled: "Pusherman" by Curtis Mayfield.

Soon his tiny, Japanese mother entered the garage just as he had expected, with a small bowl in one hand and a small box wrapped in brown shipping paper in the other hand. She offered the bowl to her son, setting the box on the worktable. Even though he was a full-grown man, she still loved to cater to him.

"Hungry?" she said.

Conchino nodded, sucking one of the steamed dumplings into his mouth. The slurping noise that escaped from his lips pleased his mother. He raised the box closer to his face so he could read the label.

"It's from your grandfather," she sighed. "He's not doing so well."

Conchino examined the shipping label and stickers on the box, emblazoned with both Japanese and English letters, then set it on the workbench.

"We'll get him here one day to live with us," she said, patting her son's back. He grunted. "Don't say anything. I know how much it hurts you to know he's suffering. But he likes sending you these mementos. Enjoy them!"

She beamed a smile for her son and then left him alone in the garage: his sanctuary. Outside in the front yard, lightning bugs began floating above the grass, their rear ends illuminating their night dance. Crickets continued playing the night song where the cicadas left off, chirping and creaking.

Sitting on a stool at his workbench, Conchino stared at the small box, pondering if he should open it or save it for another time. He decided to open it and sliced it apart with a razor blade. Inside the box were things he immediately loved— precious, vintage Honda accessories from the 1960s and '70s: a chrome Honda emblem, a gear shifter knob, seat belt buckles, and more. *Cool,* he thought. *Maybe I can make them work.* His Honda was newer than the models these accessories were originally intended for, but that wouldn't stop him from at least trying to fit them in his car somewhere. He was too sentimental to *not* try. He envied that his grandfather was a retired autoworker from a Honda auto factory in Japan, although his working conditions were nothing to be envious of. Still, there was a romantic lilt in the way he used to describe the factory in letters to Conchino when he was a small boy. He made the factory sound like a place that Willy Wonka would have created.

Not too long after his mother disappeared into the house, his father appeared in the garage. Squat and round and hairy like an armadillo, his dad shared his son's passion for automobiles, although his love for cars skewed toward older American makes and models. His father was Latino to his core and always took the opportunity to remind his son of that, even at Conchino's expense.

"*Que paso*, homes?" he said, his accent of Spanish words morphing into a Cheech and Chong parody. Some of

Conchino's generation thought that type of accent offensive; others of his father's generation thought it endearing. Conchino's feelings about it sat on the fence. That's just the way his father was: silly. "When are going to sell your rice burner and buy *Americano*?"

Conchino was offended now, not because of the silly accent, but because of the content of the question. He preferred Japanese cars and knew his father was aware of this fact. He glared at his father.

"Don't get your *calzones* in a wad, homie," his father said, slapping him on the back. "I'm only kidding."

His dad opened the fridge and grabbed a *cerveza*. He ripped open the beer and took a swig, then said, "Your mother is worried about your grandfather. If we move him to the States, you know we'll have to put him up in *here*." He belched a hearty laugh.

He loved to prod his son with outlandish provocations, particularly when it came to cars or the garage: his favorite place. Conchino peered at his dad, daggers shooting from his eyes. His father laughed some more and then chugged his beer.

"I'm only kidding, *Conchino*. Just jokes, *mijito*. Sheesh."

Although his father was not the creator of his nickname—Conchino—he was the approver of the moniker. Conchino's elementary school classmates were the originators of the ugly nickname once they found out his mother was Japanese. Though it was intended as a malicious double-entendre, his father laughed when he heard the other kids call him that on the playground. Never one to shy away from humor—well-intended or not—his father endorsed the childish name by repeating it on the drive home, ad nauseam.

"*America's Funniest Home Videos* is about to start. Gonna come inside and watch with us?" his father said. Conchino nodded. "Great! Starts in five."

His dad disappeared into the house, leaving Conchino to himself. He picked up the chrome Honda emblem from the box and examined it. His thoughts morphed to a vision of his grandfather as a young man working in the Honda factory, welding sheets of metal together or operating power tools of various kinds. But then his grandfather's stature withered into an old man and he sat in a dilapidated wheelchair, wearing a brown robe and slippers, his back arched and bony, his hair white and thin. Conchino often wondered if his grandfather thought of him as much as he thought of his grandfather. It worried him so that his grandfather was widowed, alone, old, and frail. *How can I help move him here?* he thought. *We have plenty of room. He could live in my dad's room!* He snickered at this idea, disappointed he didn't think of it earlier while his dad was in the garage.

He decided he would go inside and prod his dad with that zinger, as well as enjoy watching *America's Funniest Home Videos* with his parents. So, he locked his car, closed the garage door, and disappeared into the house, leaving the Honda mementos on the workbench.

13.

The next morning—the day after the Schertz Beer Garten melee—Brent walked lackadaisically into Unit 3, completely forgetting that the shiner around his right eye was still there: swollen, purple, and dreadful. His damaged eye was so hideous that Rita yelped when she witnessed it while unwrapping homemade donuts at the printer table.

"Mr. Baker!" she cried out. "What happened to yo' eye?!"

"What do you mean?" he said, then realized that his hope that the others in Unit 3 simply wouldn't notice the unfortunate bruise rendered by the fists of the irritable burly man. He scrambled for an explanation. "Oh, that. Sorry. I fell down a flight of stairs yesterday. Just an accident."

Rita turned to face the others and noticed J. D.'s face was white and gaunt with shock. She assumed J. D. hadn't noticed his black eye either but, in fact, he was startled at the false explanation Brent had just given her for his shiner. He knew its real origin. Deborah and Conchino got a look, too, and were equally shocked. It was a gruesome surprise for them all, except for J. D. He clearly remembered the burly man clobbering Brent's face with his rocky fists.

"Right, J. D.?" Brent said, looking for J. D. to corroborate his excuse.

"That's right," J. D. said, reluctantly.

"It'll heal up soon," Brent said, shuffling papers on his desk as if nothing happened. Rita was still in shock.

"You should put some ice on it to help the swelling. I can get you some ice in a bag from the café downstairs."

"Thanks, Rita, but I'm really OK," he said.

Rita slowly made her way back to her desk, wincing when seeing his shiner again and then looking at Deborah for a confirmation at what she was witnessing. Deborah shrugged, then said to Brent, "Those stairs must have been angry with you. Looks like they won the argument!" She chuckled. Brent sighed.

"Ha ha," he said, annoyed.

Soon enough, Unit 3 was in the throes of data entry, busy with the morning's workload of new unemployment applications—to Brent's relief. He hoped everyone would just forget about his facial injury, although that would be hard to do. The shiner stood out like an explosion on his pale, white face. He'd also hoped that his white lie about falling down the stairs would alleviate any suspicions from the others. After a few hours of shifty glances and spontaneous giggles from his coworkers, he'd had enough.

"J. D.!" he blurted. "Come with me."

"OK, but let me finish this app. I'm almost done."

"Fine," Brent said, standing and then waiting by the door, tapping his foot impatiently.

Once J. D. completed the app, he printed it, then followed Brent into the hallway. His supervisor stomped away from Unit 3. He seemed rather upset and J. D. jogged to catch up.

"Can you believe Deborah?" Brent said, irritated. "She was giggling and gossiping all morning!"

J. D. was caught off guard. He hadn't noticed anything unusual about the way Deborah acted all morning. To him, Deborah and Rita were happily working like they always did most mornings.

"Sorry. I didn't notice."

"How could you *not* notice? She was snickering all morning!"

"Where are we going?" J. D. said, a little worried. He didn't want to fall behind in his work for a second day in a row.

"To The Warehouse."

"The warehouse?"

"That's right. It's just a few blocks away."

"I didn't know we had a warehouse," J. D. said, following his supervisor down the stairs and out the building.

"Yeppers, we do." Brent continued to mumble under his breath to himself. "All the things I do... for them... always approving their shit..."

The two coworkers trudged a few hot blocks and then reached their destination, a building similar to several they had lunched at before, this one with a sign that read, "The Warehouse." J. D. was confused, as usual.

"I thought we were going to the T-DUB warehouse," he said. Brent laughed.

"You are so literal. Are you always this way?"

"Yes," J. D. said, blankly.

"You need to stop that," Brent said, then went inside. J. D. followed.

He found himself in another pub—another time, another place, same vibe—with his supervisor. He started to wonder if this was Brent's usual routine, telling his coworkers that he had somewhere important to go, then going somewhere that was not really important at all. He also hoped to God that Brent wouldn't ask him to drink more beer with him, not because he didn't want to enjoy another freewheeling lunch, but because he wasn't used to drinking so much beer. He was tired of it and wanted nothing more than to enjoy his favorite drink: a soda. Finding himself at the bar standing behind Brent, he thought he would intervene before unwittingly being asked to drink another cheap beer.

"Can I have a root beer?" J. D. said.

"Are you sure?" Brent said, puzzled. "I am your boss, you know. You won't get in trouble."

"Root beer sounds nice."

"OK," he said, ordering their drinks and some sandwiches.

J. D. found a table to sit at. Brent soon joined him. Then what followed was something J. D. didn't expect: a catharsis from Brent. Through the course of their lunch, Brent unleashed a laundry list of pet peeves, mostly about Deborah, some about Rita, and not much about Conchino, through spittle of sandwich bits and droplets of beer. Brent was riled up and he wanted to vent. And, of course, drink more beer. J. D. was enthralled as he listened.

"She's always asking for time off, blaming her son for everything!" Brent said, while finishing his sandwich and then chugging his third beer. He raised his hand for a fourth, which came a few minutes later, courtesy of the waitress. She patted Brent on the shoulder, indicating to J. D. that they must have known each other. "And Rita has been late sooo many times. It's unbelievable!"

"I've never seen them late for work," J. D. said, surprised.

"Well, you haven't been here very long. I guess when Conchino started carpooling them, then their tardiness subsided. But for a while, it was almost *every* day. This is such bullshit!" he said, chugging his beer.

"I'm sorry you feel that way."

"Eh, whatever. Thanks for letting me vent."

"Sure!" J. D. said, proudly.

"I wish I had two or three thousand bucks so my band could hit the studio some more. That's what really makes me happy. Making music," Brent said, then belched. He waved his hand for another beer but the waitress refused him. Irritated, he paid the tab—tossing some cash on the table—then stumbled back to their building, J. D. walking next to him. Brent was thoroughly intoxicated and J. D. found himself assisting his boss, mostly keeping him from tripping and falling into the street. J. D. feared that he'd get run over on the way back to the T-DUB and didn't want to be held responsible. He helped his boss the best he could.

Once they bumbled up the stairs and reached Unit 3, Brent plopped into his chair while J. D. went back to his desk. No one else was in the office and J. D. figured the other three were still outside eating their lunch near the Vietnam Veterans Memorial, as Rita and Deborah enjoyed doing. It seemed plausible that Conchino was with them, too. J. D. promptly got his workload in order—stacking the applications and organizing them in a neat stack—while Brent laid his head on his desk. He attempted to say something and then lunged for his trashcan next to his desk, vomiting profusely in it. J. D. was horrified, and the smell of the retching made him gag. Brent wiped his mouth with his sleeve, then laid his head back on the desk, right next to his computer keyboard.

"I'm just goooing to rrrest a bit beforrre everyooone gets ba-baaack," he said, slurring his words. A moment later, he was snoring.

J. D. felt terrible for his boss but also, more than anything, didn't want to appear to his other coworkers to be Brent's accomplice. So, before the other three returned from lunch, J. D. quickly picked up the trash can Brent had barfed in and carried it to the basement garage, where he knew a dumpster sat back in one dark corner. He tossed the trash can into the gaping, black opening of the dumpster, then went back up to Unit 3 to get ready to work before everyone else returned from lunch.

***

Brent was awakened by a sharp jab to his shoulder. As he opened his eyes, he felt the pool of drool—cold, sticky, and putrid—on the desktop that his cheek swam in as well as the keys of his keyboard jabbing his face around his eye socket and forehead. The first thing he saw was Deborah's face, too close for comfort and at an unusual angle. The next thing he saw as he propped up his heavy head were unfamiliar message boxes on his computer green screen. The messages popped up in fast succession like gambling cards, riffling across the screen one over the other. He was very confused and his brain did exactly what it was used to doing in situations like this; it conjured a white lie.

Someone must have spiked my drink, he thought, then discarded that white lie as preposterous. *Epilepsy? That's it!*

Deborah spoke before he provided his excuse for sleeping on his desk: "Mr. Baker? Are you OK?"

"I think so," he said, wiping drool from his lips with his sleeve.

"Something unusual is happening," she said, frantically.

"What's happening?"

"While you were asleep, all of a sudden our computers went *crazy.* Strange messages started popping up."

"Messages we've never seen before!" Rita blurted from her desk. "And we can't stop 'em! The apps from this morning aren't printing, either." She moved her mouse as if attempting to do something helpful, then tossed the useless mouse to the side.

As the nerves in Brent's face came back to life after he had snoozed on his keyboard, an unusual sensation resonated from his brow and forehead. He rubbed his face with his hand, his fingers probing the indentations in his skin from the computers key like Braille letters etched on his face. He was out of sorts and it worried Deborah.

He's wasted! she thought. *That son of a—*

To alleviate the situation, he pressed the key combinations he knew to use to escape from troubled situations, which only frustrated Deborah more.

"I already tried that!" she barked.

"How about Ctrl + Esc?" he said, pressing those keys.

"Doesn't do nothing," she said. "Why don't you try the keys that left an impression on your face?"

"What impressions?" he said, lifting his fingers to his forehead and feeling the edge of the indentions.

"Looks like Ctrl + Shift + Tab," she said, chuckling.

Brent rolled his eyes and leaned back in his chair—sighing and running his fingers through his hair—clueless about what to do to fix this dilemma. He looked over at J. D. and Conchino. Both shrugged. Everyone in Unit 3 was at a loss for words, as if witnessing an apocalyptical moment that some worried would come true one day, that had actually come to fruition.

What the f---?! Brent thought.

Deborah returned to her desk, plopping in her chair and then rolling her eyes at Rita, who was snickering. J. D. was worried, sensing that something seriously wrong was happening. He'd never seen Deborah perplexed like this, although he had witnessed Brent hung over from drinking too much beer before. Conchino didn't appear worried at all. During this episode, he turned off his computer and was tinkering with a locking mechanism for the trunk of his car. He smiled while he tooled with it, blissfully detached. J. D. wanted to know more about the emergency.

"What do these messages mean?" he said to Brent, who was shaking his head.

"You got me," he said, then raised his voice so the women in the back of the room could hear him. "Deborah, what's the manual say about this pop-up?"

She held up her hands in frustration and said, "I can't find my manual!"

"Great," Brent whispered.

He leaned forward and read the messages as they popped up on his screen. Through the blurry, riffling boxes, he could see the same message over and over again in every box. It said: "Validating the Application for Transfer to the Comptroller." He then read the message out loud—slow and deliberate as if he'd never read out loud before—to the rest in Unit 3.

"What does *that* mean?" he said.

"You got me. In all the years I've been here at the Texas Department of Unemployment and Benefits, I've never seen that message in TAPES before," Deborah said. She looked at Rita, who was shaking her head. "It's the weirdest thing!"

"Well," Brent said. "I guess we'll just have to wait for it to finish whatever it's doing."

He leaned back in his seat, interlocking his fingers and setting his hands in his lap. The others heeded Conchino's direction, doing what they would do if it really was break time. Deborah pulled a fashion magazine from her desk and flipped through it, occasionally glancing at her computer screen to see if the messages had stopped popping up. J. D. rifled through his cache of pecan snacks in his desk drawer, selecting his new favorite to eat: a pecan praline. Rita opened her window and looked outside, wishing she was back out there like she was during lunch, sitting in the grass, enjoying the breeze and sunshine.

As an hour went by, there were no signs of the messages on their computer screens stopping before Ken the paper collector burst through the door of Unit 3, panting and gasping for air. His hair stood on end and his face was bright red. It was as if he'd seen a gigantic monster stomping through the Great Lawn of the Capitol—ready to crush all the buildings and the monuments—and came to warn everyone.

"Validations is in chaos!" he said, exasperated. "They don't know what to do!" He was breathing like he had just finished a marathon.

"What do you mean?" Brent said, sitting up.

"Have you seen the messages? They have these strange messages popping up on their—"

"You mean *these* messages?" Brent said, turning his screen to Ken. The paper collector slapped his forehead.

"Well, I'll be damned. You have 'em, too!"

"And we don't know what to do. We've tried everything."

"You've gotta come with me to Validations. It's unbelievable!"

Brent did what Ken asked and followed him down the hall to Validations. J. D. was not far behind the two, tagging along out of curiosity. When Ken opened the door to the Validations Suite, Brent was shocked. The usual clickity-clack orchestra of keyboards had been replaced with whispering and sighing, hands appearing occasionally above the cubicles, releasing papers in the air as an act of frustration and surrender. Brent had never seen Validations in this state before.

"It's the damnedest thing I've ever seen!" Ken said, shaking his head in disbelief. "And none of the other data entry units are printing. All of their screens say the same thing. Validating the Application—"

"—for Transfer to the Comptroller."

Ken turned to Brent, surprised.

"That's right! That's what the messages say. All of 'em."

"Thanks, Ken," Brent said, patting his shoulder and walking back to Unit 3. J. D. followed close behind. Back in their office, J. D. sat down while Brent stood at the door, his hands on his hips. The others kept on doing what they had been doing: taking a break.

"There's only one thing left for me to do," Brent said, tapping his foot.

Deborah curiously looked up from her magazine.

"Oh yeah? And what's that?"

"I have to go talk to the Big Boss," he said, saluting his group of data entry clerks and then leaving the office, the door slamming shut behind him.

"A lot of good that'll do!" Deborah said, sarcastically.

Rita snickered, too, as she sorted through the various sections of her recipe card box, placing the money from their lottery pool in the back, then looked for her banana bread recipe in the "Quick Breads" section so she could make it for her grandchildren and coworkers that night when she got home.

14.

Brent stood in the dank alley between the rental truck and the nightclub, drinking his free beer from a plastic cup and smoking a Pall Mall cigarette. His band had just finished its sparsely attended show and he was commiserating with the bass player of the band, Chip—chubby with a long red beard that matched his thinning hair on his freckled scalp—who also drank his free beer but avoided Brent's cigarette smoke as if it was toxic.

"Can you blow that shit the other way?" he said, wafting the smoke away from his face with his free hand. Brent purposely exhaled his next nicotine cloud in Chip's direction, engulfing him in yellow smoke and infuriating him. "You son of a bitch!"

"Calm down, John Paul Jones! Don't get your panties in a wad," Brent said, sarcastically. One of Brent's favorite things to do was call his band members by the names of famous musicians who played their same instruments. It pleased him to tweak his bass player by calling him the name of Led Zeppelin's bass player. "What? Did you quit smoking again?!"

"Yes, I did actually, so I would appreciate it if you'd blow your smoke away from me," he said, sipping his beer. The pale, yellow liquid was called beer but it tasted more like urine once its temperature warmed up. "Man, this shit's disgusting, even for *free.*"

"Pretty good turnout tonight, huh?" Brent said, chugging the rest of his beer.

"If three people including the bartender is a good turnout, then we did great!"

They both laughed, although Chip's uneasiness at the poor turnout was obvious in the tenor of his laugh. Brent finished his smoke and then flicked the lit cigarette butt, its hot cherry exploding when it hit the asphalt ground. He picked up his guitar case and slid it into the back of the rental truck, next to Chip's gear, leaving room for the rest of the band's equipment.

"How's work?" Brent said. "You get that promotion you were waiting for?"

"Got laid off. I'm looking for another job."

"Shit, man." He unsheathed another cigarette from the pack in his pants pocket and placed it over his right ear.

"Yeah. The wife's pissed, too."

"I bet."

The door to the back of the club careened open, slamming against the back of the building. Out strolled Jeff, the guitar player—a guitar case in one hand and a beer in the other hand—attempting to drink and walk at the same time. Before he could get to the truck, half of his beer spilled down the front of his black T-shirt. He stopped and watched the spilled liquid absorb into the material.

"Figures," he said, sighing.

"Nice job, Eddie Van Halen!"

"Fuck you," Jeff said, sliding his guitar in the truck and turning to the others, attempting to wipe the stinky beer from his T-shirt. It was futile. "Did Ralph tell you guys yet?"

"Tell us what?" Brent said. He pulled another cigarette out from his pack and handed it to Jeff, who gladly took it and lit it with his own lighter, standing next to his two bandmates. Tall and lanky with a round gut like a basketball shoved under his wet shirt—his freshly shaved pate concealing the fact that his hairline receded sometime in his mid-twenties—his six-and-a-half-foot frame towered over his friends.

"He's quitting the band now that Jackie had the baby."

Jackie was Ralph's pestering wife and the nemesis of the band, although their enemy only through Ralph's messages from his distant wife. She never came out to watch them play anymore and finally had gotten the upper hand by giving birth to their second child.

"Shit," Brent said, looking at Chip, who returned a limp shrug. "He can't quit. He's our secret weapon!"

"I know," Jeff said, exhaling smoke over Brent and Chip, who swatted at the toxic cloud. "You quit smoking again?" he said to Chip.

"Yes, damn it!"

"Sorry," he said, continuing to smoke. "I'm sure he'll tell you more about it when he comes out. I'm going in to help him pack up his kit."

Jeff walked back into the club, his stride long and sweeping like a giraffe. Chip glared at Brent, his eyes transmitting his displeasure.

"That's not good, man. You know how hard it is to find a shit-hot drummer like Ralph? We're screwed if he quits."

"Our album will go down the toilet, too," Brent said, lighting the cigarette that was perched above his ear. He tipped the plastic cup to his lips for more beer to guzzle, but soon discovered his cup was empty. He crumpled it and then tossed it to the ground. "What a waste of five thousand bucks!"

"At least you have a good job. And with a pension to boot!"

"Yeah," Brent sighed. "A good, *boring* job."

"I'd take a good, boring job with a pension any day!"

"Yeah."

"How's it going, anyway?" Chip said, sipping his stinky beer. Brent eyed him as he drank it. "There's more beer *inside*. You know?"

"I know. It's just sooo far."

Chip finished his precious, free beer and then tossed the crumpled cup to the ground next to Brent's, then said, "The job? How's it going?"

"It's fine. Although, the weirdest thing happened the other day."

"Oh yeah?" Chip said, his interest piqued. "What happened?"

"I accidently pressed some random key combination on my computer and the system went crazy! Messages no one had ever seen before were popping up on everybody's screens."

"Oh shit!" Chip blurted. He knew just how many people worked at the T-DUB. The idea that this mistake affected all those employees astounded him. "Did you get in trouble?"

"Not really. At first, I thought I would get in trouble so I went to talk to the Big Boss. He was really freaked out!"

"I bet! Then what happened?"

Brent sucked on his smoke and exhaled straight up into the sky, away from Chip. Then he continued.

"So, my Big Boss started calling around, freaking the shit out 'cause no one at our agency understood what was going on. But then someone suggested he call the Comptroller and see what was going on at their end. The weird messages said that data was being verified to send over there and he wanted to see if they received anything."

Brent slowly sucked on his cigarette some more. Chip grew impatient for his story to continue.

"Well? Did they receive anything?!"

"Turns out they did. Millions of backlogged applications were sent straight to the Comptroller without printing on our end or going through Validations or being mailed."

"Wait a minute," Chip said, confounded, putting his hands on his hips. "You're telling me that your random, fat-fingered keyboard flub bypassed all those departments at your agency?"

Brent finished his cigarette and flicked it on the ground, then said, "That's what the Big Boss told me."

"Sounds like you accidentally are going to save your agency *millions* of dollars. Did your Big Boss tell you *that*?"

Brent absorbed what his bass player had told him in his slightly intoxicated brain. *Millions of dollars? Millions??* he thought.

"You think so?" Brent said, scratching his scalp.

"Yep. Millions. Think about it. All of those people in all of those departments? And your key combo bypassed them all? And no one knew about it? Wow!"

"Crazy, right?" Brent said, uneasy.

"Totally. It doesn't suck to be *you* right now," Chip said, patting Brent on the back and then walking back to the club. "I'm getting another beer before we go home. Want one?"

"Yeah," Brent said, looking up at the night sky, an illuminated plane flying above the clouds, and the pale yellow moon glowing brightly. "I'll be right there."

Chip disappeared inside the club, leaving Brent to himself. He thought of what he would say to his drummer, Ralph, about the rumor that he was quitting the band, then thought about what Chip said to him.

Millions? he thought. *Millions!*

It had been several years since just the idea of going to work the next day excited him, but that's just how Brent felt at that moment. He thought about strolling into the Big Boss's office to find out if this was true. Would this fortunate accident save the Texas Department of Unemployment and Benefits millions of dollars? He couldn't wait to find out.

Feeling renewed, he skipped back inside the club for another free beer and to ask his drummer if he was really going to quit the band or stay on to finish what they had all started: their rock and roll dream.

PART II.

15.

The gaggle of reporters waited patiently for the governor of Texas, Dwayne Bennett, to make his highly anticipated appearance at the press conference. It had been a few months since the governor had spoken to the press, and the anticipation of what he might say was palpable. The reporters sat in metallic gold folding chairs with navy blue seat cushions in the lavishly furnished conference room, the podium surrounded by navy blue curtains of velvet, two over-sized ferns in gilded pots, two flags (one for Texas—of course—and one for the United States) on golden rods, and a gold plaque of the Texas seal mounted high behind the podium with the name "BENNETT" emblazoned under the shiny emblem of Texas. The gaudiness of the faux gold accompaniments still made the reporters laugh, even a year after Governor Bennett miraculously won the hotly contested election by a slim margin. He had aggressively campaigned that he would do things differently if he was elected governor and he kept that promise, throwing out longstanding institutional rituals and decorum and replacing them with the ways and means of how he ran his family business. Bennett was known to say, "They will think you're successful as long as you make them *believe* you're successful!" That's when the faux gold fixtures began to appear everywhere in the Governor's Mansion and, to this day, it irked reporter Esther Jean Stinson.

Not one to fall prey to fool's gold, Esther Jean scoffed at the governor's gaudy interior design choices. She leaned over to the reporter sitting next to her and said, "I bet his toilet is gold-plated."

The reporter—Bob Davis from the weekly alternative newspaper—chuckled. The gold folding chairs in the conference room were tightly set together and Bob struggled to keep his limbs from accidentally touching Esther Jean as he folded his scrawny, hairy arms across his Western-styled shirt with pearl snaps.

"With a velvet-covered toilet seat!" he blurted.

Esther Jean laughed as she leaned back in her seat, crossed her long, slender legs, and pushed a chunk of her straight brunette hair from her elegantly made-up face, a few strands having stuck to her freshly applied lip balm. She preferred glossy lips to tinted lips for occasions like this. She had decided earlier that morning to wear her immaculately tailored, dark gray suit but was irritated that she unconsciously chose a navy blue silk shirt to accompany it, not thinking at the time—while standing drowsily in her closet—that she would match the fixtures and dressings of the conference room, an error she chalked up to a lack of adequate caffeine to kickstart her brain. Bob noticed the similarity in color of her blouse to the curtains and prodded her.

"Are you kissing up to Bennett's people?" he said, elbowing her.

"Whatever," she scoffed. "I'd rather offer sexual favors than *appear* complicit with these people."

"Hmm," he replied, then suddenly sat up. A commotion at the front of the room excited the gaggle of reporters, stirring the conference room to life. "He's coming in."

All the reporters stood and watched Governor Bennett entering the room, driving his gold-plated, leather-clad wheelchair—his trademark mode of transportation that gave him the appearance of gliding across the room—up a small ramp. He parked behind the podium, accidentally bumping it and knocking it askew, then barked at an unsuspecting assistant to put it back in place. He didn't stand due to paralysis in both of his legs, an infirmity whose origin was related to an unknown childhood illness that was never revealed during the campaign, but which didn't impede him from ascending to the highest office in the State of Texas. A smattering of applause and camera flashes greeted the governor, who returned a toothy smile to the room full of reporters, one of his front teeth capped in gold. His pitch black hair—dark and glossy like newly laid asphalt glimmering in the summer heat of west Texas—crested high on his head, reminiscent of the hairstyles popular during his youth in the 1950s, his puerile notion of cool a permanent fixture of his adulthood.

"Good morning," he said to the reporters. "Please be seated. Now, let's hope this press conference doesn't turn out like the last one. You vultures better behave yourselves!" He wagged an indignant index finger at the gaggle of reporters, which was met with equal parts gasps and snickers. All soon sat down and then raised their reporting tool of choice: cell phone, tape recorder, legal pad, and the like. Governor Bennett cleared his phlegmy throat and then spit on one of the potted ferns. The vulgar gesture didn't seem to surprise the reporters, who were used to such ugly mannerisms from the boorish politician. "Who's first?"

Many hands rose, some more enthusiastic than others, but Bennett's eyes were trained on a black woman wearing a red business suit with Afrocentric flourishes, a green and yellow handkerchief blossoming from her breast pocket, her hair plucked tall into a large afro. Her hand was not raised to ask a question—she sat in her chair with her arms and legs crossed in a self-protective, defensive posture like a turtle bracing for a predator's attack—but Governor Bennett called on her anyway.

"You there—Frizzy! You ask the first question."

The woman was embarrassed and not prepared at all to ask the odious politician a question of any sort. Consequently, she slowly stood and asked the first thing that popped into her head, something that most in the room were curious about.

"Governor Bennett, what is your strategy for increasing your historically low poll numbers? It seems—"

"Ah, I see where this is already going. I will not give your stupid question the dignity of an answer. And your press pass is revoked immediately. Get her out of here!"

Before the woman could take a seat, she was accosted by a security guard, who tore the lanyard containing the press pass from her neck and unceremoniously escorted her from the conference room, leaving her folding chair empty with the green and yellow handkerchief stranded on the seat cushion. Esther Jean and her cohort Bob looked at each other, both their eyebrows raised in astonishment.

"He's like a mob boss!" Bob said to Esther Jean. She nodded.

"Are you going to ask a question?" she whispered to him.

He returned a disgusted look and shook his head, as if she had requested he taste something he already knew to be foul to his palate. Unfortunately for Bob, Governor Bennett called on him, pointing his chubby finger at the unprepared reporter.

"You there, Pencil Neck! You! Got a question? Remember, Frizzy swung for the fence and struck out. Three strikes for the group and you're all out!"

Nervous, Bob didn't have a prepared question to ask. Not wanting to be called on in the first place, his presence at the press conference was more an obligation to his employer than an opportunity for notoriety. He stammered as he stood there, causing Governor Bennett's eyes to wander to his compadre: Esther Jean. Pleased with her attractive appearance, then smiling as if recognizing her, he decided to prod her for a question instead.

"You there, Hot Cakes! Do you have a question for me?"

Esther Jean was used to the name-calling and was not surprised one bit at the callous manner in which he spoke to her, having covered the governor extensively over the past year for the prominent city newspaper she worked for. Her political columns were often the talk of the town, and she was always prepared to ask a politician a pointed question, particularly the gruff and crude Governor Bennett. She was well aware that his reputation for bad behavior fueled her career, one that provided her a small amount of celebrity and job stability in return.

"Yes, I do," she said, standing up while her embarrassed cohort quickly sat back down. "There are reports coming from many border towns that the citizens there are quite pleased with the presence of the newly deployed National Guard, as well as contracted security details, to curtail the rash of invading illegal immigrants. Can you give us more information about your exciting yet controversial border security plans?"

This question pleased Bennett and he commenced to give a rambling answer, one without cohesion or substance. When Esther Jean sat down, her cohort elbowed her again.

"Exciting?!" he said to her, his face twisted with irritation. She rolled her eyes. Esther knew there wasn't much truth in her question but she asked it anyway, hoping the press conference would continue without any more strikes against the group.

"I got his attention, didn't I?" she said.

The governor rambled for a few minutes, spouting unproven statistics and recounting campaign transgressions by his treasonous political opponent that were irrelevant to Esther Jean's question. But she didn't care about the content of his answer. She smiled at her confused colleague, then said, "Check this out."

Wanting to end the press conference on a high note, Governor Bennett wrapped up without soliciting any more questions or giving any specifics about solutions to the current ills of the State of Texas, most of which were of greater importance than supposed immigrants supposedly flooding the border towns. He waved goodbye—projecting both thumbs up triumphantly in the air—and drove down the small ramp, exiting behind the navy blue velvet curtains like a genie retreating back into its bottle. Not long after his disappearance, a security guard approached Esther Jean and asked her to follow him. Bob was shocked.

"Sexual favors, indeed," he said, sarcastically.

Esther Jean winked at him and then followed the security guard.

Walking around the throng of reporters and behind the velvet curtains, she was surprised to see that the opulent decorations enveloping the conference room were simply propped up by planks of wood and duct tape, a façade so weak, fragile, and shoddy that a breeze from the Hill Country could knock it over effortlessly. She followed the security guard—his hulking frame and buzz-cut hair raising her hackles—down a long corridor whose windows offered a glimpse of the manicured lawn and garden outside. She soon found herself in Governor Bennett's office, deep inside the Governor's Mansion, though the governor himself was not present. The security guard insisted she sit in a leather-covered, wood chair in front of his massive, wood desk. As the guard retreated from the governor's office to stand watch outside (leaving the door cracked open a skosh), Esther Jean attempted to make herself comfortable in the stiff, navy blue chair, but found herself irked once again that her silk blouse matched the décor of the gaudy office.

Dammit! she thought, attempting to conceal the blouse under her jacket, but doing so made it appear as if she wasn't wearing a shirt at all, so she decided to leave it be.

Interrupting her preening was the sound of a toilet flush. Governor Bennett soon emerged from a door to a private bathroom, drove his gold-plated wheelchair to his massive desk, then parked behind it. To get the chair close enough to the desk, he had to raise one arm of the motorized chair, the one with the remote control on it. He then laid the arm on top of the desk, awkwardly pointing upwards. Esther Jean craned her neck to see if she could catch a glimpse of the bathroom, but she could only see the door ajar and a small section of white floor tile. Governor Bennett set his hands on his glass desktop, his fingers interlaced.

"Nice to see you again, Esther," he said. He smirked, flashing his gold-capped tooth wedged within a row of brown kernels.

"Likewise. And you can call me Ms. Stinson," she said, crossing her legs and setting a notepad on them, ready to jot notes.

"Why the formalities? We're *friends* here, am I right?" he said, leaning back in his wheelchair.

"You didn't have to throw Patty out of the news conference," she said, referring to the reporter whom Bennett had called Frizzy, offering him a glimpse of the camaraderie she shared with the other reporters. "What she asked wasn't false. Your poll numbers are low—in the basement, in fact."

"Semantics. Isn't that what they say?" he said, maneuvering his wheelchair backwards, the jutting arm falling back into place. He then turned it to go around the desk. "My office is doing great things, you know!"

He drove his wheelchair slowly in circles around Esther Jean and his desk, as if corralling her and the furniture for an attack.

"I don't believe your constituents think you're doing *great* things. Texans just hear you spouting ugliness. You promised change in your campaign, yet you're the same as the rest."

"And how is that?" he said, still circling her, keeping his eyes trained on her.

"It's just self-serving B.S."

"B.S.? Ha!"

This exchange excited Governor Bennett. He raced his wheelchair back behind the desk and parked it, lifting the controlling arm again to get close. He leaned forward, his arms propped on his desktop.

"Don't fool yourself, Esther. We all are self-serving. Everyone projects what they want the people around them to believe. Even you, I'm sure."

Esther Jean wriggled uncomfortably in her chair, an air of truth in his declaration. She then sat up, jotting notes on her notepad.

"What great things are you referring to, then?" she quipped.

"You'll see in due time."

"Mmm-hmm."

"What can I do to get you on my side? What can I do to... get you on *my* team?"

"What do you mean?" she said, curiously looking up from her notepad.

"You know, my father used to say, 'Make your friends a cocktail, but make your enemies *three* cocktails.'"

"Excuse me?"

"Do you like whiskey?" he said, extending his arm to reveal a bar under a window at the side of his office. "You know, Austin is a cesspool of progressives and liberals! But, where you find liberals, you will also find *craft products*. And liberals distill a fine whiskey. Would you like to try some?"

Esther Jean hesitated. On the one hand, a glass of whiskey sounded very appealing, a nice way to ease the tension. On the other hand, it seemed duplicitous and cloaked in sleaziness. She demurred, to Governor Bennett's displeasure.

"Tell you what. If, in the future, you have something special for me, something really great for Texans, a great exclusive story for me to tell, then call me. I'll gladly cover that story," she said, pulling a business card from her coat breast pocket. She placed the card on the desktop, just out of reach of the governor.

"Alrighty then," he said, smirking. "Then I guess we're done here. Anything else I can do for you?"

"Can I use your restroom before I go?" she said, standing up and extending her hand for a shake. The skeptical governor did not shake her hand but did offer her his restroom. She quickly used the palatial facility, then left his office. The hulking security guard escorted her out of the Governor's Mansion through a back entrance, then immediately returned to his post inside the office. Governor Bennett called him to his desk, then commanded, "Keep an eye on her. However you need to do it, just do it!"

The security guard nodded. His name was Frank, as it said on a gold name tag pinned to the lapel of his navy blue blazer, and he dutifully did *whatever* Governor Bennett asked of him.

Outside the Governor's Mansion, Esther Jean walked a few blocks under the warm sun to her favorite café, the one with exceptional espresso and affectionate cats roaming around inside. She loved to park her weary butt there in the afternoon sometimes, refilling her caffeine levels and stroking a pussycat or three. She ordered an espresso and sat down, spotting her favorite kitty—the one named Rascal—as well as a few familiar human faces from the press conference, including Bob the alt-weekly reporter. When he saw her, he raced over to her table and took a seat.

"Well?!" he said, excited. "Did you get an exclusive?"

"Not yet. Just the usual B.S."

"Ah," he said, sitting back and sipping his latte. Rascal the kitty hopped on their table and sniffed his latte, then plopped in Esther Jean's lap, making himself a nest to snooze in.

"But," she started, then sipped her espresso, "I did go in his royal bathroom."

"And?" he said, excited again. Her pronouncement had promise. "Gold-plated crapper?!"

Esther Jean laughed, then said, "No, just a regular crapper. An unremarkably regular one at that."

"Figures," he scoffed, disappointed. "Are you going back anytime soon?"

"Maybe," she said, stroking Rascal in her lap. He wound himself tight like a cinnamon bun. "Not sure."

The two reporters drank their coffees, surrounded by chatting patrons and desperate house cats waiting to be adopted.

16.

Esther Jean sat on her couch—one leg sprawled the length of the overstuffed cushions, the other stretched over the leather ottoman where her cat, Bartholomew, napped on a fuzzy blanket—in her downtown apartment while reading emails on her laptop computer. She took a break from applying makeup and choosing an outfit for the evening to reply to a few pressing emails from her boss, D. Jameson, the editor of the Texas News & Politics section of the city paper, *The Austin Journal.* He sent her emails at all hours of the day—some in an effort to micromanage her assignments, others like tiny revelations sent to her confessional inbox—but she didn't mind the deluge of information and oversharing. She liked chatting with her boss. He had been kind with the shepherding he provided her career, and the fatherly tenor of his advice and instructions provided her the mentorship she had desired from her own father, but had never received.

As she typed on her computer, she stroked her cat with her bare foot. He purred vigorously, flipping on his side so she could reach his soft belly, his favorite place for her to pet him. His aggressive harlotry amused Esther Jean very much.

"You're such a whore, Mew!" she squealed, calling him by his nickname, the last syllable of his full name: Bartholomew. Her saucy declaration didn't hurt his feline pride. He continued to shamelessly flip over to expose his belly and purr. "But you're distracting me."

Entertainment Districts (which included the rowdy bars of 6th Street, the gay warehouse district of 4th Street, and the upscale, gentrified Rainey Street). Being so close to work and leisure made signing the lease for the 5th Street apartment seem like a no-brainer. She could practically walk anywhere she needed to go, both day or night. *Why would I not live here? It's perfect!* she thought, touring the apartment building at the time with the landlord—a Lebanese man named Ahmad with a sketchy demeanor. And it certainly seemed perfect to her, with just a few, tiny imperfections, which she corrected with a smattering of chic furnishings and vibrant wall paint.

As she walked down the stairs to leave her building, one of those burdens of living downtown made itself known: the homeless population. At first, their presence around her apartment building was unfortunate but inconsequential. The homeless people rarely bugged her. But as the months of her lease went by, the hostility the homeless expressed to Esther Jean and the other tenants became more aggressive and she dreaded walking past one of them in fear that they would accost her. One filthy man, his persistent begging spurned by Esther Jean, yelled and spat on her when she refused to give him a dollar. From that point forward, seeing him or the other vagrants again made her anxious. She knew that he was probably mentally ill, and was on the street most likely because his family couldn't take care of him properly, and there was nowhere else for him to go. The State of Texas had cut back on all mental health services over the last decade in an effort to "save money" and there weren't many mental health facilities anymore. Just jails would take them in, or set them adrift into vagrancy.

Maybe a story about the neglect of the mentally ill by the current administration would make a splash? she thought. *Would that bring more website traffic? I'll have to propose it to D.*

So, as she gently stepped down the stairs, the sight of a homeless person crumpled at the bottom of the stairwell—

completely covered with a dirty bed comforter and sitting among an array of homeless necessities like a tattered suitcase on wheels, a dingy jug of water, a tall boy of beer, and a trash bag filled with aluminum cans—gave her pause. Would he confront her for money? Worse, would he scream at her? She wasn't sure but didn't want to find out. She convinced herself to tiptoe quietly. She examined the vagrant and his belongings as she gently glided past him, and was struck by the good condition of the man's athletic shoes.

Those sneakers look brand new, she thought, as she raced down the sidewalk toward the bars and nightclubs of 6th Street.

When the clacking of her stiletto heels blew away with the night breeze, the homeless person uncovered his head, revealing a hulking man much cleaner than Esther Jean would have expected, his buzz-cut hairdo mostly in place except for a few strands pushed askew by the weight of the dirty comforter. She most certainly would have recognized him, being that he had escorted her to and from the governor's office after the press conference earlier that day.

Shit, I better catch up to her, he thought, pulling the comforter around his neck like a cape, leaving his collection of props behind. *She runs like a man!*

The governor's security guard, Frank—disguised as a homeless person—trotted after Esther Jean and followed her from nightclub to nightclub for the rest of the night, gathering surveillance for his boss: Governor Bennett.

17.

Conchino surprised Rita and Deborah by adding an additional stop on their morning commute to work. When he picked them up at their homes, they both seemed down, a weight on their shoulders that he had never noticed before. Deborah wasn't her normal, cheery self. And Rita—usually gleefully effusive with a baked treat for her coworkers in tow—was empty-handed and dour. So rather than pry into their business, he stopped at a donut shop on the way to work and bought all his coworkers a dozen donuts and a dozen kolaches, a sweet surprise that pleased Rita and Deborah when he handed them the boxes in the car.

"You just made our morning!" Deborah said, patting his shoulder from the back seat. He could see the grin on her face in the rearview mirror.

"I meant to bake a pineapple upside-down cake last night but that boy Malik kept me up late. He sick as a dog!" Rita said, then took a whiff of the freshly baked goods. "Thanks for thinking of us, Conchino."

It warmed his heart that he could lift their spirits by simply buying donuts and kolaches, knowing that their home life was sometimes not ideal. And things at work had not been the same since Brent was caught sleeping on his keyboard, an unfortunate event that caused so many problems—not just for their unit, but for the entire agency. An agency-wide audit began the day after the "Incident" and their usual, daily routine was disrupted. Deborah angrily cursed Brent to his face, which was an additional kerfuffle that added to the uneasiness they all felt at work. The transmission of data to the Comptroller initiated by Brent's drunken nap was still in progress, rendering the printers in Unit 3 useless for the time being, at least until the agency-wide audit was complete and a remedy put in place.

So, when the carpool group arrived at work, Rita happily placed the donuts and kolaches on the printer table with the sleeping computer peripherals, as if she had baked them herself and brought them to work. As usual. J. D. was already in the office and met Rita at the printer table, ready to pluck a treat from one of the boxes. He danced around her— excited and hungry—just like her grandchildren did in her kitchen when she baked a cake or a pie or muffins. She playfully swatted at her pesky coworker.

"Give me room to breathe!" she said, chuckling. "Step off!"

"I just want a donut," J. D. said. "You got any maple ones?"

"I don't know. You'll have to look for yo'self. I didn't pick 'em. Conchino bought 'em."

He peered around at Conchino, only to discover his quiescent coworker already munching on a glazed donut while sitting at his desk. He wasn't entering data into his computer; no one could perform their work. It afforded him the opportunity to eat his breakfast at his desk without having to type with his other hand. He leaned back in his chair and propped his feet on his desk, just like Brent would do.

"Who do you think *you* are? The Boss?!" J. D. said, sarcastically.

And as soon as his playful tease fell from his lips, Brent burst into Unit 3, the door slamming against the wall, sheets of paper in his hand that he shook above his head as if he had just discovered something miraculous, like a long-lost papyrus found in the dunes of a desert.

"No, *I'm* the Boss!" he declared, triumphantly. "And you all are going to *love* me!" He plopped down in his chair, slapping the desktop with the papers in his hand, a big grin on his face.

Deborah, still irritated with her so-called superior, rolled her eyes.

"Doubt it," she scoffed, setting her purse on her desk, then partaking from the treats on the printer table. "What do you have? A treasure map?!"

"Even better," he said, leaning back in his squeaky office chair, placing his hands behind his head as if lounging in a hammock. "Are those *donuts*?!"

"Yes," Rita replied. "Conchino bought them for us."

Brent quickly scavenged for a donut of his preference but decided on a kolache instead—the kind stuffed with processed cheese and jalapenos and were guaranteed to give their consumer vicious flatulence. After returning to his desk and scarfing down his kolache, he wiped his mouth with his sleeve, then said, "This here, on my desk, in the presence of all of you—my employees, my coworkers, *mis compradres*—is the application for..."

He hesitated—for dramatic effect—which of course, irritated Deborah to no end.

"Get on with it, man!" she barked.

"The State Employees Cost-Savings Suggestion Program!" he said, grinning at his coworkers. They were shocked, to say the least, not knowing if he was joking or insane, either of which was plausible to them. "With a reward of $10,000! Ha!"

Rita was skeptical. She sat behind her desk eating a chocolate eclair, some of the creamy filling oozing out of a crack in the side of it, making a mess in her lap. Her curious skepticism distracted her from the dripping disaster.

"Wha choo talkin' about, Mr. Baker? You have an idea good enough to win the prize?"

"Yup," he said, scribbling on the paper application. As he wrote, he said, "Deborah? Do you remember that key combination from the other day?"

"What key combination?" she said, finishing her donut, contemplating selecting another like the one Rita was enjoying.

"The combination that caused this mess?"

"What *mess*?!" she said, baffled.

Brent stopped scribbling, realizing that he wasn't communicating effectively with his employees, something he was vaguely aware was an issue for him sometimes. He gently set his pen down on his desk and turned his chair to the rest of Unit 3. They all stared blankly at him, equally as baffled as Deborah, and he was confused as to why they weren't on the same page as he was, so he clarified it for them.

"The pop-ups on the screen mess. Duh," he said. The others still didn't get what he was trying to say and it hurt his feelings at the thought that he was going to have to recap everything he had learned about "The Incident" to his employees. There was a rather long explanation to be given, and the idea of explaining it all sounded about as fun as a root canal or a prostate exam. But just like these unpleasant medical procedures, he knew he would just have to suck it up and do it, so he did. "All right, all right. Let me explain it to you."

The others gathered around their supervisor, huddled with donuts and kolaches in their hands, listening to Brent retell the night he hung out with his bandmates and how his bass player, Chip, planted the seed of excitement in his mind about how the simple mistake of sleeping on his keyboard could possibly save the State of Texas *millions* of dollars. So, he went to the Big Boss as soon as he could to see if what Chip said could possibly be true. At first, the Big Boss was skeptical, only seeing the problems right in front of him that were challenging the agency: applications not printing, printed applications not being verified, verified applications not being mailed, received applications at the Comptroller not being reentered, and unemployment benefit checks for suffering Texans not being mailed. But then, a funny thing happened. A colleague at the Comptroller informed the Big Boss that the transmission of data from the Texas Department of Unemployment and Benefits initiated a process on their end that triggered the printing of checks, completely bypassing all their manual procedures. It seemed too good to be true that this unexpected catastrophe had a silver lining—a gold lining, even.

"And what could that be?" Deborah said.

"Yes, what is it?!" Rita chimed in.

Brent continued. Subsequent calls from the Big Boss to his colleague unearthed a problem. Would bypassing all of these manual processes put hundreds, maybe thousands of employees out of work? It seemed that might be the case, but further analysis proved that many of these employees—the full-timers—could be retrained to input more applications at T-DUB, increasing efficiency and speed on the data entry side, and that many of the validation and mailroom employees were unnecessary contractors that the agency could release, saving T-DUB millions of dollars in labor expenses. Hence, a gold lining.

"As you can now see, we got ourselves a cost-savings winner!" Brent said, clapping self-congratulatorily.

The others were stunned. It just didn't seem possible that something amazing (and potentially award-winning) like that would come out of their humble, data entry unit.

"Holy shit," Deborah said, confounded.

"My Lord, Sweet Jesus!" Rita said, clasping her hands together and gazing above her at the dingy white tiles in the ceiling. "Do you see this, Reggie? It's a miracle! Tell your sweet mama that we struck gold today!"

Not able to contain his excitement, J. D. slapped Conchino on the back, which caught his humongous coworker off guard. He immediately glared at J. D. before realizing the slap was congratulatory, not hostile in any way. He acknowledged J. D.'s gesture with a wink. Brent took his place behind his desk, continuing to fill out the application for the cost-savings prize.

"I need to submit this application before someone else tries to take credit for it," he said, scribbling on the paper application. "So Deborah, what was that key combo again? Do you remember?"

"Ctrl + Shift + Tab! That's the key combo. It was imprinted right there on your noggin'," Deborah said.

"Like you were branded!" Rita said, snickering.

"You got that right!" Deborah squawked.

The dark cloud over Unit 3 lifted and it pleased Conchino to see his motherly coworkers—who were so down in the dumps earlier that morning—back to their normal, jovial selves. With the prospect of a nice payout in the foreseeable future to be shared by the group, the spirits of Unit 3 were noticeably higher than earlier in the day. *Funny how things happen,* Conchino thought, but he didn't share his thought with the others. He preferred to let his actions speak for him, so he slapped J. D. on the back and gave him a fist bump, then hugged Deborah and Rita by wrapping his long arms around both of them. They enjoyed the rare display of emotion from stoic Conchino. But Deborah then unexpectedly realized something and she just had to speak her mind.

She walked over to Brent's desk, her fists firmly planted in her hips, then said, "That was the key combination but you don't know *why* it did what it did."

Brent looked up at her, perplexed.

"So?" he said, then returned to filling out the application.

"I'm certain they'll want more details than just 'Press Ctrl + Shift + Tab in TAPES.' Don't you think?"

"I guess," he said, unfazed by her inquisition. "You and I can figure that out later. It doesn't ask for step-by-step directions here in the application for the prize. It just asks for a brief summary of the cost-savings suggestion."

This explanation seemed plausible to her since Brent was well-versed in the intricate bureaucratic procedures of state government, so she decided not to worry about it any further.

"Great!" she said, going back to her desk. "Let me know when you want to figure it out."

"I will!" he said, finishing the application.

"So, what do we do while all these message boxes keep poppin' up on our screens?" Rita said, opening a window to the outside world and letting the warm morning breeze slither into the office space. "We can't do our work still."

"Just keep your butts in your seats and man those desks. I'm going to run this up to the Big Boss so he can sign it!"

And with that, Brent was out the door and on his way upstairs to see the Big Boss. He had already confirmed to Brent that he would sign the application for the State Employees Cost-Savings Suggestion Program; Brent just needed to fill it out and bring it to him. So that's what he did.

The others in Unit 3 stayed behind, sitting in their seats and enjoying their peaceful morning, without much work to do. After eating all the donuts and kolaches, their bodies were experiencing a widespread sugar crash. Conchino laid his head on his desk. J. D. contemplated writing his parents a letter on agency stationery, explaining the fortunate turn of events that had come to pass for Unit 3, but the thought of handwriting a letter wore him out, plus the lethargic effects of the sugar crash made doing anything seem downright criminal. So he, too, laid his head on his desk. Deborah and Rita continued to chat.

"You gonna pay off that title loan with your portion?" Rita said to her friend.

"You know it, sister," Deborah replied. "Quicker than a jackrabbit in heat!"

"Amen!"

"What about you?" Deborah said, smoothing her nails with a nail file she had stowed in a desk drawer. "You never did say what you would buy if we won that $10,000 prize."

Rita thought about this for a moment and realized that, although she had high hopes for winning that prize, the idea of actually winning it never seemed possible. But now that it *did* seem in the realm of possibility, she didn't know what to make of it. *What would I buy myself?* she thought. *There's so much I want to do!*

"Tell you what," Rita said, leaning back in her seat and gazing out the window at the baby blue, cloudless sky. "If we do win that prize, then I will let you know. I don't wanna jinx it!"

Deborah laughed, then continued to file her fingernails. She debated about filing her toenails as well before concluding that *that* would be a little much for the office. She didn't want to gross out her coworkers with her yellow toenails.

"I can't wait for you to tell me!" she said, then traded her nail file for a fashion magazine that she had been saving for a peaceful morning, just like that one.

18.

Rita sat at her kitchen table with an assortment of scratch-off and lottery tickets spread out across the patchwork tablecloth—one her mother had sewn decades ago for a family reunion, stains from many dinners over the years connecting the patches. She ate dinner with eleven of her thirteen grandchildren until they were all full; the two missing—Aliyah and Destiny—would be over later with their mother, Janice, who was enjoying a rare night off from work. Janice took her children to Walmart for new shoes that they desperately needed and said she'd drop by after they were done shopping to eat dinner. Rita wasn't worried, though. She baked a whole chicken, mashed a whole bag of potatoes, and steamed a pound of green beans, so there was plenty to eat. She also wanted to bake a pineapple upside-down cake for her coworkers like she had promised. After the grandkids were done eating and helped clean up the table and kitchen (Rita insisted they help her clean up even though they complained incessantly since they didn't do that at their own homes), Rita enjoyed organizing her lottery tickets at the table by herself, although her house was not a peaceful place since her grandkids rampaged through the hallways and various rooms, enjoying free reign of the entire house.

She grouped the lottery tickets into distinct groups— some newly purchased, some small-time winners yet to be claimed, some to submit to second-chance drawings, and some that appeared to be losers but she wanted to check a second time, just in case—and like a Vegas card dealer, she fanned them out across the table with aplomb and skill. It was an impressive array of time and investment, and their bright, playful graphics and logos instilled an exciting hopefulness inside her that was inexplicable yet powerful. The prospect of Brent's keyboard blunder winning the coworkers of Unit 3 the $10,000 prize was nice (*very* nice, in fact), but the thought of her actually winning a larger prize for Unit 3 was even nicer. She hoped to win a large jackpot someday and daydreamed about helping her coworkers as well as her children, even though she wished that her kids could eventually be self-sufficient. She witnessed their struggle firsthand and knew full well that it was hard to pull yourself up by bootstraps when you couldn't afford the boots to wear in the first place.

She didn't dwell on the fate of her grown children for too long; she had work to do, sorting her lottery tickets and being available for her grandkids, if needed. Mostly, they played among themselves, affording Rita the time to sit at her kitchen table alone. She could hear them in her house as they played their games—some played tag, others teased each other, and a few even read books out loud. This pleased her the most, the ones who read books. She hoped that all her grandchildren would be studious and motivated, some of them even displaying this recessive trait despite their lack of parental support. She had kept a small library of childhood, hardcover favorites including *Nancy Drew Mystery Stories* and *Hardy Boys* collections for them to read.

But one of her grandchildren was quite irascible and mischievous, causing her much trouble and consternation: that boy Malik. He had developed a taste for rebelliousness and enjoyed the attention he received from acting out. Rita knew it must have been frustrating for the grandchildren to compete for her affection—being that there were just so many of them—but causing her unnecessary trouble was just not the best way to garner her favor. Even so, Malik persisted. She could recognize the distinctive pitch and tenor of his voice, like the

TO SQUEEZE A PRAIRIE DOG

squeal of an air horn piercing through the din of a large crowd. His protestations against his siblings and cousins pricked up Rita's ears.

That boy gots the Devil in him! she thought, sighing. *He gonna be the death of me, fo' sure.*

But as long as she didn't hear any kids crying or furniture crashing or upholstery ripping, she assumed Malik was just being a pest, and a pest was better than a vandal or anarchist in her opinion.

As she sat at her table, the grandkids would float in and out of the kitchen, hoping to be the first one to get a slice of the delicious-smelling cake, but Rita dashed their hopes. She repeatedly told all of them that the cake was for her coworkers—not them—and when they asked her why she wasn't baking a cake for them, she said, "'Cause Grandma don't feel like it!'"

She eventually tired of their implorations and placed a bowl of leftover Easter candies on the kitchen table for her grandchildren to pillage, which, of course, they did. Whenever she told them that the cake was not for them, they would ransack the bowl, taking fistfuls of candy with them to wherever they were playing. Suddenly, her intuition got the best of her when Malik's voice went silent, and she didn't see him partake from the candy bowl. So, when his sister Makayla came into the kitchen—singing a Janet Jackson song as loud as she could—Rita grabbed her by the wrist and pulled her close.

"Ay! What did I do, Grandma?!" she said, wiggling as if ready to duck a blow to the head from her stern grandmother.

Rita chuckled, then said, "Nothing yet. Where's your brother at?"

"He in the back tryin' to get Anthony to challenge him in an eatin' contest."

"An eatin' contest? Wha choo talkin' about, Makayla?"

"I already told ya'. Am I in trouble?" she said, trying to escape from Rita's grasp.

"You will be if you don't tell Malik to come see his Grandma. Got it?"

"Yes, Grandma? Can I have more candy?" She scanned the bowl for her favorite candy: jellybeans.

"Of course, baby," she said, releasing Makayla from her grasp, then smiling. The grandchild plunged her hand in the candy bowl before sprinting out of the kitchen to tell her brother what her grandmother commanded him to do.

I hope she don't catch what her brother has, she thought. *He's a rascal!*

But Malik didn't come into the kitchen as she wanted. She quickly lost interest in her wily grandson as the minutes went by. She had more important things to do like sort her lottery tickets and pull the cake from the oven when it was done. And before another thought of Malik entered her mind, her two absent granddaughters—Aliyah and Destiny— suddenly appeared in the kitchen. They ambushed their grandmother—hugging and kissing her—before grabbing some candy and joining their cousins on the other side of the house. She didn't even have time to tell them about the leftover dinner in the refrigerator, which she had thoughtfully saved for them and their mother, Janice, who wearily entered the kitchen, looking tired as if she had hiked to her mother's house from Walmart instead of driving her car. She plopped in a chair at the kitchen table, exasperated and panting. Rita was surprised at her daughter's distress.

"What's wrong wit' you?" she said, gathering all of her lottery tickets and placing them in her recipe card box, to organize another time. She quickly closed the box. "I thought you just goin' to Walmart. You look like you been runnin' from the po-po."

Rita laughed while her daughter gave her some sassy side-eye. They could have passed for sisters, being that they looked so similar in size, with comparable facial features and skin tone. Only their radically different hairstyles gave away their age difference, as well as a few of Rita's errant gray hairs.

"Real funny, Mama," she said, rolling her eyes. "Any dinner left over?"

"Of course, my dear. In the fridge."

Janice went to the fridge and pulled out a plate, then put it in the microwave to warm it up. She turned to face her mother, her arms crossed and her backside resting against the counter.

"How's work?" she said to her mother.

"Fine. Just fine. That wise-ass, Mr. Baker, say our unit may win a prize for saving the state money. I'm praying to our sweet Lord that it come true."

"That's amazing, Mama!" Janice said, pulling her plate from the microwave, then joining Rita at the kitchen table. "How much ya' gonna get?"

"The prize is $10,000."

"$10,000?! That's dope," she said, a bit of food clinging to the corner of her mouth.

"Yup," Rita said, sitting back in her chair, enjoying the rare company of one of her children. Usually, they didn't spend much time with her anymore. Most of her familial company was with grandchildren, but she craved the company of her own babies. "I'm glad you're here tonight."

"Me too, Mama," she said, devouring the plate of lovingly prepared food, like she hadn't had a homecooked meal in months. "These kids drivin' you crazy?"

"Nah," she said, then paused, rubbing her chin with her hand, contemplating a delicate method to inform Janice of an indiscretion since she knew her children regularly spoke to each other through social media. "Well, except that boy Malik. He's a handful."

Janice snickered, then said, "True dat. He a rascal! Just like his father."

They both laughed, enjoying a moment of solidarity.

"Speaking of Malik. Can you go check on him? I haven't heard him for a bit? Can you do that for yo' mama?"

"Sure, Mama," she said, shoveling the last bit of dinner into her mouth, then setting her plate in the sink before heading to the other side of the house, looking for Malik. When the other children discovered the presence of their aunt, they cheered and called her name, hoping to get a small amount of attention from an elder relative. This pleased Rita but she didn't get to enjoy it for long, as the children's cheers quickly turned shrill as Janice called out her nephew's name.

"Malik!" she screamed, then stomped back into the kitchen, her nephew's limp body in her arms. "Somethin' wrong, Mama!"

Rita didn't know what to make of the unfortunate turn of events but, having been through many misfortunes before with her children and other grandchildren, she instinctively ordered Janice to take the boy out to her car.

"Let me find my purse and I'll be right there!" she commanded.

Janice complied and carried her nephew outside. Rita frantically went to the living room to find her purse. All of her grandchildren swarmed her, teary and desperate, pulling on her skirt and asking for consolation. She was both flustered and concerned, but the sensory overload from twelve worried children didn't help matters. She consoled them, telling them their cousin was going to be all right, then pulled the one she thought was the oldest—Kiara—close to her and said, "Girl, make sure yo' cousins be good. And tell them to act right or they gon' get it when I get back. Ya' hear me?"

"Yes, Grandma," she said, filled with pride that her grandmother trusted her to be the responsible one from the ornery group of kids.

"We have to take Malik to the emergency room."

"Is he going to be all right, Grandma?"

"I don't know, child. I gots to go!"

Rita waddled out of the house, locked the front door behind her, then careened through the front yard to Janice's car, which sat idling at the curb. She crawled into the back seat, where her grandson laid, pink vomit stained around his mouth and nostrils. She nuzzled next to him then commanded Janice to drive to the emergency room, the one around the corner that was open twenty-four hours. Janice floored the accelerator, driving erratically through the dark streets of the sleepy, urban neighborhood. She tried to look at her mother in the rearview mirror while she drove but she couldn't see much. It was just too dark back there and the street lights were bright and distracting, shining through the tinted windows of her car.

"Is he all right?" she said, worried.

"I don't know. He breathing, though. Keep drivin'!"

Rita lifted Malik's head and examined his face, wiping his mouth clean. He sniveled.

"One of the other kids say he ate something, like soap or somethin'."

"Soap? Why would he eat soap?! That makes no sense."

"That's what they say."

While Rita looked at her grandson, memories of many calamities long since forgotten flooded her mind. There was the time her son, Reggie Jr. at nine years of age, stole a six-pack of his father's beer and drank it all as quickly as he could in the treehouse, then commenced to vomit for an hour in the bathtub. Or the time her daughter, Patti at fifteen years of age, contracted pubic lice from the quarterback of the high school football team and cried for a week from the humiliation of having to shave off all of her pubic hair in the presence of her mother. Or the time this daughter, Janice at ten years of age, snuck out of the house late at night to commit an act of vandalism with her friends, only to get caught by the police soon after throwing eggs at a neighbor's house. *Malik a Jackson, fo' sure,* she thought, as she held him. *Oh Lord, please see him through.*

Janice parked in front of the emergency room and ran around the car to help her mother carry Malik. Inside, the waiting room was empty, the large room serenaded by a flat-screen TV tuned to a Telemundo *telenovela*, suspended from the ceiling in the far corner. A nurse peacefully sitting behind a reception desk quickly jumped up from her seat and met them in front of the desk with a wheelchair, helping them sit Malik down.

"What happened?" she said, skipping all formalities.

"We think he ate soap, or something," Janice said.

"Follow me back," the nurse said. "But one of you stay here to fill out paperwork."

Rita offered to stay up front while Janice followed the nurse through a secured door, pushing Malik back to where he could receive medical care. Rita found herself alone in the waiting room, looking over at the TV, Spanish-speaking actors embracing each other to kiss on the screen. She lifted her purse and rifled through it for her wallet, knowing she was going to need her identification card and her medical insurance cards. She was soon greeted by a different nurse, a young Latina with her hair cut in a bob of jet black and a name tag on a floral-patterned, medical shirt that said, "Lorena." She clicked a remote to mute the TV; the show she had peacefully been watching was too boisterous for dealing with clients and patients. She set a clipboard on the counter, a stack of papers and a ballpoint pen under the clip, and pushed it toward poor Rita.

"Please fill these out, then bring it back to me. Coffee?" she said, matter-of-factly.

"That would be nice. Black coffee," Rita said, then found a vinyl chair to sit in. She flipped through the ream of paper; a heavy sigh escaped from her lips.

This gonna take an hour, she thought. *Damn.*

She began filling out the forms when Lorena returned with a hot cup of coffee. She smiled as she held it out to Rita.

"Is that your son in there?" Lorena said. Rita took the cup of coffee, chuckling.

"Oh, sweet Lord, no! That one of my grandchildren. His name is Malik. He's on my naughty list!"

"I'm sorry to hear that," Lorena said, standing up. Rita grabbed her arm to keep her from walking away.

"Do you take my insurance? I'm a state employee," she said, handing Lorena her medical insurance cards.

"Is your grandson on your policy? Because grandchildren usually are not covered, unless you are the ward of the child. Are you the ward?"

Rita paused, knowing Malik wasn't on her policy, and also knowing she wasn't the legal guardian of any of her grandchildren.

"No, I'm just his grandmother."

"I see," Lorena said, placing her hand on Rita's hand. "Then you'll have to pay cash or pay with a credit card."

"Pay?" Rita blurted. "How much it gonna be?" She returned an inquisitive yet worried look.

"Minor emergencies are usually at least a grand. More serious ones can be two or more."

"Two thousand dollars!" Rita cried. "You hear that, Reggie?" She looked up to the ceiling, hoping to see her kind husband's face gazing back at her. All she saw was a white ceiling with one of the ceiling tiles stained brown from a leak in the roof. She was inconsolable.

"No worries. Our finance department can work with you. We'll make it right," she said, patting Rita on the shoulder and then returning to the reception desk. She lifted the remote, clicking the TV's volume to its previous level.

Rita began filling out the paperwork, not knowing how she was going to pay for Malik's care, or what she was going to say to Malik's father, Michael, about what had transpired under her watch. She still didn't know for sure what had happened to her grandson and was too consumed with knowing that she would receive a bill in the mail from the emergency room for what could be thousands of dollars, a very unfortunate turn of events for her. As she filled out the paperwork, Lorena sat behind her desk, filing her nails and watching her *telenovela*.

"If you need more coffee, let me know. I'll be glad to get you some."

"Thank you," Rita said.

Then she began to cry.

19.

The Big Boss had an actual name, but J. D. hadn't heard him called by his real name before. Brent always referred to him as the Big Boss—no matter what, like he was a guru or shaman perched in a throne in an executive suite up on the fourth floor—and J. D. had never met, seen, or interacted with him. So, when the four data entry clerks in Unit 3 received an important email from Ted Schneidermann, J. D. didn't know who he was.

"Who is Ted Schneidermann?" J. D. said, turning around to Rita and Deborah. "And why does he want to talk to us?"

"What choo talkin' about?" Rita said. "Mr. Schneidermann don't want to talk to us. He never come down here."

"Read the email. You were CC'd."

Rita opened her dormant email program, read the email, then said, "Well, I'll be."

"Maybe we're all getting fired!" Deborah squawked.

"Finally!" Rita said, snickering. "I'm gettin' tired of coming downtown every day. I need to retire and drink some lemonade on my front porch. Kicking my feet up!"

"Amen, sister!" Deborah sang.

J. D. wasn't satisfied with their silly exchange, mainly because he wasn't ready to retire from work; he was just too young. He looked over at Conchino, hoping to get some kind of explanation about why Mr. Schneidermann wanted to come down and speak with them, but Conchino wouldn't give him one, which frustrated J. D. He knew Conchino could talk (Deborah and Rita had confirmed as much to him) and it hurt his feelings that his giant coworker chose *not* to communicate in a meaningful way with him, not even through text messaging. All he ever did in J. D.'s presence was shrug his shoulders or chuckle to himself or any number of a variety of nonverbal tics and mannerisms. It was maddening to poor J. D.

I'll get him to talk to me one day, he thought. *Someday!*

So, when Brent finally came into Unit 3, J. D. immediately accosted him for any explanation concerning the email from Mr. Schneidermann.

"The Big Boss is coming down here?" he said, pleased. "He must want to make the announcement *in person.*"

"What announcement?"

"You'll see!"

J. D. returned to his desk and sulked in his chair. He watched his boss bounce in his office chair, happier than a grackle bathing in a puddle of muddy water. J. D. wasn't quite sure what to make of all this, but Brent's excitement was contagious and he soon found himself bouncing in his own seat, looking forward to the announcement from Mr. Schneidermann.

Soon enough, a slender man in a tan suit with a balding pate and a bushy moustache came into Unit 3, his skin worn like tanned leather from hours in the Texas sun, from hunting deer on leased land in the Hill Country. It could only have been Mr. Schneidermann, the man everyone had been waiting for with anticipation: the Big Boss. He stood by Brent's desk, his hands plundering the depths of his pants pockets, a politician's smile stretched across his furrowed face.

"Good morning!" he said. Unit 3 replied the same. "Please excuse my presence. I know you have lots of important work to do. Data entry is the *cornerstone* of what we do here at the Texas Department of Unemployment and Benefits."

"You got that right!" Deborah chimed in. The outburst caught Mr. Schneidermann off guard and he stumbled to restart his carefully prepared speech. A little flustered, he carried on.

"As you may know, your supervisor—the esteemed Mr. Baker," he said, extending his arm like a TV game show hostess to Brent. "He is submitting a cost-savings idea to the State Employees Cost-Savings Suggestion Program and I'm certain it will be a winner!"

The four clerks in Unit 3 clapped somewhat enthusiastically, like the audience of a high school talent show, both enthused and obligated to cheer. Brent beamed from the attention, with a grin so wide it barely could be contained within the contours of his face. Mr. Schneidermann pulled an envelope from one of his pants pockets, holding it up for all to see.

"I've signed the application for the State Employees Cost-Savings Suggestion Program and I'm certain—without a doubt—that Mr. Baker's suggestion will win, as well as receive the prize of $10,000! And bring great honor to himself, as well as to *all* the employees of the Texas Department of Unemployment and Benefits, including those of you here in Unit 3."

The four clerks clapped again, this time with more enthusiasm since, in essence, they were clapping for themselves.

"Or, as I call it, my *best* unit! Let's hear it for Mr. Brent Baker!"

Brent stood up and took in the smattering of applause from his employees, bowing first to Conchino and Deborah on his left, then to J. D. and Rita on his right. After a few more seconds, he motioned for them to stop as if pushing the applause down into a quiet place.

"Thank you, Mr. Schneidermann," he said to the Big Boss.

"No problem, my boy. Now, I'm off to submit the application to the Cost-Savings Committee."

He waved to everyone in Unit 3, shoved the envelope back in his pocket, and left the office, the door slamming after him.

Brent plopped down in his chair and smiled as he swiveled it, pleased with himself. Deborah glared at him. When he noticed her mean eyes burning through him, he said, "Can I help you, Deborah?"

"You're gonna *share* that prize with the rest of us, aren't you?" she said, tapping her desktop with an agitated index finger.

"Of course, I will! That's our pact, right?"

"That's right," Rita said. "We gots a pact."

"I will. I *will*," Brent said, shuffling some papers on his desk. "Sheesh."

Rita sighed. Deborah looked over at her friend, noticing weariness and discomfort in Rita's posture, and felt compelled to ask her what was the matter.

"You OK?" she said, concerned. "You look worn out."

"I'm fine. Just stayed up past my bedtime... again."

"Malik?"

"Yup."

Deborah didn't prod further. She knew the toll family could take on your soul—children and grandchildren alike—so she simply nodded and the two friends continued their work, the clickity-clacking of the five keyboards in Unit 3 percussing their work song.

At that moment outside their building, Mr. Schneidermann walked hastily across the Great Lawn of the Capitol, the envelope in his clinched fist, toward the Governor's Mansion, which sat across the street on the other side of the Capitol Building. He traversed the lawn as fast as he could, or to put it more plainly, as fast as his hips would allow. A lingering sports injury kept him from jogging and made him feel older than he was, but he marched through the pain. He just had to see Governor Bennett that very moment, if possible.

At the security desk inside the Governor's Mansion, Mr. Schneidermann explained to the security guard why he was there, flashing his state-issued badge. When the guard scoffed and began his routine of stating how busy the governor was and how people—even state employees with state-issued badges—couldn't just walk in unsolicited, Mr. Schneidermann interrupted him.

"I'm on the list," he said, winking.

"The list?"

"Yes, the *list*," he said, winking again. He leaned closer.

The security guard rolled his eyes, then grabbed a clipboard from a shelf behind him and scanned through the pages, flipping through sheet after sheet, looking for Mr. Schneiderman's name. Finding something, he picked up the phone to make a call. When the person on the other end confirmed his request, the security guard hung up the phone.

"Someone will come escort you shortly to the Governor's Office."

"Thank you," Mr. Schneidermann said, looking around the small lobby decorated in navy blue and gold and ferns. He decided to take a seat on a leather settee, but before his butt hit the seat cushion, Frank the security guard opened a secured door and waved him over. Startled, Mr. Schneidermann stumbled to regain his footing, then followed him through the door.

Frank didn't speak to Mr. Schneidermann as they walked down a long corridor—whose windows offered the loyal bureaucrat (who rarely spent time in the Governor's Mansion) a glimpse at the manicured lawn and garden outside—toward the Governor's Office. Once inside the palatial suite, Frank the security guard motioned for Mr. Schneidermann to take a seat, which he dutifully did. Frank returned to his post outside the door, keeping it cracked open a bit, leaving Mr. Schneidermann to himself. He gandered at the large, oak desk, its presence in the middle of the grand office like an anchored battleship in a small port. He was admiring the desk and wondering how one similar to it would look in his own office when Governor Bennett disturbed the tranquility of his daydream. The governor drove his gold-plated wheelchair from the private bathroom to his place behind his desk, a short length of toilet paper slithering from the base of the wheelchair as he drove.

"Well, look who we have here," Bennett called out. "It's our friendly, neighborhood Schneidermann!"

Mr. Schneidermann squirmed in his seat, a little uncomfortable with the *Spider-Man* reference that the uncouth governor seemed so enamored with. After all, it wasn't the first time Bennett called out this Marvel Comics motto for the popular superhero to poor Mr. Schneidermann, who chuckled and thought, *The things you have to do these days to get ahead.* But Schneidermann knew better than to complain.

"Good morning, Governor," he said, forcing a smile.

"Same to you, Schneidey. How's the wife?"

"Good. She's good."

"And the kiddo? Is he still busting your balls?"

"Well..." Schneidermann paused, thinking of a diplomatic way to reply. "I don't have any kids, sir."

Bennett laughed it off, chalking it up as a minor transgression.

"That's right. That's right. No worries. What can I do for you on this fine day?"

Schneidermann pulled the envelope with the application for the State Employees Cost-Savings Suggestion Program from a pocket inside his tan suit jacket and placed it on the desk for Governor Bennett, who picked it up and opened it, reading the piece of paper inside.

"This might interest you," Schneidermann said, smirking.

Bennett immediately tossed the application and envelope on his desk, then set his hands in his lap, his fingers interlaced.

"There are too many words for me to read on this piece of paper and I'm a very busy man. So, give me your pitch."

"My *pitch*?" Schneidermann said, confused.

"Yes, think of me like a movie producer and give me a thirty-second pitch like this will be the grandest movie of all time," he said, his hands setting a cinematic scene in the air above his head. "Go!"

Schneidermann sat up, mulling over what to say and how to say it, not prepared to give the governor a pitch to an imaginary movie, but he did his best.

"Well, as you may know, the State of Texas has a State Employees Cost-Savings Suggestion Program where state employees can offer suggestions to save the state money. And I have an employee who has one that could save the state a *lot* of money."

This pricked the governor's curiosity. He leaned forward and said, "I see. How much is a lot?"

"Millions," Schneidermann said. "Possibly tens of millions, maybe hundreds."

"Hundreds of *millions*?!" Bennett blurted. "Are you sure?"

"Yes, an internal audit at our agency was conducted and confirmed this."

Bennett picked up the application and pretended to read the information on it, then eyed his loyal crony. Schneidermann continued enthusiastically.

"This could be a huge political win for you. Saving the State of Texas hundreds of millions of taxpayer dollars would make a great headline. Don't you think?"

"Yes," Bennett confirmed, rubbing his dimpled chin. "Yes, it would be fabulous for my poll numbers."

Schneidermann gleefully continued.

"And since you appointed the members of the committee who select the cost-savings suggestion, I'm sure you could suggest to them who the winner this year *should* be."

"Yeees," Bennett hissed. "I could do that, Schneidey. I could!"

Schneidermann sat there, pleased with himself. He smiled at the governor, who was also pleased, and the two sat there briefly, gazing at each other, with an air of self-esteem and importance circulating around them.

"I hope this helps your... poll numbers."

"And I'm sure this means you would like something in return for your loyalty."

Schneidermann grinned, then said, "Well, that would be totally up to you. It's not for me to suggest."

"You know what sounds nice to me?"

"No, sir. What would that be?" Schneidermann said, leaning forward with anticipation.

"Commissioner Schneidermann. Do you like the sound of that?"

"Oh yes, sir! Most definitely!" Schneidermann beamed.

"There is an opening for a commissioner over at the Railroad Commission."

"Thank you, sir!" Schneidermann said, popping up from his seat, extending his hand to Governor Bennett for a shake, but Bennett didn't shake it.

"Germs," he simply said to Schneidermann, wincing.

"That's fine," Schneidermann replied, putting his hands in his pockets.

"Have a good day," Bennett said. "My security guard will see you out."

Schneidermann bowed to Governor Bennett, then quickly left his office, the door closing behind him. Alone, Bennett opened a drawer to his desk and rifled through it, looking for something. He soon found what he was looking for, a business card with a reporter's name on it: Esther Jean Stinson.

A naughty smile slid across his face as he thought of the svelte, beautiful reporter, and he knew his phone call to the city newspaper reporter would be unexpected and intriguing. So, he dialed the phone number on the business card. Esther Jean answered.

"Governor?" she said.

"I have a great, exclusive story just for you," he said. "Interested?"

20.

Brent didn't ask J. D. to lunch for the first time in a while, and J. D. found that he didn't quite know what to do with himself. He hadn't packed his lunch that morning, figuring he'd accompany Brent to a bar or pub or café that served beer—their usual lunchtime routine. So, while Deborah, Rita, and Conchino were gathering their lunches to go eat outside by the Vietnam Veterans Memorial, J. D. sulked at his desk. Deborah eventually noticed his despair.

"You meeting Mr. Baker for lunch?" she said, logging out from her computer, then picking up her purse.

"No. He said he had something important to do. And I didn't bring my lunch today," he grumbled. He reached for a brown box with shipping labels on it that had been sitting on his desk, then placed it on his lap. "I do have some pecan snacks from my folks, though. It came in the mail yesterday. I guess I'll just eat them for lunch."

Surprised, Rita stood next to J. D., then said, "You can't eat pecan snacks for lunch! But if you share them with me, then I'll share my chicken salad with you. Deal?"

J. D. was caught off guard by Rita's unsolicited act of charity. He looked at Deborah and Conchino, both of whom seemed to agree with Rita, as they stood there waiting for him to respond. Conchino even nodded his head, as if to say, "Come on, homie." J. D. jumped at the chance, wedging the box from his parents under his right arm, ready to join them for lunch.

"Deal!" he said, beaming. "I love chicken salad!"

Rita cackled, then said, "Who doesn't love my chicken salad?!"

They walked out of Unit 3 together.

Outside behind their building, they found a spot near the Vietnam Veterans Memorial and all four coworkers sat in a shady place in the grass. The lawn was so lush and soft that they didn't even need a picnic blanket. They sat in a loose circle, all their lunch items in the middle. Deborah, Rita, and Conchino unpacked their lunches while J. D. flipped open a pocketknife from his pants pocket (a Buck knife he got for a Christmas gift from his grandfather many years earlier), then surgically sliced the packing tape apart. He opened the top of the box to reveal a large stash of pecan desserts from his parents all the way from Brady, Texas: roasted and salted pecans, pecan rolls, pecan logs, pecan pralines, and a number of other treats made with or topped with pecans. He marveled at his fortune. Rita did, too.

"Save me one of them pecan logs, will ya?" she said, handing J. D. half of her chicken salad sandwich. "Those are my favorite!"

"Some potato chips for a pecan praline?" Deborah said, offering J. D. some of her chips.

"OK!" he said, trading with her. Deborah gleefully placed her treasure on her lap.

Conchino, curious if he could get in on this deal, raised his lunch to J. D., offering a bit of what he had in a bento box his mother had prepared for him earlier that day. J. D. looked at the bento box, puzzled with the balls of rice inside— exquisitely decorated with sesame seeds, splinters of carrots, and carved cucumber to look like a small animal.

The rice looks like a bunny rabbit! J. D. thought. He had never seen food fashioned into bite-sized pieces like miniature sculptures before. He didn't know what to make of it. Conchino offered again but didn't say anything, of course. Deborah decided to translate for Conchino.

"It's a bento box. His mother made it. He wants to trade with you."

"What is it?" J. D. said, skeptically.

"Rice balls with vegetables," she said.

"Rice balls?" J. D. examined the bento box some more and concluded that if Conchino's mother had made it, then there was a pretty good chance that it was delicious. He approved of the trade. "Sure, I'll try one."

He pinched a rice ball and sniffed it, while Conchino excavated in the box for a pecan snack of his liking. Finding a cinnamon bun topped with pecan pieces, he gladly traded a rice ball for some dessert. But rather than eat his lunch first, he devoured the cinnamon bun. J. D. watched him eat it, pleased with their trade. And then—out of nowhere—the unspeakable happened.

"Mmm," Conchino said. "That's good!"

J. D.'s eyes widened as if he had seen a ghost or some other frightening apparition. Seeing his shock, Rita burst out in laughter, slapping her knee, her head flying back as she bellowed to the sky, her hands over her stomach. She laughed so hard that Deborah laughed, too. Conchino sheepishly smirked with his mouth full of food.

"See! He *talks*," Rita said, snickering some more. "It took a dessert to make him do it!"

"Well, I'll be," J. D. said, smacking his forehead. "I never thought I'd see the day."

Conchino's smirk morphed into a grin as he finished the cinnamon bun, licking his fingers and wiping the crumbs from his lap.

"I talk when I feel like it," he said, his voice low in volume, barely audible.

This made J. D. smile from the satisfaction of knowing he had witnessed something special, like a birdwatcher spotting a rare, reclusive warbler. And as he munched on his chicken salad sandwich, Rita spotted a letter within the box between the snacks. She pointed to it.

"You get a letter, J. D.?" she said.

Curious, J. D. pulled the letter from the box and quickly read it, then folded it back up, placing it back where it was.

"Yeah," he said, eating some more of his sandwich.

"Everything all right with your folks?" she said.

"Their business isn't doing so good. They *really* want me to go home."

"Go home?!" she said, spitting out bits of bread and chicken salad. "You can't go home. You're part of our team!"

"I don't want to go home," he sulked. "I just feel bad, that's all."

Rita patted his shoulder.

"You're a good boy, J. D. You know that?"

This made him smile a bit. It had been a while since he was praised for being himself and it pleased him to hear her say it out loud.

"Thank you," he said.

"Well, maybe if we win that prize, then you can send them some money," Rita said, comforting him some more. "Lord knows. I could use it, too."

"That would be nice."

"I'm sure we'll find out sometime soon. Mr. Baker been hot to trot to win it!"

"Ain't that the truth!" Deborah said. "He's like a vulture circling roadkill!" She and Rita cackled; even Conchino chuckled a bit. They enjoyed razzing Brent, especially when he wasn't around to defend himself.

"When we go back inside, let's ax him. Maybe he know somethin'."

"OK," J. D. said, finishing his sandwich and eyeing a pecan log in the box.

When they were done with lunch and dessert, they moseyed back up to Unit 3, trudging up the stairs and walking the halls together in a small herd. Once inside their office, they all sat at their desks and began to work. Since the "Incident"—the apocalyptic event instigated by Brent Baker sleeping on his keyboard—they were informed that they were to select "Submit data" instead of "Save and print" after entering unemployment applications, a simple alteration to their longstanding procedure, something easy enough for J. D. to change since he was new. But, for the other three, it was an irritable adjustment. They had been at the T-DUB for many, many years and the keystrokes used to "Save and print" had been imprinted into their muscle memory, so it took some effort and concentration as well as quite a few flubs and frustrating mornings to change their data entry routine. They soon got the hang of it, though. Once they all submitted the data as the new procedure required, the applications waited in a queue for a manager—like Brent—to send the applications to the Comptroller with the miraculous, new keystroke combination.

One beneficial side effect of the "Incident" was the unceremonious removal of most of the printers from Unit 3. Since they weren't all needed anymore, Ken the paper collector dutifully came by Unit 3 and removed them all, except for one. Fortunately for Ken, he was transferred to the Network Support Department from the Validations Department after receiving a bit of training; he was perfectly suited to support the remaining printers in the building and didn't seem to mind the change in employment position—a lateral move that didn't affect his paycheck or his longevity at all. The Unit 3 printer table—once a crammed, unsightly place covered with four large printers, bundles of cables, stacks of printer paper, and network routers—transformed into their cozy break area. Rita and Deborah brought spare small appliances from their homes for their coworkers to use at work—like a coffeepot, a toaster, a microwave oven, and a mini refrigerator—and before long, morning and afternoon rituals were created around making coffee or tea for all in Unit 3. They needed something to drink,

Rita surmised, to go along with the treats she baked or the snacks J. D. brought. Everyone in Unit 3 amiably agreed that this was an excellent idea.

So, after an hour or so of data entry, Rita approached their break area to make coffee, initiating the afternoon break, while J. D. set the box of snacks from his parents on the break table. They hadn't seen Brent Baker all morning through the afternoon and didn't seem to care one way or the other. They enjoyed the serenity that came from working without the nervous energy he sometimes brought to work. But the tranquility didn't last long. Brent burst into Unit 3—almost as if on cue—as soon as the coffee began to drip. The door slammed against the wall and Brent stood there, his arms above his head triumphantly, a piece of paper in one hand.

"They picked my—I mean OUR—suggestion! We won the prize!"

Everyone in Unit 3 cheered, even stoic Conchino. It was good news worth cheering about, for all of them. Brent stomped over to the bulletin board, removed a red thumbtack that held a to-go menu for a Chinese food restaurant in place, and stuck the piece of paper he was holding over the flyer for the State Employees Cost-Savings Suggestion Program. He was quite pleased with himself and enjoyed the last smattering of applause from his employees.

"Great work, Mr. Baker!" Rita said.

"Hooray!" Deborah agreed.

"When do we get the prize money?" J. D. said. The others listened curiously. This quandary was on all their minds as well.

"Patience. All I can say is have patience. What I pinned to the board is a press release from the Office of the Governor of the State of Texas. We have all been invited to a press conference that will be happening at the Governor's Mansion in the next few days. We all need to dress to impress," Brent said, sitting at his desk, then propping his legs up on the desktop.

"Impress?!" Rita squawked. "I'm gon' wear my Sunday church outfit!"

"Amen, sister!" Deborah cheered. "I'd wear mine, too, but I don't go to church."

"You can wear your datin' outfit, then," Rita replied.

"Are we gonna be on TV?" J. D. said.

"Probably," Brent said, eyeing the snacks and coffee on the break table. He decided to indulge in the treats.

"My parents are gonna see me on TV!" J. D. beamed.

"You're going to be famous like me!" Brent said, back at his desk, stuffing his face with a muffin topped with crumbled pecan bits and cinnamon.

Still curious, Rita said, "So, *when* are we gonna get that cash prize money?"

"The Big Boss didn't say. He just said my suggestion won and that we were going to have to be at a press conference. I imagine on my next paycheck."

Deborah sneered at him while he finished his muffin. Her stare burned through him and he quickly felt the heat of her contempt, but he was in too good of a mood to bicker with her. He acquiesced.

"Don't worry. I'm sharing with all of you," he said. Unit 3 clapped and Brent enjoyed the last bit of adulation for the day. "We had a pact. Right?"

"Damn right!" Rita agreed.

"Thank you, Mr. Baker," Deborah said.

Her soothing gratefulness pleased Brent, who wasn't used to hearing Deborah thank him—for anything. The four data entry clerks began working again while Brent shuffled some papers on his desk, pretending to do something.

"Now, the important question is...," he said, pulling his chair closer to his desk. "Should I bring my acoustic guitar or not?"

"Why would you bring a guitar?" J. D. said, curiously.

"To play a song to my largest audience *ever*, of course!"

21.

Deborah stood on her front lawn, eyeballing some prickly sow-thistle invading her grass, a glass of wine in one hand and her water hose in the other. The sight of the weeds worried her, mainly because the cost of weed killer was an expense she didn't want to incur. She knew she could squat in the grass and pull the weeds, but she could think of a hundred things she'd rather do than pull weeds with thorny leaves and goopy stalks. The year before, she spent an entire weekend in the grass pulling prickly sow-thistle—hundreds and hundreds of them in the front and back yards—only to watch them reappear just one month later, invading her poor grass as if she had never done the grueling work in the first place.

Why even bother? she thought, ignoring the weeds. *They just come back again.*

She sipped some red wine and sprayed water away from the weeds, hoping to encourage the grass to overtake the prickly sow-thistle. The sun was setting and she watched several of her neighbors come home from work or the grocery store, some carrying laptop computer bags and others carrying grocery bags. She hoped maybe one of her neighbors would mosey on over and chat with her, but no one did. They all scurried into their homes to eat dinner with their families or watch TV with their spouses or drink beer by themselves. Even Steve—the computer programmer with the beautiful wife and two adorable kids who lived a few houses down—simply waved at her when he arrived home, then quickly retreated inside his house. The lack of neighborhood friends to talk to at times like this depressed her. She even thought of calling Rita and inviting her over, but she knew Rita was busy watching her grandkids and she would see her the next morning at work anyway.

I'll just drink my loneliness away, she thought, gulping the last of her wine.

As soon as she finished it, two cars pulled up to her house and parked: a police cruiser and an unmarked police car. Two police officers—one male and one female—got out of the cruiser and two men dressed in inexpensive suits got out of the other car. They all quickly approached Deborah, and she immediately knew who they were looking for: her son, Ricky.

"Good evening," she said to them. "He's not home."

The two men in cheap suits stood close to her. The other two officers lingered back a few feet, their hands on their utility belts as if ready to pull a weapon, if necessary—maybe a stun gun or maybe pepper spray. The two men—one Latino and the other black, both slender and tall, both with very short, cropped hair, both in their mid-thirties—had no discernible expression on their faces; they looked serious and bored simultaneously. The Latino man pulled a folded piece of paper from the inside pocket of his suit coat, holding it up for Deborah to see. She didn't need to read it, nor did she want to hold it.

"We have a warrant for Ricky Martinez. Do you know his whereabouts?" the Latino man said, his voice deep and gravelly, his breath thick with nicotine and caffeine.

The black man stood stiffly, almost unnaturally, like someone was holding a knife to his back.

"No, I don't know where he is. I haven't seen him in a couple of days," Deborah said, holding her empty wine glass behind her, their presence in her peaceful yard making her uncomfortable.

"Do you know when he'll be back?" the Latino man said.

"No," she said, looking over their shoulders as if a neighbor was there, even though there wasn't.

"Do you mind if we look inside?"

"Go ahead. His room is the front one. The door in the garage is unlocked."

The Latino man nodded to the black man, who turned to the male police officer and nodded to him. The three walked into the garage, leaving the police officer to guard the door while the two men in suits went inside the house. The female police officer approached Deborah, then stood next to her.

"Good evening, ma'am," she said to Deborah. A name tag on her shirt said "Kapersky." She looked to Deborah to be in her late thirties, her short brunette hair cut in the style of a man except for a wavy bit right above her forehead that twerked in the night breeze. She was extremely fit like the gladiators on the television show Deborah was obsessed with a couple of years before. Deborah wasn't one bit intimidated by a female police officer, but the male ones were another story.

"What has my son done *now*?" Deborah said, then sighed.

"Sorry, ma'am, but you'll have to wait for the detectives to tell you."

"OK."

Deborah turned to look at the window of Ricky's bedroom, the one at the front of the house, and she could see the shadowy silhouettes of the two detectives looking for something in his bedroom, first near his dresser, then around his bed.

Good luck finding anything in there! she thought. *His room is a pigsty!*

Then all she could think about was drinking more wine, or maybe even smoking the joint she had hidden inside a small Tupperware container stashed in the freezer. The thought of Ricky committing a crime disgusted her, and her disgust for her no-good son fed her contempt. But, even when she was angry with him, the thought of his cute little face—the way it appeared in her mind from when he was a little boy—filled her with equal amounts of nostalgia and joy. She often wrestled with several feelings all at once when it concerned her son.

Deborah turned to Officer Kapersky, then said, "Do you have children?"

Officer Kapersky didn't respond, looking off in the distance as if monitoring the horizon for incoming enemy planes or unidentified flying objects.

"That's OK. You don't have to tell me about yourself. We can just stand here in uncomfortable silence," Deborah said. She examined her empty wine glass and decided it was pointless to hold it anymore, so she set it in the grass. She wiped her hands, removing the last atoms of the glass's presence from her skin. "Hopefully this will be over soon."

"Sorry," Officer Kapersky said, abjectly. "I'm not trying to be rude. Just following procedures."

"Your procedure is to ignore people?" Deborah said, chuckling. "That's rich."

"No, just not to say too much to citizens."

"I see. I'm a government employee, too. You know?"

"Really?"

"Yep, State," she said, then punctuated her admission by clicking her tongue.

"I see. And yes, I'm a mother. My son is three."

"Three?!" Deborah said, excited. "I *loved* that age. My son was so cute. He's not so cute anymore."

They both laughed, slightly uncomfortable yet amiable enough for the circumstance. Officer Kapersky loosened up a bit and shook out her stiffness.

"My son is adorable. Looks just like his father. He's a miniature version of him."

"Is that where your son is right now? With his father?"

"Yep. He's a stay-at-home dad."

"Stay-at-home dad?!" Deborah squawked. "I've heard of those but I've never met one before. Must be nice. My son's father was a piece of work. A real loser."

Officer Kapersky felt a little guilty after hearing that. She knew she was lucky to have found such a good man for a husband. But she still felt the need to gloat, even just a little, because most women responded positively to her fortunate familial situation.

"Yes, I'm a lucky woman," Officer Kapersky said, smiling. "He's a good man."

"But just you wait!" Deborah blurted, wagging an indignant index finger. "Those cute children grow up to be scoundrels. I would take dirty diapers any day over warrants. Trust me!"

"I'm sorry, ma'am," Officer Kapersky said. "I really am."

Without warning, Deborah began to cry. The weight of the situation in combination with the frustration and guilt she felt was just too much for her to take. It was so unbearable that her eyes sprung a leak. Officer Kapersky didn't know if she should console her or just stand to the side and let Deborah cry. She decided to console her, against her better judgment. She put her arms around Deborah and hugged her.

"Is he going to jail?" Deborah said, talking into Officer Kapersky's chest.

"When we find him—yes."

"Then what?" she said, muffled.

"Well, you can bail him out till the court date."

"Bail him out?!" Deborah blurted. She laughed uncontrollably, wiping tears from her cheeks, then sighing. "I can't even afford to fix my car. If he goes to jail, then that's just where he'll be. Can't do nothin' about that."

Officer Kapersky soon realized that there was a reason for the police procedures as she watched Deborah's mood swing back and forth from hysteria to anger to resentment to sadness.

They were told in training that citizens like Deborah could be unpredictable and that they shouldn't engage with them. She regretted starting a conversation with Deborah. Her motherly instincts got the best of her.

But soon enough, the two men in cheap suits and the other police officer came out of the garage. The Latino man carried a plastic bag full of things from Ricky's bedroom. The black man scribbled something on a piece of paper, then handed it to Deborah.

"If you find out where your son is, then please call us."

"Sure. Whatever," she said, irritated.

The two men hopped in their car. The male police officer got in his car, and before Officer Kapersky joined him, she turned to Deborah and said, "Good evening, ma'am. Nice talking to you, from one mother to another."

"Good evening," Deborah said.

Officer Kapersky joined her partner in the car, then both cars disappeared down the dark street. Deborah picked up her wine glass, wiping blades of grass from its misty exterior. When she stood up completely, she saw her neighbor, Steve, standing on the sidewalk in front of his house. He eagerly waved to her. But, rather than walk down the street to talk to him like she usually would, she turned and walked inside her house. The shame she felt was just too much to take and she didn't feel like socializing or explaining to Steve just how awful her son, Ricky, was for the hundredth time. She decided it would be better to go inside and drink herself to sleep.

So she did, closing the garage door behind her.

22.

The way the sunlight sparkled on the surface of Town Lake mesmerized Esther Jean, and as she stood on the Congress Avenue Bridge, watching the ducks and paddle-boaters maneuver through the illuminated ripples of the lake, she ruminated about her love life, or lack thereof. She often wondered when love from another would consume her, whether from a man or a woman. She didn't have a preference; she just wanted to be loved. She often pined for love, and it frustrated her that she was denied the intoxicating emotion. The irony of this wasn't lost on the strong-willed, feminist reporter. She didn't want this desire to consume her world but, sometimes, it just did. She couldn't help but think about it.

My broad shoulders are a turn-off, she thought, watching a duck pursue his potential mate through the glistening water. *Maybe I should work out less.*

As she stood there—consumed in her thoughts and hypnotized by the view—Bob the alt-weekly reporter snuck up behind her unnoticed. He had the advantage of the lake's incantation, which distracted Esther Jean. He enjoyed teasing or pranking her at any possible moment like an older yet pesky brother. So when he jabbed her in the ribs—a high-pitched squeal unintentionally released from her lips—she wasn't ultimately surprised that the unsuspecting assailant was her journalistic cohort. She clinched her fists after he poked her, and the sight of Esther Jean raising her dukes amused him.

"Whoa there, Punchy McGee!" he hooted. "Careful with those things!"

Esther Jean realized she was being ridiculously defensive. She unclenched her fists, then chuckled.

"I almost punched you!" she said, adjusting her disheveled outfit.

"I have no doubt you would have *destroyed* me."

"Totally. Without remorse."

"Good thing I can run fast. Ready for coffee and cats?"

"As ready as I'll ever be."

The two reporters walked the seven or eight blocks to the Cheshire Cat Café, the one with terrific espresso and affectionate cats roaming around inside: Esther Jean's favorite place. Once they arrived, Bob laughed at the sign above the entrance, something he did every time he saw it, the titular feline face grinning at customers as they went inside. Bob held the door open for her like a gentleman and she found her favorite table was unoccupied. They made themselves comfortable and ordered two cups of espresso from a friendly waitress.

Esther Jean looked for her favorite kitty—the one named Rascal—but didn't see him anywhere, so she asked the waitress of his whereabouts.

"You got me," the waitress said, miffed. "He's named Rascal for a reason."

Esther Jean nodded an affirmation at the waitress, who ran off to give the barista their order.

"Hi, how are you?" she said to Bob, sitting across from her. He wore a cream-colored T-shirt with the "Hi, how are you" alien frog on the front, a caricature famously drawn by the schizophrenic Texas musician Daniel Johnston, who painted a mural of it on the wall outside of a now-defunct record store. Bob liked wearing T-shirts with historic punk rock landmarks on them. It made him feel clever or, better yet, hip, even though he disagreed with the moniker of "hipster." He chuckled at Esther Jean's referential salutation.

"Hi, how are *you*?"

"Good. Ready for coffee. And Rascal."

Bob swiveled his head, looking around for the reclusive cat.

"I don't see him yet. Maybe someone adopted him," he said, nonchalantly.

"You shut your mouth!" she cried out with mock anger. "No one is adopting that pussy but me."

"Fine," he said, getting more comfortable in his chair.

"I'm just not sure if Mew would get along with Rascal, though," she mused, scratching her head.

"Mew?" he said, confused.

"My cat Mew. His full name is Bartholomew."

"Ah."

The waitress returned, two espressos to deliver, then disappeared again. The two friends quickly sipped their delicious caffeine delivery systems.

"Wha cha covering these days?" she said, curiously.

"Mostly city council stuff. Not too exciting, except for that new parking ordinance downtown for musicians who need to unload their vans for live gigs. That's got quite a few folks riled up. Causes a shit-ton of traffic. What about you?"

"Mostly state ledge stuff, except when Governor Bennett news comes around. That maniac sells news. I can't get away from him!" she said, finishing her espresso. She raised her hand for the waitress to return, and she promptly did. They both ordered another cup of espresso.

"His ugly mug is everywhere. I heard a rumor that he has only one testicle," he teased.

"Really?!" she said, her curiosity piqued. "Do tell!"

"That's all I've heard on that one."

"What else have you heard, then?"

"Hmmm," he said, stroking his chin, setting up a funny premise. "I heard that he grew up in a polygamist cult in West Texas."

"I've heard that one, too. Not true. I looked into it. He did spend time in El Paso as a kid, though."

"Right. I was just joking anyway."

As Bob finished his espresso, Esther Jean rummaged through her memories for a rumor about a local politician that she knew to be true, but wasn't sure if Bob knew its validity or not. She thought of it as a simple test to see just how deeply embedded he was in the local political scene. She quickly thought of one and initiated her test.

"I heard Councilman Waterson enjoys hanging out at the bondage club on 4th Street and is a founding member of the Austin Grizzly Bears Society."

Bob spit out the last sip of his espresso onto the front of his T-shirt. He quickly sat up and attempted to clean his prized shirt, but it was already ruined.

"Damn it! This T-shirt is vintage and hard to find."

Esther Jean laughed at his misfortune.

"Well? Is it true?" she prodded.

The waitress arrived with their second round of espressos and scrutinized Bob's attempt to save his T-shirt from ruin.

"You should dab, not wipe," she said, setting their espressos on the table. Esther Jean tipped her five dollars and winked. The waitress happily retreated to the coffee bar with a skip in her step.

"She's right. Gotta dab, not wipe."

"Yeah, yeah," he said, annoyed. Seeing his efforts were futile, he tossed the napkin onto the table. "Shit. I loved this shirt."

"So? Is it true?" she said. She knew the rumor was true—having witnessed Councilman Waterson rubbing the bare belly of a large, hairy gay man at a late-night event at the bondage club—but wanted to see what Bob personally knew.

"I've heard that one but don't know if it's true or not," he said, carefully sipping his new drink.

"It would be crazy if it *was*, riiight?" she said, extending the last syllable, then going up an octave.

"I guess."

Bob was still sad about his vintage shirt. Not only was it ruined, but so was his morning.

"Are you going to the governor's press conference tomorrow?" she said, then sipped her espresso.

"Of course. I wouldn't miss it."

"Want to meet up beforehand? Maybe outside the Governor's Mansion?"

"Sure," he said, standing up, rifling through his pocket for money for a tip.

"Are you leaving?" she said, surprised.

"Yeah, gonna go home and change," he said, bluntly.

"Really? I can barely see the stain."

"It's going to bug me all day."

"But I was going to tell you that Bennett called me about an exclusive story."

"Really?" he said, slightly interested but still distracted. "Sounds cool."

"I was going to tell you all about it."

"Tell me tomorrow. I gotta go change." As he walked away, he called back to her, "There's Rascal over there." Then he left the café.

Esther Jean spotted Rascal the pussycat in the corner. He appeared to limp a few steps before their waitress appeared and sprinkled some catnip on the floor for him to sniff and nibble. Concerned, Esther Jean jogged over to the waitress to see what the matter was with her favorite cat. Noticing her approach, Rascal puffed up his fur and then ran as he normally would. Esther Jean was baffled that he was not limping anymore.

"I thought I saw Rascal limping," she said to the waitress.

"Pshaw!" the waitress scoffed. "He learned to do that. It gets him attention. He's fine."

"Really?"

"Yep. I told you he was named Rascal for a reason."

The waitress left Esther Jean alone. She spotted Rascal across the café, licking his paw and then combing the fur on his head, completely normal without signs of an injury.

A rascal indeed, she thought. *So cute!*

She went back to her table, then sat down to finish her espresso. After a few minutes, Rascal made his way over to her, jumping in her lap. He curled up in a swirl of fur and whiskers, then fell asleep.

23.

It was the big day. An electric buzz coursed through Unit 3 as the data entry clerks and their supervisor ate breakfast at their desks. Rita had baked buttermilk biscuits early in the morning—some of which she gave to her grandchildren, if they were finished getting ready for school—and brought the rest along with a boat of white gravy for her friends at work. J. D. brought a container filled with pecan snacks and proudly displayed them on the break table: cinnamon muffins with pecans, mini pecan pies, and fudge squares with a pecan on top of each. Deborah made coffee and tea for her coworkers since she couldn't afford to bring anything to contribute for the breakfast, nor had the strength to make anything from the few ingredients she had in her house. Conchino uncovered a plastic container filled with scrambled eggs and bacon—his contribution that his mother had made and lovingly packed for him before he left to pick up Deborah and Rita for their morning commute—setting the container on the break table as well. And Brent plucked on his beat-up, acoustic guitar, attempting to tune it while he ate his food.

"Are you really going to take that to the press conference?" J. D. said, his mouth full of bacon and eggs.

"Hell yeah, I'm taking it!" Brent chirped. "Why wouldn't I?"

"No one wants to hear you pick and strum that thing!" Deborah said from her desk at the back of the office space. Rita snickered at her friend's spunk and audacity to goad their supervisor on this important day. "It sounds like a sick cat."

"You gonna dance a jig for the governor, too?" Rita added.

"Very funny," Brent said, annoyed. "We should finish up and walk over soon. The Big Boss said for us to be there by 9:30. He'll be waiting for us down in the lobby."

Despite their playful resentment toward their supervisor, the four clerks quickly finished their breakfast as he asked, thoroughly cleaned up the break table, and followed Brent (guitar in hand, inside a bumper sticker-clad guitar case) out of Unit 3 down to the lobby. When they emerged down there, Emmitt the security guard was glad to see them, knowing full well where they were going. He was also enamored to see Rita, with whom he enjoyed a flirtatious, single-sided rapport.

"Well, if it isn't the Heroes of Unit 3!" he said, clapping enthusiastically as they approached him. "And the *beautiful* Ms. Rita Jackson as well."

Emmitt winked at Rita, who smiled uncomfortably at his unwelcomed compliment. She knew of Emmitt's desire for her (he plainly made it known on a daily basis whenever she walked by) but it could never replace her love for her late husband, Reggie Sr., whom she still missed dearly. The thought of spending time with another man filled her with acute guilt.

"I'm married!" Rita yelped, ignoring his extended hand, hoping he could kiss hers.

"Your husband is *dead*, Ms. Rita! Has been for a while," Emmitt said, dejected.

"My love for him still strong!" She quickly skirted past the infatuated security guard over to where the Big Boss, Mr. Schneidermann, was patiently waiting for them. Emmitt greeted the others as they walked by.

"My man, J. D. Wiswall! And Brent Baker, the man of the hour! And Conchino, the quiet giant!" He emphatically shook all of their hands except for Deborah's. He ignored her completely but that didn't bother Deborah. She was suspicious of his overzealous behavior anyway and hissed at him when she passed.

Mr. Schneidermann smiled as they gathered around him.

"Everyone ready?" he said, looking each and every one of them in the eyes. To him, they seemed as ready as could be, which was fine by him. "Good, let's go!"

Outside, the four data entry clerks followed Brent, who carried his guitar case in front of him like a marching band field commander, pumping it up and down as he marched across the Great Lawn of the Capitol Building, embodying the essence of the Pied Piper of yore. Mr. Schneidermann straggled behind, examining his cell phone for messages while he walked, bumbling through the grass. Nonetheless, Brent proudly led the group.

"I bet my hand is going to hurt from all the autographs I sign!" he said, a skip in his step.

The four clerks looked at each other, punctuated by Deborah's sarcastic eyeroll.

"I bet your butt is going to hurt from all the bending over you will be doing!" she squawked. The other three clerks snickered. But Brent didn't care. He was in too good of a mood to be bothered by Deborah's resentment or asinine commentary. For all he knew, it was going to be the best day ever. And he couldn't wait for it to start.

They all followed Brent Baker across the Great Lawn, around the Capitol Building, to the Governor's Mansion.

***

Esther Jean waited near the entrance of the Governor's Mansion for Bob the alt-weekly reporter a few yards away from the throng of reporters waiting to go inside, under a tall magnolia tree. She was smartly dressed in a tan business suit with a baby blue silk blouse that she purposefully ensured did not match anything inside the Governor's Mansion, although she struggled to stand in the grass under the tree since the matching stiletto heels jabbed into the St. Augustine lawn.

Damn it! she thought, as she struggled to stand in the grass. She debated stepping closer to the throng of reporters on the walkway, but preferred the shade of the tree, a cooler environment that was more favorable to her meticulously applied makeup. Fortunately for her, she could see Bob crossing the street toward the Governor's Mansion and looked forward to bolstering her stance in the grass with his tall frame. He quickly joined her under the tree.

"Finally!" she said, putting her hands on his shoulder, propping herself up.

"Why are you standing under this tree?" he said, looking casual in a denim, button-down, short-sleeve shirt and tan slacks. He noticed the colors of his clothes matched hers, quite well in fact, like they were wearing similar uniforms. "Ha! We look like teammates or something."

"Damn it!" she cried out. "I tried hard not to match anything or anybody today."

"You failed," he said. "Bennett must have a big announcement. All the outlets are here. Look at all those people!"

They watched the throng of reporters push and shove each other, some jockeying for position at the front of the group to get inside first. Esther Jean scoffed at their in-fighting.

"I told you Bennett called me, right?" she said to Bob.

"He did?" he said, looking blankly at her. "Why am I surprised? He *likes* you."

"I guess."

"He doesn't call *me*," he said, dismissively. "He barely even looks at me. Why did he call you?"

"He said he had an exclusive for me."

"You're lucky."

"Maybe."

The doors at the entrance of the Governor's Mansion slowly opened and the group of shoving reporters flowed inside, flashing their media credentials to unimpressed security guards. Esther Jean and Bob watched them ooze into the building while they stayed back in the safety of the tree shade.

"Any idea what he wants to tell you?" he said. "Shall we go inside?"

He motioned for her to lead the way and he followed behind out of the grass, then walked next to her on the walkway, his arm near her back, almost touching it.

"No idea. He said he'd invite me back to his office after the press conference."

"Again with the sexual favors!" he blurted.

Esther Jean laughed. Then they went inside the Governor's Mansion.

***

Governor Bennett sat behind his desk—surrounded by his makeup and hair and publicity people—getting ready for the press conference. On his desktop sat a large, round, gold-plated, illuminated mirror. He peeked at his reflection whenever he had the chance. His appearance during publicity events was of the utmost importance to him, knowing that his face would be splattered across all the media outlets the very second it was over: television, newspapers, websites, everywhere. He wasn't the most handsome man in the State of Texas but, if he could help it, he wanted to be the best groomed. There wasn't much he could do about his ugly mug (except for plastic surgery, which he was vehemently opposed to, thinking it made people look unnatural and freakish), but he had full control of his presentation, at least. He knew he was ugly but didn't dwell on his God-given visage.

Frank the security guard stood watch by the door of the palatial office, occasionally taking a gander at the scrum around the governor's desk. It amused him that his boss was so concerned about his appearance, maybe more so than any of his other gubernatorial duties. The only thing he cared about more than his appearance was his popularity, which, at that moment, was at the bottom of the toilet of public opinion.

At least he can easily fix his hair, Frank thought to himself. *His poll numbers are another story.*

"Fix it! Fix it!" Governor Bennett barked at his hair stylist. The old woman in the brown smock—her body brittle and frail like a dried leaf—tried to set Bennett's hair into its odd style, but she was having trouble molding his hair. He shimmied back and forth in his wheelchair, making it difficult for her to work. "It needs to swoop up and be pitch black like an oil slick on the Galveston coast!"

"Yes, sir," she said, meekly. "I'm trying."

"You better get it right or you'll be out on the street. Pronto!"

The frail hair stylist scooped a handful of pomade out of a white container and attempted to fix his hairdo, but he wouldn't sit still. A younger makeup artist patted powder on his face, dancing around the hair stylist. The governor squirmed like a precocious child, too impatient to sit still. The publicist stood a few feet away, pecking at the screen of her cell phone, which, of course, irritated the governor.

"Hey, you! Pecker McCell-Phone! Go see if they're here!"

The publicist—a young, smartly dressed woman in her mid-twenties who appeared shocked at his brazen oafishness—retreated to the door, which Frank the security guard graciously opened for her. But before he could close it, the governor commanded, "Make sure she finds them!"

So Frank followed her, closing the door behind him.

"Slackers!" he muttered to himself.

A moment later, the door reopened. The publicist and Frank the security guard were followed in by two individuals, the guests of honor: Mr. Ted Schneidermann and Brent Baker.

Governor Bennett waved them over to his desk and they sat down in two chairs in front of it, amazed at the attention the governor was receiving from his staff. Brent set his guitar case on the floor against the front of the desk.

"Schneidey!" Governor Bennett called out, then grinned, exposing his gold tooth. "How's the kiddo?"

Mr. Schneidermann uncomfortably shifted in his seat, crossing his legs.

"As I told you, sir, I do not—"

"Yes, I know. You don't have any kids. I'm just busting your balls, Schneidey! Sheesh!"

"Oh... right," Mr. Schneidermann said, nervously chuckling. He peered over at Brent Baker, who was aghast. He stared at the governor, who in turn noticed the guitar case leaning against his desk.

"And this must be—" the governor began.

"Brent Baker!" Brent said, extending his hand for a shake, standing up slightly to reach him, but the governor didn't shake it. Brent slowly retracted his congenial hand.

"I know who you are, young man. Did you bring a *guitar* to my press conference?"

"Why, yes. I thought I might play a—"

"Oh, you're not playing anything, my boy. This press conference is more about *me* than you," he said, thumbing his chest.

"Uhhh," Brent said, taken aback. "I see. Well, can I keep it here until it's over?"

"I don't care what you do with it."

"Okey dokey, sir."

Brent sat back down, interlacing his fingers and then setting his hands in his lap. Governor Bennett clapped his hands and waved off his staff. They weren't quite done but he had grown impatient, wanting to start the press conference and get it over with as soon as possible.

"Enough! I look perfect!" he yelled, examining himself in the mirror, then sliding it to the side of the desktop. His staff scurried like ants, retreating from an attack by a hungry beast. He leaned forward with both his palms on the desk, leering at his two guests. "I will give an introduction to the media and then introduce you both. It'll be short but sweet. You don't need to say much—if anything at all. Then I'll ask for questions to wrap this thing up. Got it?!"

The governor leaned back, examining his guests. Ted Schneidermann and Brent Baker nodded.

"Perfect!" he said, snapping his fingers at Frank the security guard, who promptly came to the desk. "Take these two to the launch pad. I'll be out shortly."

The two reluctant guests of honor followed the hulking security guard, who directed them out of the office while he held the door open for the governor. Bennett backed up his gold-plated wheelchair, then maneuvered it around the desk so he could join them on the launch pad: the staging area behind the curtain where the podium stood before the gaggle of reporters.

"It's go time!" he said, then drove out of the office. Frank closed the door behind them.

* * *

The conference room was filled to capacity, all the seats taken, and the standing area at the back was filled with photographers, videographers, and their equipment. Brent's four data entry clerks sat in the front row in a section reserved just for them, clumped together with reporters surrounding them. Esther Jean and Bob sat in the back row—a defensive move on Bob's part—in hopes of avoiding verbal shrapnel from the governor. Curiosity and apprehension filled the air like static electricity, as each and every one in the packed room wondered what the impromptu press conference was about, knowing only that the governor wanted to announce something "big and marvelous for the State of Texas," but also aware that the governor was not a pleasant orator to listen to as well as to query. The governor was just too irritable and cantankerous for most of them, except maybe Esther Jean.

Bob leaned over to her, then whispered, "This might be a shit show."

Esther Jean surveyed the room, noticing the adversarial reporters from competing outlets, then replied, "Just might be."

"Remember when he called Patty 'Frizzy' at the last press conference, then threw her out?" he said, his face contorting into an expression of bewilderment mixed with disgust.

"Yep."

She craned her head to catch a glimpse of the four data clerks in the front row—obviously VIPs from their position in the room—and she couldn't register in her mind if she had ever seen them before. Then she turned to Bob, noticing the worry manifested on his face.

"I'm not going to ask him a question. I don't want to get thrown out, too," he said.

"Suit yourself," she said, then noticed some commotion by the podium at the front of the room.

Governor Bennett unceremoniously maneuvered his gold-plated wheelchair from behind the curtain up a ramp to the podium, which lowered by hydraulics to accommodate his stature in the wheelchair. Two men flanked him to the left: Ted Schneidermann and Brent Baker. They stiffly stood there like two cadavers, propped up by fear. A toothy grin appeared on Governor Bennett's face. He was pleased with the turnout and hoped for a bump in his poll numbers by the end of the day. He tapped the microphone with his index finger, sending an amplified knock to the back of the room.

"Good morning!" he said, then peered around the room. "We have a mighty fine turnout here on this momentous day. I see a lot of smiling faces in the room!"

All the reporters in attendance gazed at each other, only seeing grimaces and fear and confusion; there were no smiles to be found. Governor Bennett continued.

"You know, my great-grandfather was a *great* man. He became filthy rich as a prospector of precious metals. He once said, 'To find gold, one must turn every stone, one must look in every nook and cranny, one must extinguish all possibilities, to discover it!' And he meant what he said. He had a saying, 'You just might have to squeeze a prairie dog to find the gold you are looking for!' And I abide by that tenet to this very day. It's how I live my life and how I run this great state of ours: the State of Texas!" he said, raising the index finger of his right hand for emphasis.

The gaggle of reporters were thoroughly confused and a grumble filled the air, followed by scribbles on paper and the tapping of electronic screens. Bob gave Esther Jean an expression that said, 'What the hell?!' The governor continued, undeterred by the reporters' confusion.

"One of my campaign promises was to find ways to save this great state of ours money, to save your tax dollars from being wasted. And that's why I've called you here today. I want to tell you something monumental, momentous, and magnificent!"

He raised both index fingers high like an honor guard firing volleys from bolt-action rifles at a funeral.

"As you may or may not know, your state government is constantly trying to find ways to save money and has a program for its employees, The State Employees Cost-Savings Suggestion Program, where any employee of the State of Texas can submit a suggestion that could possibly save the state money. And boy, do we have a doozy for you! I have personally selected this year's cost-saving suggestion from a pile of many worthy suggestions."

He paused briefly to pull a postcard from his inside coat pocket. He scanned a few lines on the card, cleared his throat, then continued.

"Ah yes, behind me stand two men from the Texas Department of Unemployment and Benefits. We have Brent Baker, the man of the hour!"

A smattering of applause greeted Brent, who then raised both arms triumphantly, which of course annoyed Governor Bennett, who didn't waste the opportunity to retrieve the spotlight back from Brent.

"Calm down, Rocky Balboa!" the governor barked, at the expense of Brent's pride. "Next to him is his supervisor, Ted Schneidermann."

Schneidermann raised both hands in front of him like a defeated soldier surrendering to his captors, unwilling to fight them. He didn't dare irk the governor or hurt his chances of being a commissioner one day. Having introduced his two guests, the governor flicked away the postcard into one of the ferns next to the podium, then continued his speech.

"Mr. Baker discovered a solution in the data entry software that will save the State of Texas hundreds of millions of dollars!"

The gaggle of reporters marveled at this declaration, releasing a sound of awe from their collective mouths. Governor Bennett smiled at their reaction, contemplating just how high his poll numbers would climb the following day.

"That's right, folks. Hundreds of *millions* of dollars! The savings will be seen by year's end with the expiration of several large employment contracts. It's monumental, I tell you!"

The room exploded in applause, particularly from the front row, where Brent's coworkers sat, beaming at their supervisor. Even Deborah enthusiastically applauded him, which was a surprise to Brent considering he was used to contempt shooting from her eyeballs at him. The reporters were impressed too, for once, witnessing a real person doing some good for the State of Texas. Brent bowed to the reporters and his coworkers. Governor Bennett was pleased with how the press conference was unfolding and, without really thinking, offered the podium to his star employee.

"Want to introduce yourself?" he said, backing up his wheelchair, his arm extended to offer the microphone.

Brent stepped to the podium, its height reaching only to his waist. He started to bend down, as if to get on his knees, when the podium hydraulically raised itself, someone controlling it off-stage somewhere. Once in place, he tapped the microphone with his finger.

"Yo! Microphone check, one, two... what is this?!" he rapped, then extended his arms out as if to say, 'Check me out!' He was greeted with silence. "Oh, OK. Ummm, I'd like to thank the governor for selecting my cost-savings suggestion. I'd like to thank my coworkers for believing in me... and they're all right here in the front row!"

He indicated where they were sitting, then motioned for them to stand. They reluctantly stood up. Brent applauded them which, in turn, encouraged the reporters to applaud them, too.

"There they are: Rita, Deborah, Conchino, and J. D. My crew!" he said, then clapped some more for them. His coworkers absorbed the adulation from the room for a moment, then sat down. Brent continued.

"I'd also like to thank my band, who are playing tonight at the—"

Governor Bennett quickly tired of Brent's acceptance speech. He drove his wheelchair into the back of Brent's legs, almost toppling him to the floor. Once out of the way and back by Schneidermann's side, the governor motioned for the podium to be lowered to his preferred height. It slowly descended back into the stage.

"All right, that's enough of that. Thank you, Mr. Schneidermann and Mr. Baker. You can leave now."

They both skirted around the curtain, out of sight. Governor Bennett adjusted his jacket, which wiggled out of place during the unrehearsed confusion.

"Let's hear it for them one more time."

The clerks of Unit 3 clapped enthusiastically while the reporters readied their questions.

"Any questions?"

Several hands shot up and Governor Bennett scanned the room for his preferred inquisitors. He pointed to a young, attractive blond woman in front from a local TV station. She stood to ask her question.

"Good morning, Governor. Do you have any more details about this cost-saving suggestion?" she said, lifting her pad and pencil as if shielding herself from an attack.

"Not at the moment but there will be specifics in the press release we send out this afternoon. Next!"

Esther Jean peered at Bob, prodding him with her eyes to ask a question, but Bob silently refused, shaking his head. More hands in the room raised and the governor pointed at a different attractive young woman, his preferred gender and age of reporter.

"You had mentioned something your great-grandfather used to say about a prairie dog. What does it mean again?" she said, lifting a microphone up to record his response.

"It's pretty self-evident what it means. My great-grandfather was very successful so you will have to infer its wisdom yourself. Next!"

Esther Jean raised her hand, catching Bennett's eye. He pointed to her, then she stood up, all eyes in the room turning to her.

"Governor, what does this employee receive for saving the State of Texas hundreds of *millions* of dollars?"

Knowing the answer was on the postcard, Governor Bennett reached into his coat to retrieve it, but realized that he had discarded it in the fern, so he snapped his fingers, notifying

Frank the security guard to assist him. He emerged from behind the curtain to fetch the card from the fern. Once he gave it to the governor, he quickly returned back behind the curtain. Bennett read a few lines on the postcard to himself, then cleared his throat and answered the question.

"The selected employee suggestion nets Mr. Baker $10,000 on his next paycheck, before taxes of course. What a fine way to thank him for his suggestion and his service. Next!"

But rather than sit down and allow another reporter to ask a question, Esther Jean continued.

"What exactly did Mr. Baker suggest that would save the State of Texas so much money? Surely, you have a few details for us..."

"Again, it'll be in the press release this afternoon. I want to thank you all for your time but I'm a busy man. Until next time!" he said, then unceremoniously backed up his wheelchair, stopped, and raised both index fingers triumphantly in the air. He then maneuvered his wheelchair off the stage, disappearing behind the curtain.

And just like that, the important press conference was over. The four clerks of Unit 3 stood up and received handshakes from some reporters while the rest of the media slowly filed out of the conference room, except for Esther Jean and Bob. They continued to sit and watch the mob of reporters exit. She examined the clerks from Unit 3, curious if they would be willing to talk to her on the record. Bob noticed her watching them.

"Are you going to talk to them?" he said, elbowing her. "The black lady looks nice."

"I want to but I'm supposed to meet with Mr. Bennett after the press conference."

"When are you meeting him?"

"I have no idea. Hopefully soon."

As the last few reporters left, the clerks of Unit 3 congratulated each other with handshakes and back slaps, then milled about for a few, brief minutes. With no one left in the room but Esther Jean and Bob, they looked around for their supervisor. Not finding him, they decided to leave. Esther Jean waved at them. J. D. returned an enthusiastic wave, then followed his coworkers back to work.

Esther Jean and Bob sat in the conference room alone, except for a janitor who entered with a vacuum, wearing the motor on his back like a backpack and sucking up remnants of the press conference from the floor with a vacuum hose.

"How long are we going to wait?" Bob said to Esther Jean.

"As long as I have to."

Eventually, Frank the security guard emerged from behind the curtain and approached the two reporters. Stopping in front of them, he towered high above their heads. They tilted their heads back to look up at him.

"Mr. Bennett told me to tell you that he will contact you another time. Something important has come up."

"Oh, OK," Esther Jean said, nudging Bob. "Then I'll wait for his call."

The two reporters stood up and quickly left the conference room. Frank watched until they were gone, then turned around to head back to the Governor's Office. As he passed the janitor, he pointed to the ground and said, "You missed a spot."

Once behind the curtain, the janitor raised his hand in Frank's direction, stiffly extended his profane middle finger, then continued his duty the way he preferred to do it.

24.

All the members of the North Austin Racing Club parked their cars in the front row of the Wells Port Shopping Center at midnight. With their hoods propped up, some of the members milled about inspecting the modified engines of their fellow members' cars, while others drank beer in red plastic cups pumped from a pony keg hidden in the trunk of a 1999 Honda Prelude. Conchino stood next to his car at the end of the row, sipping a beer. A few minutes earlier, he had enviously gawked at a custom air intake system in a 2000 BMW 540i and his jealousy festered, so he walked back to his car to ponder how to get the money to install a similar one in his Honda Accord. He knew money from Brent's cost-savings suggestion prize would eventually make its way to him, but he had a couple of things to consider when the money finally hit his bank account. He had been pining for a performance chip for his car but, also, his mother had been worrying about her ailing father in Japan. Two thousand dollars would go a long way in helping his parents bring his grandfather to the United States to live with them. Still, he wrestled with what to do: auto performance or familial responsibility? Both were tantalizing prospects in equal measures.

Should I invest in performance upgrades? he thought, while sipping beer. *Or help my mom bring granddad over from Japan? Either way, I'd win.*

He soon finished his beer and tossed the cup into the backseat of his car. He didn't want to drink too much beer, just in case he was picked later to race, something he desperately wanted to do. He was in a celebratory mood, having witnessed his boss receive some recognition at the Governor's Mansion earlier that day, even though the press conference wasn't all it was cracked up to be. No matter, he enjoyed watching his coworkers have fun—even if the governor wasn't very accommodating—because Rita, Deborah, and J. D. had a ball being in close proximity to the famous politician as well as sharing Brent's newfound notoriety and accomplishment. They all felt they shared what Brent was luckily being given. In actuality, Brent really didn't do anything except drunkenly sleep in the right place at the right time, but their pact intrinsically tied them all together. Being a part of this all excited Conchino more than he realized, and he needed a way to let off steam. Street racing was his way of doing just that.

He constantly checked his phone to see if there was a message about a new race. The North Austin Racing Club had an elaborate yet secretive procedure for organizing, setting up, announcing, then proceeding with a street race in order to avoid problems with law enforcement. The worst thing that could happen would be an arrest of a member and impoundment of their car. To minimize risk, the high-ranking members of the club spent the week before a meet concocting an elaborate bait and switch for the police. Then once the police were distracted, they had an additional elaborate plan to cordon traffic so no one could interfere with the race. Conchino heard rumors that three members would be randomly selected to be in a race on the interstate highway, an idea that was completely bonkers since so many eighteen-wheelers traveled north and south on it. He was excited to see if he would be selected.

As he stood by his car, checking his phone, he was approached by the owner of the car parked next to his. Raul was his name and he was a new member in the club. He hadn't been selected for a race yet and probably wouldn't be for a while; new members had to wait to race. His diminutive size comically contrasted with Conchino's massive stature. Dressed in tan chinos and a T-shirt with short-cropped hair—similar to Conchino—Raul offered a fist bump, which Conchino quickly acknowledged with a tap of his fist. In another life, they could have been brothers from the looks of them.

"You see that air intake on that Beamer?" Raul said, sipping beer. "Makes my K&N filter look like shit."

Conchino chuckled, then looked at his phone again.

"You think you'll race tonight?" Raul added, finishing his beer, then crumpling the cup.

Conchino shrugged.

"Don't talk much, do you?"

Conchino smiled, then his phone dinged a notification. He looked at it and flashed a toothy grin. Raul knew exactly what that meant.

"Oh shit! You're up!" Raul said, offering a hand so Conchino could give him some skin. He slapped Raul's hand before hopping in his car.

He cranked the ignition—his engine rumbling to life and then idling like a hungry jungle cat—and waited for the phone call to tell him what to do. As he waited, a bright red, 1998 Toyota Supra pulled in front of his car—its windows tinted black with a massive spoiler mounted on the trunk— then stopped briefly. Its engine rumbled and its muffler gurgled as the car idled in place, the driver wearing mirrored sunglasses and his hair gelled tall and prickly. Then without warning, the driver tore out of the parking lot, leaving burnt rubber on the asphalt as it turned sharply on the frontage road of the highway, speeding into the distance, the car swallowed by darkness. Soon after, a few police cruisers appeared from nowhere and pursued the decoy, leaving the club members alone. As soon as the cruisers were out of sight, they all ran to their cars, starting them as soon as they jumped in. While Conchino watched them, his phone rang. He placed a receiver in his ear, then answered the phone.

"Yeah?" he said, his voice deep and gravelly.

"Go to I-35 and Rundberg. The race starts there. You're driver number three. The finish line is at I-35 and Wells Port Boulevard. Got it?"

"Yeah," Conchino said, then hung up the phone.

He put his car in first gear, stomped the accelerator, and tore out of the parking lot. Most of the club members followed him in their street racers, just a few staying behind in case the police came back. Conchino knew what the instructions meant: Driver #3 was to occupy the far-right lane on the highway, while driver #2 occupied the middle lane, and driver #1 occupied the far-left lane. He knew that section of I-35 very well and also knew from documents and memorandum circulated within the club that a decoy would stop traffic before the Rundberg Overpass. He was to enter the highway after the overpass and wait for the other drivers on the highway. The decoy was usually a pickup truck or van disguised as a service vehicle from the city or county, and it would stop traffic with orange cones and flares as if it was protecting construction workers (other club members disguised in overalls or workmen body suits). It was an effective decoy at such a late hour, not being unusual that construction work would be done at night on the dilapidated highway. Conchino sped to his destination as fast as his car could go.

Once on the frontage road near where he needed to be, he could see a white van and people disguised as a city construction crew. The highway was backed up due to flares and flags, and he knew he had to get on the far end of the overpass as soon as he could. There wasn't much time. He turned onto the entrance ramp, then parked at the starting position in the far-right lane of the empty highway. As he waited, he watched the fake construction crew block the highway in his rearview mirror, irritated drivers honking their horns and flashing their high beams. Within seconds, his competitors appeared, one parking in the middle lane, the other in the far lane. He looked over at the car in the middle and discovered Raul in the car with an excited look on his face. Conchino tilted his head back, as if to say, "I see you." Raul revved his car's engine in acknowledgment, the souped-up four-cylinder motor screaming. The early '90s Mustang in the far-left lane was Bob or Bill's; Conchino couldn't remember his exact name or see his face.

At the side of the road, a pickup truck appeared from the top of the grassy embankment, tearing down through the grass and screeching to a stop on the highway shoulder. A burly man wearing sunglasses jumped out of the pickup truck with two red bandanas in his hands. He ran out onto the highway. Standing on the lane divider line between the middle and far-left lane, he raised the bandanas above his head. Conchino watched the bandanas as they blew in the wind. He gripped his steering wheel tightly with his left hand and squeezed the knob of his shifter with his right hand. When the bandanas fell, Conchino stomped on his accelerator, his car roaring to life. He felt the rear of his car swerve slightly as the front wheels plowed up the highway, gravel and smoke shooting out the back. His heart pounded as his car sped down the highway, the yellow divider lines shooting past him in a blur. He glanced to the left and could see both cars trying to gain on him, so he stomped the clutch and shifted with purpose. He wanted to win, and as his car's engine escalated past 4,000 RPMs, he could feel the power generated by his engine modifications. His car was performing better than he had hoped. He looked in the driver-side mirror. As the two competing cars fell behind him, a rush of pride overtook him. He couldn't help but smile, watching the two cars shrink in the mirror, the street lights whizzing past in pulsing bursts of yellow-tinted illumination, his car roaring as his speed increased.

Something nagged at him, though, as he drove over the next overpass. As he came down the other side, flashing blue and red lights reflected in his rearview mirror, police cruisers careening on the highway from the next entrance ramp—three of them, maybe four. His two competitors were no longer visible from his driver-side mirror and he couldn't help but think they saw the cruisers before he did, being he was too consumed with pride and adrenaline to notice. He decided right then and there that he would take the next exit and evade them by driving through Deborah's neighborhood, which wasn't too far away, a section of town he knew quite well, maybe even hide in her garage if he could get there fast enough. He quickly turned off the highway at the next exit but, as he sped down the exit ramp, he could see three police cruisers parked at the end of it, barricading the frontage road. He briefly thought of jumping the curb and driving through the grass but, for some reason not very clear to him, he slammed on his brakes. His car swerved left and right, then stopped. Without the clutch engaged, the engine hiccupped, then died.

Smoke and dust billowed around his car as the police cruisers surrounded him. He raised his hands as a sign of abdication, not wanting to get shot, or worse, beaten to death. His heart pounded in his chest, pumping his blood at a frantic pace into his neck and up to his head. The thrill of victory was gone, replaced by remorse and regret. All he had wanted to do was blow off some steam and enjoy himself, not get arrested. But it seemed his worst nightmare was coming to fruition.

One of the police officers rapped a night stick on his driver-side window, but he didn't respond or speak or even look at him. He just sat there with his hands in the air, thoughts of the next morning rushing through his mind, thoughts of Deborah and Rita waiting for him to pick them up for work, then wondering where he could be, or if something terrible had happened to him. That thought tortured him as the police officers forcibly removed Conchino from his car, then handcuffed him.

Rita's disappointed face stared back at him in his mind. He could hear her scolding him.

Boy, what's wrong with you?! she said in his head. *Street racing is for dumb-dumbs!*

25.

Governor Bennett's love of Mexican food was notorious among his staff. He was known to demand orders of *enchiladas* or *carne guisada* at all times of the day or night, whenever his appetite dictated or his stress levels were high. No one was more aware of this peccadillo than Frank the security guard. Although it was not an official job duty, it might as well have been listed as one of his daily obligations since it took up quite a bit of his time, organizing the procurement of Mexican food for his boss whenever he desired. So, it didn't surprise Frank one bit when his boss analyzed his poll numbers the day after the press conference and found that his numbers had not increased but, in fact, had gone down.

"Frank!" Governor Bennett yelled from his private bathroom. "Enchiladas! Stat!!"

His security guard was already on the case by that point, having called Miguel's Tex-Mex immediately after overhearing the publicist bemoan the tragic news.

"I will certainly be yelled at today," she moaned. Frank knew what to do upon hearing this.

When the governor angrily drove out of his bathroom, Frank was walking in with a delivery order from Miguel's, piping hot Mexican food inside the to-go containers. Governor Bennett parked his wheelchair at his desk, raising the control arm so he could get close. It pleased him that his security guard was proactive concerning his personal needs.

"You deserve a raise, my boy!" Bennett declared, unwrapping his late-morning feast, a salve for his ire.

"Thank you, sir," Frank said.

"If the state budget wasn't in such a tight spot, then I'd authorize you one this instant!" Governor Bennett placed a napkin over his shirt like a baby's bib, then commenced to stuff his face with *enchiladas* covered in *chipotle* sauce.

"I know you would, sir."

"And my damn poll numbers!" he cried out, pounding his desk with a clenched fist. "I was certain parading those knuckleheads out from the Texas Department of Unemployment and Benefits at the press conference would get me a bump. I didn't get shit!"

He angrily ate his food while Frank watched. It was a sight to behold even though he had witnessed similar chow-downs before. This time, it was clear. Governor Bennett was torturing himself.

What do those crazy priests call it when they beat themselves? Frank thought, watching Governor Bennett stuff his face. *Self-flagellation?*

"Whatever!" Bennett barked. "Next publicity stunt!"

"Anything else, sir?" Frank said, deciding it might be time to leave the governor to himself.

"Yes, let me know when that reporter is here. I want to talk to her."

"Yes, sir," Frank said, then left the office.

He walked to the front of the Governor's Mansion and found the reporter, Esther Jean, waiting at the security desk. A new security guard was checking her purse when Frank intervened.

"She's OK," Frank said, taking the purse from the inexperienced newbie. "Come with me."

Frank pressed a button behind the desk which opened the security gate. Esther Jean walked through, then followed Frank. They walked down a familiar corridor, and Esther Jean once again gazed out at the manicured garden, watching two grackles dance their mating ritual in the lush grass. The sight of the poofy male bird amused her, causing Frank to turn and look at her when she giggled. Frank didn't even crack a smile.

What a sourpuss! she thought, as she followed him into the palatial office.

She was greeted by the gorging governor, his mouth filled with food. He waved her over to his desk and offered her a seat, which she took. Her presence did not impede his gluttonous behavior.

"Don't mind *me*," he said, wiping his mouth with a napkin. "Just getting a quick snack in. The day just flies by!"

"I don't mind," she said, crossing her bare legs. She noticed he watched her as she did that, so she made an effort to fix her skirt as to not inadvertently flash him her private parts. "Finish your meal."

"I'm done. No worries," he said, shoving the plastic and aluminum containers to the side of the desktop. He finished wiping his mouth and hands, then tossed the wadded napkin on the floor. "Now, what can I do for you?"

This question caught Esther Jean off guard.

"What can you do? You invited me here."

"I did?!" he said, confused, sitting up in his wheelchair. He looked over at Frank the security guard, who nodded in agreement with Esther Jean. "Oh, yes, YES! I did."

"You said you had an exclusive for me," she said, setting a legal pad on her legs and readying a pen. "Something monumental. Or was it *momentous*? I can't remember the exact word. It started with an 'M.'"

"Yes, of course," he said, probing his mind for something juicy to tell the overzealous reporter. "Marvelous! I have a story for you. New methods of deterring illegal immigration. Interested?"

"Hmmm," she said, bewildered.

"We have a contractor that has developed machinery that uses motion detectors to launch webs to contain illegals at the border. It really is amazing!"

"You do realize...," she said, sitting up in her seat, then crossing her legs in the opposite direction, "...most illegal immigration occurs nowhere near the borders. Forged documents are a bigger problem than border jumpers."

"But these web cannons. They're amazing! You have to see them to believe it. Really!"

"Not interested," she said, sighing.

"Then what are you looking for?" he said, waving to Frank the security guard to come over, then directing him to clear the to-go containers from his desk. Frank reluctantly did as he was commanded. "A feel-good story in your newspaper would be great! How about stray animal euthanasia?"

"Ewww," she said, disgusted.

"Closing of several abortion clinics?!" he hollered.

"I never saw the press releases for the press conference the other day."

"Excuse me?"

"The press conference? The one where the state employee discovered a solution that will save the State of Texas hundreds of *millions* of dollars?"

"Right," he said, remembering why he originally requested their meeting—the feel-good story about Brent Baker's cost-savings suggestion—although he had hoped she had forgotten all about that. Unfortunately for him, she didn't. "That's yesterday's news."

"I'd like to talk to him. Interview... uh..." She flipped through some pages in her legal pad, then found what she was looking for. "I mean them. Brent Baker. And Ted Schneidermann."

"Ah," he said, leaning back in the seat of his wheelchair, interlacing his fingers, then setting his hands in his lap. He thought of other prime topics he could suggest that he wanted more visibility for: arming teachers with machine guns to prevent mass murders, additional discoveries of fossil fuels by fracking in state parks, or the eradication of pesky, endangered salamanders just down the street at the natural spring. But he decided to acquiesce. The press conference hadn't provided a bump in his poll numbers. Maybe a feel-good story in a prominent city paper would do just that.

"Fine. Fine," he said, leaning forward on his desk. "I'll get you an interview with our prized employee, Bren—"

The governor grabbed his midsection, then groaned loudly, his gut rumbling and gurgling so loud that it sounded like he was going to defecate in his pants. Governor Bennett blushed with embarrassment and held his arms across his stomach, as if to shield the reporter from any further gastronomical detonations. His go-to snack was revolting in his stomach and he didn't know what to do. Without thinking, he placed his hands on the wheelchair armrests, then began to push himself up, as if to stand. He immediately stopped, noticing the reporter was staring at him, then quickly sat back down.

"Please excuse me," he said, backing his chair away from the desk. "I need to use the restroom. I'll be right back."

He maneuvered his wheelchair around his desk, went into the private bathroom, then closed the door behind him, although the door didn't close all the way. Esther Jean was a little stunned and didn't know quite what to make of what she had just witnessed.

Did he just try to stand up? she thought to herself. *No way!*

She looked around the office to see if Frank the security guard was around but didn't see him. So, she decided—right then and there—to sneak over to the bathroom door and take a quick peek. She tiptoed over to the door, quiet as a mouse. When she reached it, she looked within the crack. Inside, the Governor was standing by his own will—not using a cane or crutches or holding onto anything—and wiping his backside.

He delicately cleaned his rear end by patting it, as if it had been dipped in acid, the Mexican food from the night before surely burning on exit. It was a shocking sight to see—not his bare genitals dangling like a withered carrot between his legs, but the governor standing and not appearing handicapped at all. She didn't know what to make of what she was witnessing, but she knew she needed proof if she was going to tell anyone. She quickly reached in her purse for a small camera she carried around with her, just in case of situations just like this. She held up the camera then held down the shutter button, silently snapping a dozen photos in that brief second, then tiptoed back to her chair. Just as she sat down, Frank the security guard entered the room, standing by the door. Governor Bennett soon drove back out to his desk, pretending that he was OK, even though beads of sweat clung to his forehead.

"Where were we?" he said, wiping his brow with a navy blue, silk handkerchief. "Oh, yes! I'll call good ol' Schneidey and set up an appointment for you to interview Brent Baker. Does that work for you?"

"Yes. Yes, of course," she said, shifting uncomfortably in her seat, worried he might have seen her peeking through the door crack. But he didn't give her any indication that he saw her.

"And I hope to see a feel-good story in your newspaper," he said, dialing a number into the phone. He waited while the phone rang, then blurted, "Schneidey! It's Bennett! Governor Bennett. Yes... Yes, it's *me*. Listen Schneidey. I'm going to send over a reporter tomorrow to interview your man, Baker. OK? Give her access to his unit. Got it? Good. Don't let me down, Schneidey. OK? Great! God bless you, too."

He hung up the phone, then accidentally farted.

26.

Emmitt the security guard had only been at work for an hour and already he was bored. There was always a flurry of activity first thing in the morning in the lobby of the Texas Department of Unemployment and Benefits since everyone was arriving for their workday, but that usually died down quickly and his typical routine of manning the security desk and answering the phone began its glacial pace into his workday. He thought of dusting off the desk, a task he didn't find much pleasure in, or maybe wiping the vinyl covers of the various binders that contained the visitor logs. But neither of these tasks sparked his interest. It wasn't until Esther Jean entered the lobby that his morning seemed brighter and less tedious. She wore a tight-fitting pencil skirt and matching blazer, and her hair was shiny and coiffed to perfection. Her high heels clicked and clacked on the tile floor as she approached the security desk.

"Good morning!" he said to Esther Jean, flashing his bright, toothy smile. "Can I help you?"

"I have an appointment with Brent Baker," she said, rummaging through her purse for an identification card. Emmitt waved off her search.

"No need. I was told you were coming. Let me ring Mr. Baker," he said, picking up his phone receiver and dialing Brent's number. After a brief moment, he said, "Mr. Baker, that reporter is here to see you. Right... OK. I'll let her know." He hung up the phone. "He'll be down in a few minutes."

"Thank you," Esther Jean said, flipping her hair over her shoulder, then absorbing the adulation emanating from Emmitt's adoring eyes. She enjoyed the attention first thing in the morning, something she wasn't expecting at all.

"It's a fine morning, innit?" he said, opening the visitor log, then setting it in front of the reporter. "Just need you to sign in here."

"It is a *glorious* morning. The weather is perfect," she said, signing the visitor log. She handed the pen to Emmitt, who smiled mischievously at her.

"Must be exciting working for the city paper! And getting to interview the fine folks at the Texas Department of Unemployment and Benefits, too! That Mr. Baker... he a fine individual. A fine state employee! You'll like him and everyone in Unit 3. Good people up in there!"

Esther Jean returned a curt smirk, then adjusted her jacket. Emmitt continued.

"And let me tell you somethin' else—"

Before he could spill the beans about his personal feelings for Governor Bennett and the political rancor pertaining to that terrible man, Brent Baker emerged from the elevator.

"Well, speak of the devil! Here he is right now!"

Brent extended his hand to the reporter for a shake, which Esther Jean enthusiastically returned.

"Whoa! Quite a *grip* you got there," he said, shaking the pain from his hand.

"I work out," she replied.

"I can see that. Follow me," he said, then led her inside the elevator.

"The security guard is friendly," she remarked.

"Emmitt's the best!"

When the elevator reached the third floor, it dinged. Esther Jean followed Brent out. The interrogation immediately started.

"How long have you worked here?" she said, after pulling out a tape recorder, then clicking the record button. Brent eyeballed the tape recorder. "Do you mind if I record our conversation?"

"Not at all! I love being recorded," he said, continuing down the hall. Esther Jean followed closely.

"OK then. How long have you worked here?"

"Oh, fifteen, maybe twenty years. I can't remember."

They continued down the beige hall and across the skywalk. She watched people scurry about on the ground outside, small as ants from her vantage point.

"That's a long time," she said.

When they reached the door to Unit 3, Brent stopped, smiling broadly, then gripped the door handle.

"Here's where the *magic* happens!"

He opened the door to let her in the office. Inside, J. D. and Deborah were performing their usual morning routine of entering unemployment applications into TAPES. Rita was at the break table, making coffee and arranging their morning snacks into a presentable offering of hospitality.

"Welcome to Unit 3," he said, extending his arm to introduce his employees. "This here is J. D., Deborah, and Rita. Our fourth data entry clerk is out today."

"You mean *arrested!*" Rita squawked. "He was street racing again!"

Esther Jean's eyebrows involuntarily raised like fighting caterpillars, her brain always ready for unsolicited bits of newsworthy information. Brent scowled at Rita.

"Well, we don't know for sure yet if he *was* arrested but—"

"Oh, he's in jail for sure," Deborah continued. "And we didn't get a ride to work this morning. I had to ask my neighbor, Steve, to give us a ride. I was so embarrassed." Her eyes locked with Esther Jean's as they both examined each other.

Brent offered a chair for Esther Jean to sit down next to his desk. She accepted, sitting quickly, then crossing her bare legs. She noticed J. D. looking at her legs, which pleased her. But once he saw that she noticed him taking a peek, he quickly looked away. His face turned red with embarrassment.

"Anyway...," Brent said, sitting behind his desk. "This is where the magic happens."

"You said that already."

"Yes, so I did."

"Tell me more about this cost-saving suggestion, the one that will save the State of Texas hundreds of *millions* of dollars."

She tilted her tape recorder toward Brent, who noticed the recording device more prominently than before, then out of the blue he became filled with self-awareness and anxiety and apprehension, a rare case of stage fright for the attention-hungry rock 'n' roller/supervisor. He thought about the prophetic day when he drank too much beer and stumbled back to work with J. D., but he didn't remember laying his head down or falling asleep on his keyboard. His lack of a meaningful answer in his brain shocked his nervous system into action, in turn activating the sweat glands in his armpits to excrete liquid at an alarming rate. Beads of sweat also appeared on his forehead, which he promptly wiped with his forearm. Esther Jean noticed his reticence.

"Well...," he stammered, looking over at J. D., trying to subconsciously signal him for help, but J. D. didn't get the signal. He just stared blankly back at Brent.

Esther Jean attempted to prod an answer from him.

"Did you correct procedures for the data entry application? Or did you update code for the... What's it called? The Texas Application Processing Entry System?"

"TAPES!" Deborah barked from her desk. "We call it TAPES around here, for short."

Esther Jean turned to see where the comment came from, then saw Deborah in the back of the office peering back at her.

"Cute acronym!" she said, forcing a smile, then turned back to Brent. "Like she said—for TAPES. What exactly did you suggest?"

Brent couldn't control his anxiety much more and all he could think about was smoking a cigarette or downing a beer or anything—ANYTHING—besides sitting in the hot seat with an inquisitive reporter from the city paper. He decided without much thought that it would be OK to take a break from the interview for a respite in the parking garage down in the basement, possibly to smoke a cigarette. At the least, he could think of a reasonable answer to the reporter's question instead of the truth, which was unsavory and infantile and, most of all, ridiculous.

"Do you mind excusing me and..." He looked over to J. D. "Excusing me *and* J. D. for a moment. I just remembered we have an important meeting to attend with the Big Boss. Do you mind?"

Caught a little off guard by the quick interruption, Esther Jean said, "Oh, I don't mind."

"We'll be right back. Promise," he said, pushing papers around on his desk.

"That's OK. Can I chat with these ladies while I wait?"

"That's fine by me," he said, standing at his desk, then indicating with a tilt of his head that it was time for him and J. D. to evacuate. J. D. jumped up from his desk and followed his supervisor out the door of Unit 3, leaving Esther Jean behind with Rita and Deborah, who were dutifully entering unemployment applications into TAPES.

Esther Jean sat her tape recorder on Brent's desk but didn't press the stop button. She pulled a pad of paper from her bag and scribbled down some notes. Rita peeked around her computer monitor and noticed that Esther Jean was without a cup of coffee or a morning beverage of any kind. The genial host in her was appalled that they had not greeted their guest in a proper manner, so she completed the application she was entering, then stood up to approach the break table.

"Would you like some coffee?" she said to Esther Jean.

"That would be fantastic," she replied, placing the pad of paper back in her bag, then meeting Rita at the table. She discovered the plethora of snacks and break-time accompaniments and it pleased her that she would be receiving an additional dose of caffeine. Being that Esther Jean preferred the night life, it was still just too early in the morning for her to think straight. Rita loaded up the coffee maker to start the morning brew.

"Want a sweet treat to go along with it? There's plenty. I brought banana bread. My grandkids don't like it 'cause I put nuts in it. They crazy!"

"I would love some," she said, smiling.

Rita cut her a slice, then said, "Must be exciting working for the city paper. The most excitement we get around here is meeting the governor the other day. That was excitin'!"

"Well, you did mention that one of your coworkers was in jail for street racing," Esther Jean said, taking a bite of her bread, then covering her mouth as she chewed. "That sounds pretty exciting to me."

At this point, Deborah just couldn't stay away from the conversation between the two women, or from the banana bread and fresh coffee. She hadn't received a piece of bread yet and was ready to partake, as well as gossip with Rita and their guest. It was a rare event having anyone in their office besides the five coworkers, or maybe Ken, the former paper collector, who didn't come around much anymore.

"It's just our suspicion about Conchino but it seems plausible to us. He never forgets to pick us up for work. He once joked that if he wasn't there to pick us up, then that meant he was in jail. So, we just figured that's what happened to him."

"I see," Esther Jean said, finishing her piece of banana bread. Rita handed her a cup of coffee, which Esther Jean proceeded to put three large spoonfuls of sugar into. Rita was astonished.

"Girl! How do you stay thin putting that much sugar in your coffee?" Rita squawked. "I'd weigh a ton with that much in my cup."

"I work out a lot," Esther Jean said, flattered.

"We workout our keyboards a lot," Deborah chimed in. "Our hands are in great shape!"

The three laughed and the tension in the air dissipated. The apprehension that Rita and Deborah initially had about their inquisitive guest slowly disappeared with each sip of coffee and bite of banana bread. They enjoyed the respite from their daily morning routine of monotonously entering data into TAPES. Chatting at the break table was much more fun.

"So," Esther Jean started. "How long have you ladies worked here?"

Deborah sighed, then said, "We've been here since the beginning of time. We're ready to retire!"

"Ain't that the truth!" Rita said. They both cackled.

"What's keeping you from retiring then?"

"We're broke," Deborah said.

"And we have mouths to feed," Rita added.

"We simply can't retire. That prize money will be nice, though," Deborah said.

"Prize money?" Esther Jean said, curiously.

"Yeah, the money Mr. Baker is receiving. We gonna share it. We've got a pact!" Rita said. "If any of us won that money, we'd all share it."

"Interesting," Esther Jean said. "That's a generous pact."

"We're just shocked Brent Baker was the one to win it," Deborah said, eating her slice of bread and sipping her coffee, then looking at Rita for confirmation. "Really shocked!"

"Never would have guessed!" Rita added.

"Why is that?" Esther Jean said.

With this question, something snapped inside of Deborah. She had felt resentment toward Brent—resentment tinged with jealousy and a bit of disgust—a feeling that had been festering for quite some time. She and Rita had been at the Texas Department of Unemployment and Benefits for a very long time, had worked hard, and had been model employees—in her opinion. Never in that time had they received the recognition that Brent was receiving, and for doing nothing really. The scorn in Deborah bubbled to the surface.

"Well," Deborah started. "He only figured it out by *accident*. He came back from lunch drunk and fell asleep on his keyboard."

"Those two like to drink beer during their lunch!" Rita added joyfully, feeling free from Brent's presence.

"Those two?" Esther Jean said.

"Brent and J. D. *Those* two. Brent has a spell on J. D., who is from a small town. That's probably what they are doing now. Drinking beer," Deborah scoffed.

"It's nine in the morning," Esther Jean said, surprised.

"So?" Deborah replied, finishing her bread and coffee. "Trouble is always looking for trouble."

Esther Jean quickly noticed two things. First, she knew she didn't have all morning to tend to this blossoming news story, being that she was told on the phone by Mr. Schneidermann that she had thirty minutes to spend with Unit 3. Second, the unnaturally red blush of Deborah's cheeks told Esther Jean that Deborah must have been nursing a hangover, which gave her an idea.

"Would you mind telling me more over a glass of wine?" Esther Jean said to Deborah, who was flattered by the social invitation. "Maybe both of you?"

"I would love that!" Deborah said.

"I can't," Rita added. "I have to watch my grandchildren after work."

"I can bring a bottle of red to your house," Esther Jean said, turning to Deborah. "Is it a date?"

"Sounds fun!"

Esther Jean reached into her jacket pocket and pulled out a business card, handing it to Deborah, then added, "Give me your address."

As Deborah wrote it down to give to the reporter, Brent and J. D. returned to the office, smelling of cigarette smoke. Brent quickly noticed they were all standing at the table, drinking coffee and eating banana bread, which of course excited him.

"Is it break time?" he quipped, pouring himself coffee.

J. D. partook in the banana bread by taking a slice.

"Looks that way," Deborah said.

Brent turned to Esther Jean, then said, "I'm ready for the interview."

"That's too bad," she said. "I have to get going shortly."

"Oh," Brent said, excited. "Maybe another time."

"Maybe," Esther Jean said. "Nice talking to you all. I hope you have a great day."

She gathered her things, including the tape recorder that had been recording since she arrived, shook all their hands, then left Unit 3.

"That was easy," Brent said.

"Yep," J. D. said.

"You have no idea," Deborah said.

They all soon finished their morning break, then returned to their desks and continued entering unemployment applications into TAPES—their usual morning routine.

27.

Brent drank his free beer at the bar while his bass player, Chip, waved at the bartender to hopefully bring him another free beer. The bartender ignored him as much as possible, knowing full well that he wasn't going to get a tip worth bragging about from Chip, or from Brent for that matter. Jeff the guitar player was in the bathroom, taking a pre-show piss, a ritual he never abandoned, believing it kept him from distraction during a show. The bandmates were meeting before they played to discuss what to do moving forward, since they were abruptly downgraded to a three-piece from a four-piece earlier in the day. It was an unfortunate circumstance, since Ralph the drummer's wife recently gave birth to their second child. The arrival of this baby was the harbinger of doom for their band. Ralph told them that the baby's name was Ricardo, named after his great-grandfather on his mother's side. Brent joked to Ralph that the baby should have been named Lucifer after its mother. Ralph didn't find that very amusing.

Chip continued to unsuccessfully commandeer the bartender's attention.

"I think he's ignoring me on purpose!"

"I don't blame him. You're cheaper than a polyester leisure suit," Brent said, sarcastically.

"Screw you! I tip well," Chip snapped, waving some more at the bartender before he fled into the walk-in cooler. "Damn it."

"Keep your pants on. He'll be back. Here, drink some of mine."

"You have cooties," he snarled, refusing Brent's offer.

"Whatever," Brent scoffed.

"Anyway, I saw you in the newspaper at the governor's press conference. How was that shindig?"

"Lame," he said, sipping some beer. "He wouldn't let me play a song."

"Play a song?!" Chip said, laughing boisterously. "That's funny."

Brent didn't find that funny. He was serious and let Chip know with some intense side-eye. He drank more of his beer.

"When do you get that prize money?" Chip said, licking his lips while watching Brent drink his beer.

"Probably on my next paycheck."

"You still gonna share with your coworkers?"

"That's the plan, I guess."

"You know," Chip said, moving closer to Brent, lowering his voice so no one else could hear him. "You could do a lot with $10,000."

Brent turned to his bass player, giving him a curious look.

"Oh yeah? Like what?"

"We could finally finish our album, then get it mastered professionally."

"True," Brent said, guzzling the rest of his beer.

The bartender emerged from the walk-in cooler with some six-packs of beer in his arms. Brent raised his hand and the bartender promptly came over after setting down the beer, which annoyed Chip to no end. The bartender stood in front of the two friends.

"Oh! You come when *he* waves, but not me?!" he quipped.

The bartender stared blankly at Chip.

"Can you bring us two more beers?" Brent said. The bartender complied. Brent then turned to Chip. "I'm supposed to share the money. That was our pact."

"Do you have that in *writing* or something?" Chip said.

"No. Why would I have a friendly pact in writing? Our band doesn't have anything in writing."

"That's true. Maybe we should," he said, rubbing his chin.

Brent laughed. The bartender sat the two beers on the bar, then Brent quickly handed him something, releasing it like it was hot. The bartender saluted him, surprised with the gratuity, before going back to his duties.

"What did you tip him?"

"A little bud."

"Ahhh."

The two bandmates sat in silence, sipping their cold beers and looking around the empty venue from their vantage point, sitting at the bar. Playing an acoustic gig early on a weeknight certainly wouldn't attract much walk-in traffic from the street, and their army of fans was more like a small clump of friends than live music enthusiasts. But this did not intimidate Brent, or diminish the power of his dream of being a famous musician. He knew several musical cohorts who found ways to bring their dreams to fruition, whether writing music for commercials or hustling to grow their live music fan bases.

If they can do it, then I can do it, he thought.

He mulled over Chip's comment about the pact he had with his coworkers. It was a brittle covenant that hinged mostly on him actually following through—since the prize was to be given directly to him in a direct deposit. Ultimately, he did not have a legal contract to share the prize with his coworkers. He didn't mention their pact at the press conference or to his boss, Mr. Schneidermann. What would happen if he didn't share with Deborah, Rita, Conchino, and J. D.? Deborah would be furious with him, but she already gave him lots of grief regardless, whether he was kind to her or not. Conchino wouldn't say anything since he mostly never said anything, although he might wait for him in an alley somewhere. Rita would complain but she always complained about *something*. The only one he had a hard time imagining his grifting would be J. D., who he felt was more like a friend than a coworker. But even then, what would he do? Cry? Tell Mr. Schneidermann?

Why should I share with them? It really is my prize, he thought, taking another sip of beer.

Jeff the guitar player grabbed the back of their necks and surprised them, then sat at the bar, finished with his pre-gig ritual of emptying his bladder. He waved to the bartender, who promptly brought him a beer. Brent turned to him.

"What do you think the band should do if I sunk $10,000 into it? Finish the album?"

"Hmmm," Jeff said, sipping his beer, then wiping foam from his mouth with his arm. "How about a European tour? If we went over there as an acoustic three-piece, then ten grand would make a good start."

"An acoustic three-piece?" Brent mused.

"Well, Ralph is out, right? No more drummer makes us a three-piece."

Brent mulled this scenario over, then smiled.

"I've always wanted to go to Europe," he said.

"I have a shitload of vacation at work," Chip said. "Like a month!"

"That's my suggestion," Jeff said. "Why?"

"Just curious," Brent said, standing up and then putting his hands on his friends' backs. "Time for sound check. Let's do it!"

The three bandmates took their beers to the stage, picked up their instruments, and commenced strumming. They each hummed into their microphones as the soundman behind the soundboard approved their levels. As they got ready for their gig, a cute, young, blond woman wearing a halter top and tight jeans stood to the side of the stage holding a frozen strawberry margarita, ogling Brent as he plucked the strings of his guitar. He winked at her, then strummed some more as the soundman gave him a thumbs-up.

28.

Rita and Deborah gathered their lunches at their desks. They asked J. D. to join them outside because it was a beautiful day, but he wanted to finish entering the unemployment applications on his paper holder first. He had learned in the time since he had started working in Unit 3 that falling behind only made it harder when he came back from a lunch break or came in first thing the next morning. Besides, he had already promised Brent that he would go to lunch with him, so he gently informed Rita and Deborah that he would eat lunch with them another time. They gladly left him to finish his work.

Brent rolled his eyes when J. D. pronounced that he wouldn't just drop what he was doing to go to lunch, but he didn't give J. D. a hard time about it, either. He knew better than to give his crew a hard time when they worked so hard, so he decided to just let him finish his work.

"I'll wait for you down in the garage. I could use a smoke anyway," Brent said, before slamming the door behind him.

To an outsider, it would appear that the data entry clerks in Unit 3 took breaks or goofed off whenever they pleased, like Brent did. But in reality, the four clerks were just really good at their jobs. Entering unemployment applications was a task that they had all mastered, and they did it in such an efficient and adroit manner it would appear easy enough that anyone could do it. But that simply wasn't the case. There was still a lot for J. D. to learn, but what he had learned so far, he absorbed acutely.

Unfortunately, J. D. was also discovering that there was a tedium and banality to the data entry tasks that bordered on insanity; he sometimes wondered how Rita, Deborah, and Conchino had done the work so dutifully for so long. He admired his coworkers' tenacity but was beginning to wonder if he was cut out to be a vested state employee. At this rate, he could retire when he reached age fifty-two. To a young man like J. D., that seemed like forever.

Dang! he thought. *That's a long time to enter these darn applications.*

He sighed as he finished the application he was working on. As he typed the last of the data, he could hear a phone ringing in Unit 3. It was Brent's phone. It rang five or six times, then the next phone in the room rang as it was automatically transferred. Conchino's phone rang five or six times, then it moved on to Deborah's, then Rita's. To J. D.'s surprise, his phone then rang. It was strange for him to hear it ring since his phone hadn't made a peep since he started working there. In a fit of excitement (and of course duty), he answered his phone.

"Unit 3 of the Texas Department of Unemployment and Benefits," he said, as he was told to answer. There was a card with this exact phrase on it taped to the side of his phone in case he forgot.

The other end of the call crackled with static. J. D. began to repeat the approved T-DUB telephone greeting when a robotic voice began to answer.

"You – have – a – call – from..." the robotic voice said, then paused. "Ramiro – Gonzalez... from – the – Travis – County – Jail. Do – you – accept?"

"Yes!" he said, without thinking.

Ramiro? he thought. *I don't know any Ramiro.*

Some clicking and buzzing came from the other end of the line as J. D. patiently waited for a human to speak to him. Then after a final click, a deep voice answered.

"Hello?" the voice said. "Who dis?"

"This is J. D. Who is this?"

"J. D., it's Conchino."

"Oh. Hey, Conchino!" he said, then paused. It was strange hearing his stoic coworker's voice. J. D. examined the phone receiver, then placed it back to his ear. "Are you all right?"

"Yeah, I guess," he said, a sigh bubbling up from his heavy heart.

"But the robot voice said you were Ramiro, not Conchino."

"Yeah, Ramiro is my *real* name."

"Oh!" J. D. chirped with surprise and a little joy, as if a profound secret was shared with him.

"But no one calls me that, not even my parents."

"Right."

"I don't have time for this, though. Can you come down to the jail and bail me out. You got $500?"

J. D. analyzed his recent bank statement in his mind, then replied, "Yeah. I have $500."

"If you can come down here and bail me out, then I'll pay you back in cash. I got the money at home. Can you do that?"

"Sure. But why me?"

"'Cause *you* answered the phone."

J. D. had a hard time reconciling that the person with the deep voice he was speaking to on the phone was his silent yet humongous coworker, Conchino, but he wanted to help, so he got over any reticence or apprehension he felt.

"OK," J. D. said. "I'll be right over."

After he hung up the phone, J. D. finished the application he was working on as fast as he could, gathered his things, grabbed his bike helmet, and was out the door. He sprinted down the hall, across the skywalk, then careened down the stairs. When he emerged in the underground parking garage, Brent was standing by J. D.'s bike, smoking his third cigarette. It caught him off guard that J. D. was in such a frantic hurry.

"What's going on?" he said, flicking his cigarette on the ground. "Why are you running?"

"Conchino called me. He needs help!" he said, unlocking the bike chain, then stuffing it in his messenger bag.

"Conchino? Where?!"

"He called me from jail. I gotta go bail him out!" he said, mounting his bike.

"But what about lunch with me?"

"I'll have lunch with you tomorrow!" J. D. said, as he sped off on his bicycle.

Brent watched him ride away and out the garage exit, frantically pedaling like Conchino's life depended on it.

"What is going on?!" he said, smacking his forehead with his hand, then placing it next to his mouth to amplify his protestation. "You can't just leave!"

J. D. pedaled his bicycle as fast as he could the eight or so blocks it would take to get to the county jail. As he rode, he worried about all the things that could possibly happen to his coworker while being incarcerated, a succession of absolutely horrific scenarios, ideas he mostly got from watching movies and reading comic books. J. D. didn't actually know for sure what Conchino was going through. If the movies or comic books were even close to reality, then he had to bail him out as soon as possible. Saving Conchino from unwelcomed sodomy or brutal fistfights was all he could think about. He pedaled his bike like he never had before.

When he reached the Travis County Jail, rather than lock his bicycle with his chain like he normally would, he tossed it into some grass next to the building. He ran inside, then quickly realized he had to go through security, so they could check him for weapons or explosives or any illicit items. Knowing he didn't have these things made the wait even more unbearable. After passing through unscathed, he said to one of the security guards, "Where do I pay bail for a friend?"

"On the third floor," he said in a monotonous tone, as if he had already answered that question a thousand times.

J. D. found an elevator and went inside to go up to the third floor. Three convicts handcuffed together and their accompanying guard occupied most of the elevator. One of the convicts—the one with a shaved head, a wrinkled tan, a teardrop tattooed on his face, and wearing pink jail clothes—glared at J. D. as if he was going to consume him. He worried that they were on their way to confront Conchino, making the elevator ride more intense and awkward for J. D. When the bell dinged for the third floor, J. D. ran as fast as he could out of the cramped cabin lift.

With a wealth of signage to help him as he walked past courtrooms and meeting rooms and bathrooms, he eventually found where he needed to pay Conchino's bail—the cashier sitting behind a large pane of bulletproof glass. No one was waiting so J. D. approached the window, speaking into a microphone.

"I'd like to bail my friend out of jail," he said.

On the other side of the glass sat a woman in her mid-fifties, her skin tan and loose as if she had recently lost more weight than her body was prepared to relinquish, looking like a deflated balloon on her skeleton. Her nameplate read "Guadalupe." She had a folder propped up in front of her and it appeared that she was reading important documentation, but J. D. could see a copy of *People* magazine in the manila folder. She immediately reminded him of Deborah or Rita. She eventually noticed J. D. standing there and laid the folder down, making no effort to hide the magazine anymore.

"What's his name?" she said, typing something in her computer to awaken it.

"Conchino," he said, smiling.

"Is that his first or last name?"

"First, I think."

Staring at him as if she was wondering if he had a functioning brain or not, she said, "Are you sure?"

J. D. thought about this question for a bit and then realized that Conchino's real name was probably Ramiro, not Conchino, a simple mistake on his part.

"Oh! I'm sorry. His name is Ramiro. Ramiro Gonzalez," he said, smiling bigger than before.

She typed the name into her computer and read what appeared on the screen, tapping the keyboard when prompted.

"That'll be $500. Cash or check?"

"Check, I guess," he said, then rummaged through his messenger bag for his checkbook.

He wrote out the check while she typed some more, then he tore the check from the booklet and slid it to her under the glass. She stamped a series of printed receipts and various forms, then stamped the front of the check and the back. She collated all the papers into two piles—one for J. D. and one for her records—then slid the release papers under the glass to J. D.

"Wait downstairs in the lobby. He'll be out shortly," she said, checking her papers once more for accuracy.

"That's it?" he said, confused.

"That's it. Why? You want to spend extra time with me?" she said, returning a sly grin adorned with a gold tooth. J. D. demurred, laughing awkwardly.

He shoved the paperwork in his messenger bag, then went back down to the lobby. This time, the elevator was not occupied by convicts or guards or anyone else to give him hostile stares. He found an empty bench and sat down to wait for his friend. He wasn't sure how long he'd have to wait, but was prepared to wait as long as it took. He was quite pleased with himself to be helping Conchino in this honorable capacity. To his surprise, Conchino came out an exit door no more than fifteen minutes later, dressed in the clothes he had worn the night he was arrested. He walked up to J. D. and quietly stood over him. J. D. began to giggle, which surprised Conchino. He glared back at him.

"What's so funny?" he said, low and gravelly.

"Your real name is Ramiro?!" he said, giggling some more.

"Very funny," he said, his scowl slackening to a smirk.

"Come on!" J. D. said, leading his friend to the free world. Conchino lurched after him.

Outside, J. D. looked around for his bicycle, but it wasn't where he left it in the grass. He looked off into the distance with his hand shading his brow, as if maybe it was laying on the ground further down the street in a different patch of grass. The two coworkers were approached by a homeless man wearing a tattered T-shirt and jeans and smelling of musky sweat, stale beer, and a car air freshener. He stood in front of them, insidiously rubbing his hands together.

"I'll tell you where it is if you give me $20," the bum said. His two top, front teeth were missing. His tongue poked through the gap when he spoke.

"Where *what* is?" J. D. said.

"Whatever it is you're looking for," he said, cackling.

"Sorry, I don't have $20."

"Then I will not assist you in this matter," the bum said, and skipped away.

Conchino looked down at J. D., then said, "You came to pick me up on your bicycle? How were we gonna fit on your bike?"

J. D. replied while rubbing his chin, "I don't know. I didn't think about that."

They both laughed, then sighed at their unplanned dilemma.

"I guess we can take the 38 bus. It goes near my house."

"Fine with me. I haven't ridden the bus yet!" J. D. quipped.

The two coworkers huffed to the nearest bus stop.

After a silent bus ride and a short hike to his house, Conchino knelt at the front door and picked up a polished rock to reveal a hidden house key. He unlocked the door and they both went inside.

J. D. followed him through the thoughtfully decorated home. In the kitchen, Conchino found a handwritten note on the kitchen island that said:

Mijito—
Not sure where you are but we decided
to spend a few days in Fredericksburg.
There's some leftover Chinese takeout in
the fridge. See you when we get back.
Love, Mom and Dad

"That's why they wouldn't answer the phone," Conchino sighed.

"Bummer," J. D. said.

"Yeah."

"So, what happened to you?"

"Street race. Got caught."

"We knew it!" J. D. said, snapping his fingers, excited that his coworkers' premonition came true. "Well, Rita called it. She said you were in jail."

"Yeah."

"But I'm glad you're out."

"Wait here. I'll get your money."

He left J. D. to himself in the kitchen. He looked around and marveled at the new appliances and immaculate tile floor. On the refrigerator were yellowed paintings on construction paper that appeared to have been created by a small child, maybe from Conchino's elementary school years. Conchino soon came back into the kitchen and sat a cigar box on the island. He pulled out a wad of cash and counted out $500 in twenty-dollar bills for J. D.

"Thanks for bailing me out. I appreciate it," Conchino said, gruffly.

J. D. smiled back at him, then said, "No problem. I was worried about you."

Conchino stared out the kitchen window, as if solemnly revisiting his time in jail. Then the corner of his mouth perked up.

"Not much happened," he said, rapping the countertop with his fingers on one hand. "Although I did kick one guy's ass for talking shit about his mother."

"Really?" J. D. said, surprised. "Did you know this guy's mom or something?"

"Yeah," he said, rapping the countertop some more. "It was Deborah's son. What's his name?"

"Ricky? You beat up Ricky in jail?!" J. D. said, his eyes round with disbelief.

"Yeah. I recognized him from the photos on her desk. Felt good kicking his ass, too. I don't think he'll be talking bad about his mom no more," Conchino said, smirking. "Want some Chinese takeout? I'll heat some up."

J. D. looked at Conchino's hands. His knuckles were scabbed and bruised. He then looked up at his friend's smiling face. He felt strange conversing with Conchino in his family's kitchen, a mysterious place he had never been to before. In fact, he had never been to any of his coworkers' homes, not even Brent's. He felt a placid feeling emanating from within: a tranquil affection.

"Sure," he replied. "Sounds good."

While Conchino heated up some leftovers for them to share, J. D. put the cash for the bail in his pocket, then wondered how he would get home since his bicycle had been stolen at the police station.

"It's a long walk to my house from here," he sighed.

"I can give you a ride," Conchino said, pulling a plate from the microwave, then setting it on the island counter. "Come check it out."

J. D. followed Conchino through the house to the dark garage. Conchino felt along the wall in the dark for the light switch, flipping the light on when he found it. Under the bath of fluorescent lights, a shiny, like-new 1974 Chevy Impala revealed itself—metallic, lime-green paint job with a shiny, white, vinyl top and pitch-black, tinted windows. Conchino beamed at the sight of it.

"Whoa!" J. D. moaned.

"Right!" Conchino said, stepping over to the classic car. "My pops never lets me drive it, but he ain't here right now. Is he?"

J. D. shook his head.

"I'll get you home in style," Conchino said, affectionately rubbing the vinyl top.

29.

When J. D. arrived at work after the longest bus ride of his life, all his coworkers were in the office: Deborah, Rita, Conchino, and Brent. It had been a few days since they all were in the same room at the same time and it warmed his heart to see them all together. Deborah was pouring herself a cup of coffee at the break table. Conchino and Brent were elbowing for the largest cinnamon roll in a glass pan. Rita was standing behind her desk, opening the window to let some fresh air in the office.

Dang! J. D. thought. *Everyone is here!*

Rita turned to greet J. D. and said, "Mornin'! Better get a cinnamon roll before they gone."

J. D. set his lunch box and messenger bag on his desk, then stood there grinning. Deborah noticed J. D.'s odd behavior.

"She's not kidding. Don't just stand there. These two are seriously going to come to blows over cinnamon rolls!" she said, pointing her thumb at Brent and Conchino.

Brent quickly scooped the pastry on a napkin and sat at his desk, smirking and ogling the large Danish he had procured from his hulking employee. Conchino didn't seem to care, though. He simply took two smaller cinnamon rolls, which seemed to please him more than having the larger single one. Now that the break table was clear, J. D. took his turn getting breakfast, then sat at his desk. He took a bite of the cinnamon roll and marveled at its deliciousness, as well as his fortune of working with a kind bunch of folks including a wonderful baker in their midst. As he ate and drank coffee, he noticed a lavender flower petal floating over his shoulder, then landing on his desk next to his plate. He turned around to see where it originated from and spotted a few more petals blowing in through Rita's window from outside. Rita smiled as she held her hands out, hoping the petals would fall in her grasp.

"Reggie, is that you?" she said, cooing in delight. "I know you prolly miss my cinnamon rolls. You did have a sweet tooth, my dear!"

"He sure did!" Deborah agreed. "I'm surprised he didn't have dentures!"

The two friends cackled as more flower petals from the mountain laurels surrounding the building outside floated inside. J. D. looked over to Conchino for an affirmation of the natural anomaly. Conchino tilted his head back as if to say "I see you," but didn't offer a verbal acknowledgment, nor did he look at the petals floating in the office, which was strange to J. D. since they had spent the previous day together, first at the county jail, then at his family's house eating leftover Chinese food and gawking at his father's 1974 Chevy Impala like naughty children. After Conchino dropped J. D. off at his house, he had hoped that a friendship would blossom from their day together, but that morning it didn't seem that J. D.'s hopes for a new friendship would come to fruition. J. D. didn't let it bother him, though.

He'll come around, he thought, then finished his breakfast and began to work.

The other four followed suit, tossing the remnants of breakfast into the trash and beginning their workday as well. Their orchestra of keyboards played its clickity-clack symphony while Brent conducted from his desk, his feet propped on the desktop. He offered to assist his crew with entering applications into TAPES—something the others welcomed him to do—but he never seemed to get started. He just sat at his desk, doodling on a pad of paper. After a few offers of assistance that never materialized, Deborah grew irritable. She would have preferred that Brent just disappeared, as usual, and left them to work efficiently and peacefully. But he didn't. His lazy presence scorned her.

"Are you going to actually help us? Or are you just going to keep jabbering without doing anything?" she said from her desk while she furiously entered applications into her computer.

Rita mouthed her delight at Deborah's chutzpah, then cracked herself up. Deborah grinned.

Brent looked up from his doodling, then said, "I'll help in a minute. I'm in the middle of something important."

"Oh yeah?" Deborah said, then stood up from her desk. She saved the work she was doing and walked over to Brent's desk. He quickly stashed his illustrated pad of paper in the desk's middle drawer. "What are you working on that's so important?"

Brent stammered while Deborah stood over him, her fists pressing into her wide hips. She impatiently tapped one foot.

"Just a report. Nothing to concern yourself with."

"Oh yeah?" she said, irritated. "Let me see it."

"Go back to your desk," he seethed, her attitude getting under his skin.

"I'll go back after you show me that report you're working on."

J. D. and Conchino gleefully watched the two bicker while Rita vexed. She had enough stress at home to deal with and hearing her coworkers bark at each other was another layer of stress she didn't want to contend with. She pleaded with them to stop.

"Come on, you two. Let's all be friends. OK? This has been a great morning so far," she said.

Deborah wasn't having it. Her temper flared hotter with every passing minute. She continued to fume.

"And have you talked with Mr. Schneidermann about when the prize money is coming? We're all still waiting, you know."

"I talked to the Big Boss about it the other day. It's coming," he said, nervously shuffling papers on his desk, miffed that she was still hovering over him.

"You are going to share it with us, as we all agreed. Right?" she prodded, planting her feet resolutely.

"Yes, yes! Now go back to your desk," he said, glaring at her, but she wouldn't back down.

"I swear! If you don't share it with us...," she grumbled.

Rita leaned back in her chair, turning to face the window. She gazed up at the baby blue sky, a few lavender flower petals cartwheeling just outside the window. A serene smile slid across her face.

"Can I get you a cinnamon roll, my sweet Reggie?" she sang, trailing off into a sigh.

J. D. turned around, wondering what had gotten into Rita. He found her slumped in her chair, her head tilted back and resting on the chairback, and her mouth open.

"Rita?!" he said, confused.

The others took heed of his confusion, particularly Deborah, who saw her friend sitting in an unusual posture with her head at an awkward angle. She dashed from Brent's desk to Rita's, propping her head up, then shaking her shoulders.

"Rita!" she cried. "Are you all right?!"

But Rita didn't answer, her body limp and lifeless in her hands. J. D., Conchino, and Brent surrounded her, looking over her shoulder with distress and ineptness. But Deborah wanted them to help and didn't hesitate to order them into action.

"Someone, call 911! Or go get help!"

Brent jumped back to his desk to call 911. As he dialed, he barked, "Conchino, get some water! J. D., run down to the front and ask for help! Emmitt may be faster than me!"

"OK!" J. D. said.

He sprinted out the door, running down the hall, then careening down the stairs. Bursting into the lobby, he found Emmitt at his desk, wiping off three-ring binders with a rag. It shocked the security guard to see J. D. sprinting toward the security desk with his arms flailing about.

"Boy! What's wrong with you?!" he said, tossing the rag behind him. "You look like you seen a ghost!"

"Ms. Rita!" he said, huffing and puffing. "She needs an ambulance!"

Emmitt didn't ask a single question. He pressed a button on a console next to the phone, then said, "They'll be here in less than five minutes! The hospital is close! What's wrong with her?!"

"I don't know but she doesn't look good," J. D. said, worried.

"Please, Lord! Not today. Not Ms. Rita today," he said, shaking his head.

Before Emmitt could continue with his plea, three emergency medical technicians burst into the lobby, two maneuvering a gurney, one leading the way carrying a medical bag. He was surprised at their promptness.

"Damn!" he called out. "That was fast!"

The leading EMT said, "Where do we go?"

"Unit 3! Follow me!" J. D. commanded.

He led them up the stairs and down the hall to Unit 3, past Ken, the former paper collector, who was standing against the wall curiously watching. Inside, Deborah was bawling while caressing her friend's hair. Brent and Conchino stood at the side of the office, leaning against the break table. The EMTs didn't waste time, lifting Rita from her chair onto the gurney as Deborah joined her other coworkers by the break table. They all watched as the EMTs performed a number of life-saving procedures including CPR as well as checking various vital signs. They attempted to press, push, and prod the life back into Rita, but she didn't respond. She was gone.

Deborah cried some more, then turned to Conchino, who wrapped her in his arms, giving her a massive bear hug, as the EMTs pushed their friend and coworker onto the gurney and out of the office. The leader—a strapping young man in his mid-twenties with wily blond hair and lanky limbs—stood before the crew of Unit 3, tired and dejected.

"We did all we could do but she didn't make it," he said, respectfully.

Deborah cried in anguish. J. D. patted her on the back to console her.

"We'll take her to the hospital for a postmortem," he said, pulling a business card from his shirt pocket, then scribbling something on it. He handed the card to Deborah. She wiped tears from her face and accepted the card, trying to smile through the tears. "Call this number if you have questions. Do you know where her belongings are?"

Deborah nodded, then retrieved Rita's purse from her desk to give to the EMT.

"Her wallet is inside. It has her identification card and all," she whimpered.

"Thank you, ma'am. I'll make sure the family gets this," he said, forcing a smile. It was always difficult for him to appear pleasant in times like this. "Good day to you."

Then he left the office.

The four coworkers stood there in silence, with the exception of Deborah's sniffles, for a few minutes, shocked at what had just transpired. None of them could have known that Rita would pass away that morning. Deborah, in particular, was racked with guilt for her behavior. She couldn't stop thinking about her friend and wished she had conducted herself in a different manner—maybe chatted with Rita about their children, like they usually did. Instead, she had bickered with Brent over something that at that moment seemed so petty. The loss of her dear friend was unbearable. She broke free from Conchino's grasp and left the office for the restroom, where she could cry by herself inside a toilet stall.

Brent plunged his hands in his pockets, then pulled out a pack of cigarettes and a lighter.

"I need a *smoke*," he said, turning to J. D. "Want to join me in the garage?" J. D. slowly shook his head. "Suit yourself."

Then, Brent left the office. Conchino lumbered to his desk and sat down. On the desktop sat a component for his car. But since his car was still impounded, it wasn't much fun tinkering with it. One of the cinnamon rolls still sat on his desk, cold and untouched. His appetite was gone. So, rather than toss it into the trash, he gently set it on Rita's desk, where he felt like it belonged.

J. D. noticed that more flower petals were drifting into the office from outside, carried in with the warm breeze. He went over to the window to close it. After latching it shut, he picked up the lavender petals from the floor and set them on Rita's desk, too, with Conchino's cinnamon roll.

PART III.

30.

Sitting at the bar surrounding her kitchen, Esther Jean opened a new bottle of Cabernet Sauvignon while she did two things at once: worked on her latest article for the city paper about Brent Baker and Unit 3 as well as applied makeup for a night on the town. She had been furiously working on the article over the course of a week and was just about done with it. She was keenly aware of the precarious financial situation the city paper was in, being that D the editor made it painfully clear with the inundation of pleading emails filling her inbox, and she wanted to help him with this juicy story that had fallen in her lap. She also knew that news stories had a brief shelf life and the clock was ticking since the press conference held by Governor Bennett was quickly diminishing in the rearview mirror of public attention. She tried not to think about that too much, fearing that the pressure would keep her from finishing the article.

I just have to get it done and turned in, she thought, pouring herself a glass of wine, then looking in the makeup mirror sitting next to her laptop computer on the bar. *Then it's time to disco!*

Her cat, Mew, launched on the kitchen counter and then slithered onto the bar, attempting to molest her arm as she typed, almost knocking the bottle of wine over. Esther Jean swatted at him, angry with his uninvited need for attention.

"Get down, puss face!" she snapped. "You're going to ruin everything!"

He landed on the floor with a thud, glaring derisively at her, then sashayed away. She continued to type on her laptop. As she scoured through her notes on a pad of paper sitting next to her computer, she thought of her time visiting with Deborah, drinking wine together while listening to Deborah's confession in her living room. Esther Jean's visit to Deborah's house turned out to be more fruitful than she could have hoped for. All she had to do was ply Deborah with alcohol to let her guard down. After a couple of glasses of wine, Deborah gleefully confessed the whole story behind Brent's cost-saving suggestion; how he and J. D. had gotten drunk on beer one day and stumbled back to the office, and Brent's intoxicated snooze on his computer keyboard unleashed chaos throughout the Texas Department of Unemployment and Benefits, the likes of which had never been seen before. Brent knew what he was doing when he filled out the application for the coveted cost-saving prize, but he did not know the nuts and bolts of his valuable discovery. In fact, he barely knew his way around TAPES, let alone the ways and means of saving the State of Texas hundreds of *millions* of dollars. Deborah felt slighted.

"How could a drunken lout be lavished with money and publicity when he didn't deserve it? And from the governor of all people?!" Deborah confessed.

Esther Jean recorded Deborah as she vented on her couch, constantly refilling her wine glass with more truth serum. And as she later transcribed her inebriated interview from audiotape to paper, she briefly wrestled with the morality of her journalistic method.

Is this ethical? she thought, jotting down the juicy bits of Deborah's confession. *Sometimes, the ends justify the means, I guess.*

Toppling the façade of Governor Bennett's press conference—especially his cannibalistic way of using anything and anyone for political gain—was Esther Jean's goal. She relished the idea of sinking his poll numbers even deeper in the gutter of public opinion; and Deborah was helping her do it—at least that was what Esther Jean believed. The only thing she couldn't figure out was how to work in her voyeuristic discovery, with her clandestine photographs of Governor Bennett capably standing over his toilet—without the assistance of walking canes or crutches or human assistants. This revelation was straddling the line of investigative journalism and tabloid exploitation. She couldn't think of a way to work it into this story without jeopardizing her goal.

Maybe I'll hand it off to Bob, she thought, looking in the makeup mirror to finish applying eye shadow and mascara. *He would love that!*

She concluded that was the best thing to do and would message Bob the alt-weekly reporter the next day. He certainly could use the scoop, and the photographs would help. That way, Esther Jean could have her cake and eat it, too, by having coverage in two news outlets. The idea thrilled her as she saved her document, composed a quick email to D the editor, attached the article, and clicked the Send button. Her work was careening through the internet and there was nothing left to do except to party all night.

She put away her work and finished applying her makeup. Satisfied with her skills, she placed her phone and wallet along with her keys and pepper spray in a matching clutch, then left her apartment and her naughty cat behind. As she descended the stairs outside, she noticed the stairwell was free of sleeping homeless people, particularly the man with the new-looking athletic shoes who often hid under his dirty bed comforter like a tortoise hiding from the heat of the sun. She wondered where he was as she strolled briskly down 5th Street, her high heels clacking on the sidewalk and cobblestone intersections of the crossing streets. As she approached the Warehouse District, the sensual thump of techno music could be heard in the distance, along with the smell of fried foods wafting from the various food trucks in adjacent parking lots. Walking this way at night to the dance club entranced Esther Jean; a feeling of anticipation consumed her like foreplay to a night of lovemaking. She loved the feeling of entering the club like almost nothing else. At that moment, it seemed like anything was possible.

The dance club was called Xtasy and the entrance was adorned with a number of gay pride flags and posters of male exotic dancers, their oily, tanned skin glistening behind shiny glass. A long line extended down the sidewalk from the entrance, but the sight of the numerous people waiting to get in didn't discourage her. She enjoyed the anticipation of going inside, and the line afforded her a few more minutes as well as an opportunity to see who was going inside along with her. The bass of the music thumped and wobbled through the stone walls of the building. Esther Jean bobbed her head along to the beat.

The line grew behind her, and as it snaked its way down the street, she felt the presence of a tall, hulking man behind her, his sturdy stature solid like a brick wall. His musky scent beguiled her. She could make out his reflection in the poster display in the glass window of the club and thought it strange that he was wearing a flat cap, dark sunglasses, and a jacket whose style had waned in fashion by the end of the 1980s. She didn't want him to know she was checking him out, so she dared not turn around. She just continued to glance at the reflection in the glass while the line commenced through the entrance. Once the bouncer checked her identification card— examining it and then comparing the old photo on it to her current face—she scurried inside, hoping to find a place at the bar for a quick cocktail or shot before heading out on the dance floor. It was commonplace that she was offered drinks from strange men whenever she parked at the bar. All the men couldn't resist buying her drinks. Her presence was magnetic and alluring, although she wasn't necessarily interested in hooking up with any of them. Her priority was dancing, one of her greatest pleasures. So, rather than wait for a complimentary drink from a flirty man (they were all just waiting too long), she handed the bartender a twenty and ordered a shot. While he made it, she saw the tall man leaning against the far wall, his face trained on her. She pretended not to notice when the bartender set her shot on the bar.

"The first one is on me," he said to her with a wink and a grin. He handed the $20 back to her, which she tossed into the tip jar. "Come see me later."

"Of course, darling!" she said, then guzzled the shot.

She set the empty shot glass on the bar, then snaked her way through the gawking crowd to the dance floor. The music consumed her, and as the bass moved through the wood floor into her legs, she closed her eyes and swerved her hips to the rhythm of the song. When the bridge of the song came, offering her a slight reprieve, she opened her eyes and saw the tall man slowly approaching her through the dense crowd, the lights and smoke in the club enveloping him. She felt her heart beat faster, speeding up to the BPMs of the techno song. Deep down inside, she enjoyed his lurching pursuit and she wasn't going to dissuade or discourage him. At least, she may get a few complimentary drinks from him or, even better, a few minutes of heavy petting and kissing in the darker, more secluded back room.

As the song morphed and mixed into a different song, he appeared in front of her, his tall frame towering over her. Rather than look up at his face, she moved closer to him, putting one of her arms around his waist, grinding her hip into his thigh. The other dancers around them performed a similar mating ritual, one that stirred the passion within many of them, seducing some couples to the back room. Esther Jean grabbed the tall man's large hand and pulled him back there, the music louder and more intense in the smaller, darker space, absent of the spinning light machines that hung over the main dance floor. At the far end of the back room, Esther Jean stepped on a bench attached to the wall in hopes that her face would be closer to his. For the first time, she took in his shadowy presence the best she could in the darker room—the flat cap, the dark sunglasses, and his square jawline—the lights from the dance floor flashing glimpses of his face.

She wanted a better look so she reached for his glasses, then said, "Can I take these off?"

As she reached for his sunglasses, he grabbed her wrist with a tight, crushing grip, which startled her.

"Hey!" she squawked. "Not so hard!"

She lunged for his glasses, which fell from his face to the floor, revealing her worst fear.

Oh no! she thought, as she struggled to release his grip: Frank the security guard's grip.

As she wrestled with him, his flat cap bounced off his head, revealing his flattop hairdo. She tried to pry his grip from her wrist but to no avail. He lunged for her throat with his other hand, clamping it around her neck tightly. He constricted his hold on her, squeezing tighter, forcing the Adam's apple in her throat to jab at his palm. The discovery of this unexpected piece of anatomy startled Frank, and he hesitated momentarily with his attack, giving Esther Jean the time she needed to reach into her purse and pull out her defensive weapon. She blasted him in the eyes with pepper spray. The burning chemical seared his eyeballs, causing him to loosen his grip. He dropped her, then crumpled to the floor, rubbing his eyes, trying to dig out the pepper spray from his eye sockets. Esther Jean's muscle memory kicked in and she ran, back into the dance floor and through the throng of gesticulating bodies. The other gay men and queens in the dark back room called for security as Esther Jean escaped. Once outside on the street, she peeled the high heels from her aching feet and ran all the way home, her clutch bag in one hand and her high heels strung within the fingers of her other hand.

She ran as fast as she could without regard for passing cars or puzzled pedestrians. She didn't know why Frank the security guard had attacked her, but she did know one thing: Governor Bennett was worried about her for some reason. Any hesitation or reluctance about sending Bob the alt-weekly reporter the photographs she had of Governor Bennett standing in his private restroom was now gone. She knew what she was going to do the minute she got home to her apartment, but right after arming her security system.

I'm emailing those photos to Bob! she thought, sprinting harder to her apartment no more than a block away. She wanted nothing more than to curl up with her cat, Mew, and hope that Frank didn't follow her home.

31.

Standing next to Rita's coffin and surrounded by her family, friends, and coworkers, the pastor raised his hands to the sky and gazed up to the heavens. It was a pleasant day for a funeral—the weather being mild and the sky clear—although the sadness among Rita's loved ones was palpable and somber. The pastor was known to his congregation as Reverend Al Jackson and, although there was no known relation between Rita and the Reverend Jackson, she gleefully called him "cousin" whenever she was in his presence because of their shared last name. From outward appearances, it seemed there was at least a possibility that they were related; both were pleasantly plump yet compact in size. He loved her baked goods as much or more than the rest of them and couldn't help but mention their tasty pleasures.

"It goes without saying...," he said, concluding his sermon for his dear friend. "...that we will *all* miss her delicious banana bread, a treat so scrumptious that—I dare say—it could have been deemed sinful. Can I get an *amen*?!"

Rita's children and grandchildren responded, then cried. Deborah cried, too, while Conchino and J. D. comforted her. Rita was as good a friend to her as could be, and closer in commitment and loyalty than any of her own family. Her sorrow for the loss of her friend was deep and painful, causing her to wail uncontrollably. J. D. patted her back as Conchino held her, letting her cry on his shirt. Brent tried to hide his annoyance with her crying but his eyerolls gave him away.

Malik, Rita's rascally grandson, sneered at Brent as if his grandmother's untimely death was his fault alone.

"We will all miss you, dear Rita Jackson. But as we all know, you are now with our dear Lord, Jesus Christ. And, of course, your dear husband, Reggie."

Her family agreed with his assessment of her otherworldly locale, punctuated with tears and sniffles.

"I would be remiss to not mention that there will be a celebration of Rita Jackson's life at her house immediately after the conclusion of this beautiful funeral. As I understand it, there will be lovingly baked treats for all to enjoy while we regale in stories of her life. May you go in peace, in the name of the Lord. Amen!"

Reverend Jackson comforted the children in his immediate vicinity, then retreated to his Cadillac. Rita's family members each took turns touching her casket, some of them setting flowers on it, before retreating to their own cars. Her coworkers from Unit 3 were some of the last guests to linger, standing back from Rita's immediate family so they could pay their respects to their beloved matriarch. Rita's daughter, Janice, approached Deborah, Brent, J. D., and Conchino. Her eyes were red and puffy from crying.

"Are you coming by the house?" she said, sniffling, wiping a stray tear from her cheek with her hand, her fingernails manicured long, shiny, and bright red.

"Of course, dear," Deborah said, smiling. "Can we bring anything?"

"Lord no! The kitchen is full right now. I'll see you there."

She gathered her children, Aliyah and Destiny, and walked them to her car. Brent suggested to his crew that they all go in his SUV, and they agreed, especially since Conchino's car was still impounded and neither J. D. or Deborah had a car. As they walked to Brent's beat-up SUV—the perfect vehicle for him to load with instruments and gear for his gigs with his band—Deborah watched Malik run circles around Rita's casket, and even tried to descend into the hole in the ground: her final resting place.

That Malik is still a rascal even at her funeral! she thought, chuckling to herself.

They all piled into Brent's SUV and drove the few short blocks to Rita's house. The street in front of her house was packed with all the cars of her children, family, and friends, as well as Reverend Jackson's Cadillac, as everyone wanted to enjoy time in her house, the place where she loved and cared for her family. The grandchildren played in the fenced front yard as they normally did—games of tag, hide and seek, and karaoke commenced out in the grass—while Rita's grown children either sat on the front porch or milled about inside, setting out treats for family and guests. Rita's son, Reggie Jr., sat on the front porch in her favorite chair, looking entitled as he watched over all the children in the front yard. The sight of him in her chair displeased Deborah, although she didn't know why for sure. Maybe it seemed too soon for him to enjoy sitting in that chair, or maybe it was the things Rita used to share with Deborah about her troubled son.

"Let's go inside," Deborah suggested. Her coworkers agreed, so they followed her inside.

In the kitchen, family and friends served themselves baked treats and coffee, all under the dutiful watch of Rita's daughter, Janice. When she noticed Rita's coworkers come in, she teared up as she approached Deborah, embracing her with a tight hug as she cried on her shoulder.

"Mama loved you all so much!" she said, wiping tears from her cheeks. "She talked about you all the time. *All* the time! She prolly talked about you as much or more than us kids."

"Nah, girl. She loved her family most of all," Deborah said, placing her hands on both of Janice's shoulders, consoling her.

"But she told me you were like her family, too. It's true."

Deborah was pleased with this sweet revelation from her friend's daughter and felt that she was telling the truth.

Janice continued, "Do you all want some treats?"

She looked around to discover that the three men from Unit 3 had already helped themselves and were stuffing their faces with baked goods and coffee. The sight of them gorging themselves made her and Deborah laugh out loud.

"Mama would be happy seeing this!" she said.

The remainder of the family had left the kitchen for the living room—where Reverend Jackson's booming voice could be heard—while Deborah and Janice consoled each other. Janice helped herself to a piece of cake and a cup of coffee, then excused herself so she could join her family. Deborah also helped herself to a piece of cake, then sat at the kitchen table. By this time, her coworkers were done with their food and stood around, looking bored.

"I'm going out back for a smoke. Wanna join?" Brent said. J. D. and Conchino agreed to go with him but Deborah declined.

"I'm going to sit in here," she said.

Her coworkers left her alone. As she ate her cake, she thought about her friend: her kind smile, her sweet laugh, her good heart, and her caring soul. The thought of not chatting with her at work anymore made her eyes well up, but she tried not to cry. There would be plenty more time to cry. And she didn't want to wear herself out with grief. She felt the need for more coffee and wanted to get herself some more. As she stood up, one of the grandkids charged into the kitchen in a flurry of arms and legs, singing a song about flatulence. She was pretty sure it was the rascally one, the one named Malik. She sat back down, then asked him to bring her some coffee.

"You want *me* to get you some?" he said, shocked.

"Sure!" she replied. "You're big."

"I am BIG!" he gloated. "I'll get it!"

He pulled a stepping stool to the counter, then stood on it to pour her a cup of coffee. He haphazardly brought it to the table, spilling some when he set it down.

"Thank you," she said, smiling.

"What's your name, lady?" he said, curious. "Did you know my grandma?"

Deborah was pleased—and a little shocked—with his kind demeanor.

"My name is Deborah. And yes, I knew your grandma. We worked together."

"Are you the white lady from her work?!" he said, surprised.

"Yes, that's me," she said, chuckling.

"Hold up! I have something for you!"

He ran back to the stepping stool and stretched his arms up to a cabinet, opening the door and pulling out a small, metallic box. He examined it, as if making sure it was the correct one, then hopped off the stool so he could give it to her.

He placed it in her hands, then said, "My grandma always told me... if anything happens to me, then give this to you. So, here you go!"

He smiled a bright, toothy grin. Deborah examined the box, not sure if she had seen it before, then smiled back at Malik.

"I don't care what anyone says, Malik," she said. "You're the sweetest of all the grandchildren."

The compliment, at first, embarrassed him because he wasn't used to receiving them from anybody. But then he found that he was pleased with himself and beamed brightly.

"Thanks, lady!" he said, then ran out of the kitchen for the living room.

Deborah examined the outside of the box some more, then opened it. Inside, she flipped through the various cards and placards—some were labeled for recipes; others were labeled for lottery tickets. At the back of the box were more cards labeled "Winners!" and "To Check" and "Unit 3 Lottery." As she flipped through, she found lottery tickets and scratch tickets in addition to all her favorite recipes for baked goods and dinner entrees. She admired Rita's handwritten recipe cards, then pulled out the various lottery tickets and scratch games. The section for "Unit 3" contained the most, some even marked as "To Check ASAP," with doodles of stars and checkmarks and exclamation points on them.

I'll take these to the store tomorrow to have them checked, she thought, then placed the lottery tickets, scratch games, and recipe cards back in the small, metal box. *And maybe try making Rita's banana bread.*

After closing the lid, she put the recipe box into her purse, just as Janice came back into the kitchen. She looked happy and excited.

"We're all telling stories about Grandma with Reverend Jackson. Want to join us?" she said.

"Of course, dear," Deborah replied. Then she followed her out of the kitchen to the living room.

32.

It was not unusual for Brent to wake up hungover after a gig with his band. Usually, he and his bandmates guzzled as much free beer as possible, making sure they received what they perceived to be their fair share considering they weren't paid much in cash, if at all. But the previous night was not the typical bar gig. For the first time, they opened for a national, touring band at a popular amphitheater and the crowd was larger and more raucous than they were used to at the comparatively smaller bar joints they usually haunted. Instead of beer, their alcoholic drink for the night was Jägermeister, an insidious, herbal liqueur that was legendary in rock 'n' roll lore. And instead of being paid pennies for their performance, Brent's band was paid $1,000. To them, that was an outrageous fee for their services, considering that they would have normally just played for free beer and the attention of one or two women. It was a glorious night for Brent, and his ferocious hangover was proof of that.

My head feels like it's split open, he thought, rubbing his head as he rolled out of bed, silencing his rowdy alarm clock by tossing it against the wall. It stopped ringing after the batteries popped out.

He rummaged through his apartment for painkillers to ease his suffering but couldn't find any. So, he decided to take a quick shower, then buy some Motrin at the convenience store down the street from his apartment before starting his long, mind-numbing commute to work in morning rush hour traffic.

The proprietor of the Speedy Mart knew Brent well. He was one of his best customers because he shopped there frequently. The owner's name was Duong—a short and lanky man with a few wiry hairs at the corners of his mouth that masqueraded as a moustache and a hairdo that looked like a black aloe plant. He greeted Brent whenever he came into the store. Sometimes, it appeared that Brent bought his entire grocery list at the Speedy Mart. But on this particular morning, he greeted him more boisterously than usual. Brent avoided eye contact and beelined for the pharmaceutical section when he walked in, while Duong called to him from behind the checkout counter.

"Hall-oh, my famous friend!" Duong called out, excited to see Brent.

Brent was not in the mood for pleasantries.

"Yeah, yeah," he grumbled, trying to decide which painkiller would alleviate his headache the quickest. "Do you have any Motrin?"

"Yes, Motrin is *free* for famous customers! Come get it!"

Brent lurched to the checkout counter, rubbing his aching forehead, right above his left eye. He looked at Duong with his good eye, finding him congenially holding up the city newspaper. But Brent wasn't the least bit interested in the city newspaper. In fact, he never purchased or even read a copy of the newspaper. To Brent, reading a newspaper was as fashionable as purchasing snake oil from an amiable guy on the side of the road.

"I'll take some of your *free* Motrin, then."

"Is this you?" he said, jabbing at the newspaper with his bony index finger, the fingernail long and pointy. "It sure looks like you."

Brent examined the grainy, black and white photo on the front cover with the facsimile of a man that resembled him, but he wasn't buying it.

"That's not me," he scoffed. "The Motrin, please." He extended his hand, hoping to have a box of headache medicine dropped in it. Duong eagerly continued.

"It says you're a fraud? Is that true?" he said, snickering, then set the newspaper on the counter while he turned around to find where a dusty box of Motrin was hiding among the displays of cigarettes, cigars, condoms, and electronic accessories.

Brent's curiosity was piqued. He slid the newspaper closer to him so he could read it with his good eye. Above the black and white photo was a bold headline in all caps that read:

"THE COST-SAVINGS FRAUD!"

The guy in the photo certainly looked like him, standing in the same spot he did next to Mr. Schneidermann at Governor Bennett's press conference, a self-congratulatory, shit-eating grin plastered on his face. He scanned the paragraph below the large photograph and words like "drunken" and "slept" and "unwittingly" and "keyboard" immediately leapt from the page, telegraphing their journalistic intent to his still-inebriated brain. Anxiety and dread washed over his body as he pushed the newspaper away. When Duong turned around to hand Brent the free, dusty box of Motrin, he was no longer standing there. He saw Brent's car pulling out of the parking lot and speeding away, the bell on the swinging glass door still tinkling.

"You forgot your Motrin!" he cried out, waving the box of painkillers above his head.

Brent frantically merged his beat-up SUV into rush-hour traffic, tuning the FM radio to his usual morning listen: *The Doolittle and Fred Morning Show*. He had an irrational loyalty to this particular radio morning show, mostly because Fred had mentioned Brent's band during a retelling of a raucous bachelor party one night. The group of inebriated, horny men (friends of Fred the DJ) spent part of their evening at the bar where Brent's band played. Lots of beer and shots of whiskey were carelessly consumed by the groomsmen, and a bar brawl erupted over a misunderstanding from an accidental shove. Most of Fred's party escaped from the bar but not before Jeff— the guitarist in Brent's band—smashed an acoustic guitar over the head of one of the groomsmen, the one who tried to climb onstage while the band played a cover of "I Fought the Law." Fred regaled the hilarious dilemma some of the other groomsman endured carrying their large, unconscious cohort from the bar, in turn naming Brent's band on the air, and cementing his love for the radio show. Fred never, ever mentioned Brent's band again, but Brent still listened to the morning show nonetheless. But in traffic, the conversational voices of the two DJs soothed Brent's soul, distracting him from the crushing road rage of the other drivers.

Brent's headache from his hangover still pounded inside his head. He wondered if what Duong had told him was really true, or a figment of his imagination, enhanced by the alcohol still flowing in his bloodstream. It seemed unusual and highly unlikely that a nobody like himself would be on the front page of the city newspaper. Even the governor's press conference didn't garner frontpage attention. As he slowly progressed through morning traffic, the radio DJs debated the existence of a local ordinance that allowed female citizens to walk topless around the city. Brent groggily enjoyed the debate, daydreaming about topless models strolling around town, while he kept a safe distance from the cars in front of him. The debate leaned in favor of the lurid ordinance, then moved onto other political topics of the day. Fred the DJ read the headline from the front page of the city newspaper, then scolded the governor for traipsing complicit government employees onstage to promote a sham to save the State of Texas hundreds of *millions* of dollars. Fred called the government employees "lackeys," and even called them out by name.

"And look at these jokers: Schneidermann and Baker. Look at them! You can see it on their smug faces!" Fred declared, the vitriol and contempt spewing from Brent's stereo speakers.

"It's a complete joke!" Doolittle agreed. "Government corruption at its worst!"

Brent slammed on his brakes and the cars behind him honked their horns. Brent could see the faces of the angry drivers in his rearview mirror, shaking their fists at him as his SUV stalled the slow-moving traffic. Brent couldn't listen anymore, so he turned off the radio.

What is going on?! he thought, frightened and worried. *I'm not a lackey, whatever that means!*

He cranked the steering wheel hard to the right, his SUV creeping through traffic to the nearest exit. He commenced to drive slowly through the side streets of town, mesmerized with the notion that maybe he was living in an alternate reality, one where he was all over the media: newspapers, radio, the internet, and maybe even television. Normally, this fantasy would excite him, but he wasn't being covered for the right reason: his band. For the first time in a very long time, he was worried about his employment at the Texas Department of Unemployment and Benefits. When he reached his usual parking spot in the underground garage, he left his SUV without taking his messenger bag with him, or even locking it. He scurried up the stairs to the lobby.

When Brent crashed into the lobby, his worst fear was realized. There was Emmitt, sitting behind the security desk, reading the front page of that morning's edition of the city newspaper. When he saw Brent in the lobby, his eyes opened wide with astonishment and he sat up quickly, folding the newspaper in half.

"Mr. Baker! Is it true?" he said, pushing his hat back on his head and rubbing his forehead.

Brent didn't answer him. He continued back up the stairs to the third floor, bursting into the hallway and running toward Unit 3. Ken, the former paper collector, watched him approach as he gripped the wall, standing out of his way.

He smirked as Brent passed him, then said, "Governor Bennett's lackey, huh?"

Brent ignored him. He ran across the skywalk to Unit 3, slamming the door behind him after entering the small office: his comfortable place of refuge. Conchino and J. D. were already at their desks, sipping coffee and nibbling on some cookies J. D. had brought for everyone to share. Deborah was nowhere to be found. Brent plopped in his chair and covered his head, as if sheltering himself from a hailstorm. J. D. was concerned by his boss's disheveled appearance and shaky disposition.

"Are you OK?" he said, chewing on his cookie.

"No, this morning is screwy," he moaned, his voice muffled under his protective arms.

J. D. and Conchino looked at each other, baffled by Brent's behavior. They both shrugged.

"Have you seen the newspaper this morning?" Brent said, worried.

J. D. and Conchino both laughed.

"The newspaper?" J. D. said, sipping some coffee. "We don't read the newspaper. Do you?" Conchino concurred with a slow shake of his head.

Brent slowly lifted his arms from his head, then said, "You don't know?"

"Know what?" J. D. replied. "Did something happen?"

"I think so," he said, sitting up at his desk, grabbing his pad of paper for doodling. "Where's Deborah?"

"We don't know. Conchino said she wasn't at her house when he stopped to pick her up."

Surprised with this statement, Brent turned to J. D. and said, "'Conchino said'? Since when does Conchino talk to *you*?"

Conchino smirked, then picked up his cell phone and pecked something into it. A ding could be heard from within J.

D.'s desk. He opened his middle drawer and pulled out a cell phone. He pecked something back to Conchino. Brent watched their interaction with disbelief.

"You have a cell phone *now*?" he said, annoyed.

"Yep," J. D. said, finishing his text message, then placing his new cell phone on his desk. "So he can send me messages."

Brent rolled his eyes.

"You two are the new Rita and Deborah? Great!" he said, sarcastically.

"Are you calling us old ladies?" J. D. snapped.

Brent laughed it off, then began doodling on his pad of paper. Without Deborah in the office, the other data clerks didn't have a diligent lead to follow, as far as work was concerned. Entering applications into TAPES was slow-going, encouraged by Brent's indolence. The morning hours drifted by as J. D. slowly entered applications alone, while Conchino puttered around with some car parts on his desk and Brent snoozed. But their peaceful morning wouldn't last long.

Mr. Schneidermann burst into Unit 3, slamming the door against the wall, startling the three coworkers.

He turned to Brent, then snapped, "You! I want you in my office in ten minutes!"

He wagged his finger at him. Brent shriveled.

"Yes, sir," he whimpered.

"The sh—," Schneidermann stammered, then composed himself by fixing his tan and blue tie. He continued. "The *you-know-what* has hit the fan. And heads are gonna roll. I want you in my office in ten minutes! Got it?!"

"Yes, sir."

He left Unit 3, slamming the door behind him. Brent rolled his eyes, returning to form.

"Puh-lease," he scoffed. "I'm not going up there."

"You're not?" J. D. said, surprised.

"Why? What do you think will happen if I *don't* go up there? I'll get fired?!"

J. D. returned a blank stare.

"Nah," Brent said, putting away his doodling pad. "We should go grab a beer and a sandwich. Are you two in?"

"It's only 10:30 in the morning," J. D. replied.

"So what?! Let's go!"

J. D. and Conchino reluctantly agreed and followed Brent out of the office, down the hall, and into the elevator. Brent pressed the button for the basement garage, so as to avoid Emmitt or Ken or anyone else snooping in his business. They huffed it a few blocks to O'Sullivan's—the first pub Brent ever took J. D. to—and the three coworkers sat at the bar, ready for an earlier than usual lunch. J. D. was surprised that O'Sullivan's was open so early in the morning.

"This place is always open," Brent informed him.

Soon enough, P the bartender greeted them and obliged Brent's order of a round of beer for everyone. Conchino, never having gone to lunch with Brent, was surprised. J. D. consoled him with a pat on the shoulder.

"It's cool," J. D. cooed.

After setting the pints of beer in front of them, P smiled and began his morning routine of cleaning bar glasses.

"What brings you in so early?" he said, looking at Brent.

"Shitty morning," Brent replied, chugging his beer.

"Yeah, aren't they all?" P agreed.

"Have you seen the city paper?" Brent said.

"Nah, I don't read the city paper anymore. Too conservative. I stick with the *Austin Weekly Ledger*. Alt-weeklies are where it's at."

"Right," Brent said, finishing his beer.

P poured Brent another pint, then sat it on the bar.

"Did you see this morning's *Ledger*, though?! It's crazy!"

"No, haven't seen it. What's on it?"

"Check this out!"

P the bartender walked around the bar to the entrance of the pub. He snatched a copy of the *Austin Weekly Ledger* from a newspaper stand, then brought it back for the three coworkers to see. He tossed it on the bar, then jabbed at it with his knobby finger.

"Bennett is a fraud. He ain't crippled. He can walk! It's all a scam!"

The three stared at the front page of the alt-weekly newspaper and discovered Bob's handiwork. There on the cover was a large black and white photo of Governor Bennett, his withered carrot pixelated and obscured from view, standing over his toilet. The three T-DUB employees were stunned at the raw image of the governor, whom they had always known to be seated in a wheelchair of gold.

"Uh-oh," Brent said.

"You're damn straight *uh-oh*! The shit's gonna hit the fan!"

"I think you're right," Brent said, turning to his employees. "Who's hungry?"

33.

Esther Jean stood under a tree on the grass of the front lawn of the Texas Capitol, scrutinizing the Confederate Soldiers Monument, a bronze and granite vestige commemorating their battle during the Civil War and the names etched in the base of the thirteen states that withdrew from the Union. She couldn't help but wonder about the statue's relevance at this place and time in history, and also wondered if she had the power to affect change in the hearts and minds of the people responsible for the care and upkeep of the capitol grounds.

Surely, this belongs in a historical museum rather than out here, right? she thought, as she looked up at the bronze military figures gazing longingly into the distance, maybe at their cotton plantations or cattle ranches set in times long gone. She then looked around to find families and groups of tourists of many nationalities, backgrounds, and races, laughing and taking photographs. *Gentlemen, you are now irrelevant.*

She looked down the long walkway from the entrance of the Capitol to the street, past a large black family gleefully taking an assortment of family photos in various configurations, and could see Bob the alt-weekly reporter briskly walking toward her. She marveled at the bright red, Hawaiian-print, button-down shirt he wore. It was even pressed and starched, the straight creases on the sleeves stiffly connecting his protruding shoulders to his bony elbows. She patted his chest lightly, like an approving mother, when he joined her under the tree.

"You look snazzy this morning," she said, smiling at him, wiping flakes of starch from the gaudy shirt.

"You, too," he said, embarrassed from the attention. "But you always look snazzy."

"Why am I always waiting for you under trees? It's so romantic, like we're together or something."

"You are my work wife. You do know that, right?"

The corner of his mouth slinked upward. He winked awkwardly. Esther Jean laughed, then slugged his upper arm, her motherly demeanor gone, replaced with aggressive derision.

"We did good work this week, you know?" she said, grinning as he rubbed his assaulted bicep.

"Yeah, we did."

"I'm just surprised at how fast the Legislative Ethics Committee called this press conference."

"I'm not!" he said. "The Democrats *hate* Bennett. In fact, hate is not a strong enough word to describe how they feel about him."

"Want to go in and find a seat?"

"Yeah, let's do it," he said, continuing to rub his sore arm.

She held onto Bob's good arm as they walked into the Capitol Building, through security, and into the welcoming space of the rotunda. As they walked across the terrazzo floor, they both looked up at the Star of Texas etched into the ceiling of the rotunda, up almost three hundred feet above their heads.

"It still gets me every time I look at it," she said, squeezing his arm.

"Me too," he said. "Did I tell you that D. Jameson contacted me about a reporting gig?"

Esther Jean turned to her friend, a little surprised yet pleased, then said, "Really? My editor? What did he say?"

"He wants me to start covering politics for *The Austin Journal.* Maybe you and I will get to work together more."

"I don't think so," she sighed. "I may not be around in Austin too much longer."

"What?! Where are you going?" he said.

"San Francisco, I think. I need a change of scenery."

"That's too bad. The long distance will be hard on our work marriage."

"We can still have phone sex," she said. They snickered.

Having been to the committee rooms dozens of times, they knew exactly where they needed to be in the chambers underground. They hopped into an elevator and descended together below the Capitol Building. And after snaking through the office catacombs two stories below the Great Lawn, they found room 112-B, the location for all hearings for the Legislative Ethics Committee. Dozens of reporters milled about in the hall outside the room, being that the doors were still locked. Esther Jean and Bob waited together, listening to the mumblings from the other reporters, several of whom glanced longingly at them, envious of their earthshattering news articles.

"I think we have some new fans," Esther Jean whispered to Bob. He agreed.

Once the doors unlocked, all the reporters filed inside the conference room, taking the first available seats. Esther Jean and Bob sat in the back, as they usually preferred, right in front of where the photographers and videographers stood with their equipment. At the front of the room was a wooden bench where the five committee members sat, each spot with a microphone and a name plate in front of highbacked, leather chairs. At each side of the room were two large-screen televisions, both tuned to a different conference room, one that looked like it belonged to the governor. The navy blue and gold décor broadcast on the televisions was familiar to Esther Jean.

"Looks like Bennett may be on closed-circuit TV."

"Looks that way," Bob replied.

The conference room was abuzz with chatter and whispering as the reporters waited patiently for the chairman of the Legislative Ethics Committee to come in—Mr. Giuseppe DeMarco of Dallas, Texas, a far-left progressive if there ever was one and a frequent adversary of Governor Bennett—as well as the other four members of the committee (two registered Democrats and two registered Republicans). Once they came in the room through a side door and sat down, the room fell silent. DeMarco raised a small, ceremonial gavel, then whacked the bench top with it.

"Let's get down to business," DeMarco said, setting the gavel down. His accent was a mix of New York Italian bravado and Texas southern gentility that was comical to many in the public sector, one of the endearing traits that helped him ascend in political prominence in North Texas. His slicked-back, black hair and thin, stiff moustache were immaculately groomed. His black-rimmed glasses had lenses of an unusual thickness, morphing his dark eyes into large platters of brown. And his large proboscis and thin lips gave him the appearance of a west Texas tortoise, particularly when he wore suits of dark green, one like he was wearing at this press conference. He was known to be tough on corruption and never backed down from a fight for what was right, or what he liked to call "benevolent justice."

Esther Jean thought he was quite a character and enjoyed listening to him speak, as well as watching his mannerisms, which were as unusual as his accent. She leaned over to Bob, then whispered, "He looks like he's from another planet."

Bob snickered.

"All right," DeMarco said, then cleared his throat. "I've called this meeting to discuss some revelations that have appeared in two newspapers this week that I feel are of the utmost importance to the citizens of Texas. Both news articles concern our governor: Dwayne Bennett."

A collective gasp resonated throughout the room, even though no one was really surprised. Governor Bennett had a history of using his office for dubious, personal reasons, but it seemed his slippery nature, disregard for political norms, and penchant for dishonesty made him a formidable adversary for the righteous in the public sector. Despite this, DeMarco was tenacious and contentious, and took any opportunity to investigate Governor Bennett, no matter how flimsy the accusation. It was his mission in life to bring down the sleazy governor.

"It is my understanding that both reporters who wrote the articles for *The Austin Journal* and the *Austin Weekly Ledger* are present this morning," DeMarco said, looking up to the gallery of reporters and onlookers. All in attendance looked back to Esther Jean and Bob as they both stood up. "Will you be willing to testify in this hearing this morning?"

"Yes, I am," Esther Jean said.

"Yes," Bob said.

"Good! You may be seated," DeMarco said while organizing some papers sitting in front of him, including copies of *The Austin Journal* and the *Austin Weekly Ledger*.

Esther Jean and Bob sat back down. The room was mostly silent, except for the rustling of papers coming from the bench. DeMarco raised a copy of the *Austin Weekly Ledger* and scoffed at the photo of Governor Bennett on the front page standing over his toilet, his withered carrot obscured from view.

"Now, I was quite surprised to see this front-page photo and article, particularly since Governor Bennett has claimed to be unable to walk for as long as I can remember. It was a central focus of his campaign for governor. Although it isn't a crime that all of a sudden—quite miraculously it seems, even biblically miraculous I might add—he is able to walk, I find it dubious that a miracle has happened here. In fact, it seems to me that there is a misrepresentation of his political motives.

And for years, he has accepted donations as someone who is disabled as well as received work from reputable organizations and charities and government agencies in the name of the infirmed and disabled, as he claimed to be. Ladies and gentleman, that is the exact definition of *fraud.* And because of this, the citizens of Texas have an ethical dilemma."

A collective gasp filled the conference room as reporters scribbled on pads of paper and pecked notes into their mobile devices. Camera flashes popped and crackled. DeMarco shuffled the papers in front of him, grabbing the copy of *The Austin Journal* and lifting it up.

"And trust me, starting today, I will be opening an investigation pertaining to this, and *this* as well. This employee here," he said, jabbing the newspaper with his index finger. "He simply fell asleep on his computer, stone-cold drunk I might add. He didn't knowingly discover a solution to the Texas Department of Unemployment and Benefits' misguided procedures. He accidentally passed out from consuming alcoholic beverages on the job! And Governor Bennett had the nerve to parade this fool onstage at a press conference for his own political gain. More fraudulent and shameful behavior!"

As DeMarco railed against the governor from the committee bench, Bennett himself appeared on the television screens suspended on both sides of the conference room. He appeared to be screaming, his face puffy and red with spittle flying from his clenched teeth, shaking his fist at the camera projecting his visage on the television screens, but no one could hear him. He gesticulated wildly on the screens—in silence—the volume set on mute. DeMarco chuckled at what was projected on the televisions.

"Technical difficulties. We'll give the governor an opportunity to speak later. But first, I'd like to call the reporter from *The Austin Journal* to approach the bench for sworn testimony: Esther Jean Stinson."

Esther Jean turned to face Bob, who mouthed the words, "Good luck." She stood, then approached the wooden bench, all eyes in the conference room on her. As she stood before DeMarco and the four other members of the Legislative Ethics Committee, she rolled her shoulders, as if releasing tension.

DeMarco adjusted his microphone, then said, "Ms. Stinson, do you swear to tell the truth—the whole truth—so help you God?"

"Yes, I do."

"Good, then let's start from the beginning. Tell me more about this state employee—the drunk one—Mr. Brent Baker."

34.

When Brent arrived in Unit 3 first thing in the morning—nursing a new hangover for a new day, a cup of coffee in one hand and a powdered jelly donut in the other—he discovered Mr. Schneidermann sitting at his desk. He was not amused that Brent had walked into the office closer to 9:30 than his official starting time of 8:00. Deborah, Conchino, and J. D. were already at their desks, too, tranquilized with fear, because none of them were used to Mr. Schneidermann's presence in their office space. Schneidermann pulled a chair over to the side of Brent's desk and motioned for him to sit down, patting the plastic seat. Brent reluctantly sat in the chair.

"Hey, boss man!" he said, forcing a smile through the pain in his face from the hangover. "How do you like my chair? Pretty comfy, huh?"

"Is this when you usually arrive to work?" Schneidermann said, tapping an intense arpeggio on the desktop with his fingers.

"Not all the time," Brent replied, sheepishly looking to his employees for help, none of whom returned even a passing glance.

Mr. Schneidermann was already angry, so Brent's hesitant answers just made him more aggravated and impatient. On Brent's desk was a copy of *The Austin Journal*, which he turned and then slid to Brent, as if offering him a chance to casually peruse the headline. Brent already knew what it said.

"Mr. Schneidermann, I can explain!"

"Too late. As of this moment, your employment here is terminated!" He stood up and retrieved an empty cardboard box from the break table that he had brought with him when he first came into Unit 3, before Brent casually sauntered in. He set it on Brent's desk. "Here's a box for your belongings. I will watch you as you retrieve your personal items, then I will escort you out of the building."

Brent sneered at Deborah as she pretended not to notice his searing glare. She began entering unemployment applications into TAPES—as if it was any other morning—as did Conchino and J. D., following her lead. Mr. Schneidermann stepped away from Brent's desk, allowing him space to pack his belongings into the box. As he slowly loaded the box, Mr. Schneidermann retrieved one other item from the break table: a dusty, three-ring binder.

"Yesterday, I found this in a box labeled 'Unit 3' down in the basement storage room. Do you know what it is?" he said, holding it up for Brent to see. He shook his head. "It's the original manual for the TAPES application. Have you ever seen it before?"

Brent examined the binder but didn't recognize it, although Deborah did. When she saw it, she called out, "That's my manual! I've been looking for it. I had no idea where it was."

"Well, it was in the storage room downstairs," he said, then jabbed the cover of the binder with his index finger. "Do you know what it says on page 169?"

"I have no clue," Deborah said, a little miffed that he had her personal copy of the TAPES manual. She knew it was hers because a shiny gold and silver sticker of a kitten still glistened on the cover in the same place where she had originally stuck it.

"That's fine. I'll read it to you all," he said, flipping to that page, then lifting the binder closer to his face so his poor eyes could actually read it. "It says: 'Once applications have been entered into TAPES, an authorized user (like a unit manager) shall TAB to the last application, then click Ctrl + Shift + Tab to Submit data to the Office of the Comptroller.' What do you think about that?"

He closed the binder and waited. Brent knew the answer but, rather than incriminate himself, he said nothing at all and continued to pack his cardboard box. Schneidermann slammed the binder on the desk, hard. The loud bang startled everyone in Unit 3.

"It means your cost-savings suggestion was no suggestion at all. It was a process already in place. Somehow, the fact that you neglected to follow established procedures was overlooked or forgotten a long time ago. But that doesn't make a difference to me. What *does* make a difference to me is that you will not be receiving the $10,000 prize. It has been rescinded, courtesy of Governor Bennett. And yours truly: me."

The collective disappointment of the others in Unit 3 was heard in the form of a deflated sigh. Schneidermann was not aware of their pact to share the prize money, but their audible disappointment pleased him nonetheless. For a brief moment, he enjoyed his vulgar display of power over all the employees in Unit 3.

"Now, let's go. I don't want to see your face around here for another minute!"

Schneidermann opened the door, then held it for Brent, who reluctantly picked up the cardboard box and unceremoniously left Unit 3. Schneidermann followed him out, slamming the door behind him. After a few minutes of awkward silence, J. D. looked around to Conchino and Deborah, who were both as shocked as he was at what had just transpired. They knew Brent had somehow slyly escaped termination for years, and it seemed he would retire from the Texas Department of Unemployment and Benefits as a vested state retiree, but not anymore. He was no longer their supervisor or an employee of the State of Texas. The reality of this was strange to them, to say the least.

Deborah took the opportunity to retrieve her long-lost user manual. She tiptoed over to Brent's desk, picked it up, and briskly took it back to her desk. She marveled at it—opening it and then flipping through the yellowed pages—as if caressing a recovered artifact from a past lifetime. She reminisced about the early days when she first started working at the Texas Department of Unemployment and Benefits, almost three decades before, when her original supervisor gave her the manual. She couldn't remember his name but she remembered his face—pockmarked and bearded with large, tortoise-shell glasses.

Rita was already working there and took her under her protective wing, giving her sisterly advice and scribbling notes on the pages of her user manual. The inscriptions were still there in the margins of the yellowed pages—preserved in blue, ball-point pen ink—and tears appeared at the corners of her eyes as she read them. She looked over to Rita's empty desk, the framed photos of her children and grandchildren still on the desktop, then felt ashamed. She wasn't quite sure why she had felt compelled to confess to the newspaper reporter, but she did. The wine made it easy for the angry words to come out. But the loss of her friend made her reevaluate the motive of her inebriated confession.

"Rita would be upset that we didn't get that prize money," Deborah said to her coworkers, a sniffle punctuating her proclamation. "She really wanted to win that prize."

J. D. and Conchino stopped typing and turned to look at Deborah. They could see the tears in her eyes, a materialization of the sorrow they all felt, and a realization that sometimes when you wished for something beyond your means, it was easy to overlook the precious things you already possessed: family, friendship, and love.

"She would have been pissed!" J. D. squawked.

Conchino chuckled in agreement.

J. D. opened his bottom desk drawer—the one where he kept his lunch box as well as the home for an army of sugar ants—and pulled out a pecan log to share with his coworkers. He had planned to eat it after his lunch, but felt this was a better time to share and consume it. He took the treat to the break table and cut it into thirds with a butter knife.

"Anybody want a snack?" he said.

"That sounds wonderful!" Deborah said, joining him at the break table. "I'll make some coffee."

"OK," J. D. said, patting her on the shoulder. "Coffee sounds nice."

Conchino joined them at the table for their impromptu break, where they snacked and drank coffee together. Deborah was in another confessional mood.

"I'm sorry I talked to that reporter," she said to her coworkers, but they didn't seem to mind and shrugged after she conceded her error in judgment. "I feel bad that Brent got fired."

"I'm not surprised," J. D. said, wiping his mouth with his forearm. "There's always a... what do you call it?"

Deborah was confused. "I don't know. What do you mean?"

"You know. What do you call a person who is blamed for something?"

"A guilty person?!" she blurted.

"No, that's not it," J. D. said, frustrated.

"The bad guy?!" she continued.

"No, but close."

Conchino watched the two fumble for the right words. He chewed on his snack, sipping his coffee as they threw out phrase after wrong phrase. Tired of their back and forth, he decided to interject.

"Fall guy," he said, deep and resonate.

His proclamation startled J. D. and Deborah, who weren't expecting their stoic coworker to speak at all. They laughed as they finished their coffee, then sat back at their desks.

"How long do you think it'll be before we get a new supervisor?" Deborah said, typing again.

But no one answered her. There didn't seem to be an appropriate answer anyway, so they all just began to work as they were used to doing.

"Conchino?" she continued. "Can you take me by a convenience store on the way home today?"

He nodded. Then the clickity-clack of their keyboards reverberated within the walls of Unit 3, lulling them back to work.

35.

In the days following his termination from work, Brent Baker liberally drank beer and Jägermeister at all hours, starting when he first woke up in the morning through the night until he passed out. It was his way of self-medicating his wounded pride. He did not know any other way to cope with the pain he felt from the loss of his career and his main source of income. He still had the band but the money he received from playing with his *compadres* just wasn't enough to live on. But what the band lacked in earning potential, it made up for with camaraderie and commiseration. The union of misanthropic musicians excelled in anarchy and nihilism, when called upon. Whenever one of the band members expressed any kind of disenchantment or grief in their lives, the others added fuel to the fire in the form of alcohol, cigarettes, music, and anger. This suited the worst parts of Brent's personality—the parts usually suppressed from the world—to his detriment.

In turn, this naughty proclivity of his band to wreak havoc on the bars of Austin, Texas, had a finite shelf life, usually lasting only a few days. Chip the bass player, Jeff the guitar player, and new drummer Todd were all older dudes—ones with day jobs and mortgages and bills to pay—and although they were always game when it came to cheering up a depressed bandmember, they just had only so much angst in their proverbial gas tanks. They were not young men anymore. What seemed fun at first always wore out its welcome, fast. And even if Brent begged and pleaded for them to continue partying like there was no tomorrow, in reality, tomorrow always came with a new sense of urgency to "act like a grownup."

After a few days of hard drinking, playing punk rock cover songs, and flirting with tipsy waitresses, the bandmembers left Brent at his apartment with a promise to check in on him in a couple of days and maybe play another gig in a week or two. He was inconsolable and they were ready to get back to their normal lives. Brent continued drinking beer in his apartment alone and sustained his alcohol consumption with food delivery, while time slowly moved on like a placid breeze from the Texas Hill Country.

So, when Conchino banged loudly on his front door with his fists, Brent peeled open his eyes thinking it was the pizza delivery guy, not knowing that he had passed out ten hours earlier with his phone still in his hand. The banging on the door grew incessantly louder as Brent came to consciousness. He didn't know what time it was, although he was still hungry for greasy food. Rubbing the crust from his eyes and the stinky drool from the side of his mouth, he went to the door to see who it was and to silence the loud pounding. When he opened the door, the bright, morning sunlight blinded him.

He covered his eyes with his forearm, then said, "What do you want?"

The dark silhouette of a person stood motionless. He didn't know who it was at first because he couldn't see a thing. A deep voice responded from the dark figure.

"Deborah wants to talk to us," the familiar, deep voice said. He knew it was Conchino. He could feel his colossal presence.

A wet pshaw flopped out of his mouth, then he said, "I'm not talking to Deborah. You can tell her to go to hell!" Brent said, then reached for the door to slam it shut. Conchino placed his massive hand on the door, keeping it open with a stiff arm.

"She said it's *important* and that you won't regret coming," Conchino said, his words rolling off his tongue like boulders thudding down a hillside.

"What does she *want?*!" Brent insisted.

Conchino shrugged.

Brent was frustrated. On the one hand, he was curious about what important matter she wanted to talk to them about. On the other hand, he just wanted to drink more beer, wallow in his misery, then sleep. It also fascinated him to hear Conchino's distinctive voice, since he rarely heard the young man speak out loud—for almost any reason, important or not. If he was speaking to him at his place (somewhere Conchino or his other coworkers had never been), then it must have been important.

"I have a question for you. Why don't you ever speak?" Brent mused.

"'Cause I don't feel like it."

"Oh," Brent said, surprised with the simplicity of his answer.

"You coming?"

Brent knew he had nothing better to do, then said, "Yeah, let me find my sunglasses."

Conchino waited at the door while Brent plodded to his bathroom to gargle some mouthwash, put on a T-shirt he had retrieved from his bedroom floor, and looked for his sunglasses in the kitchen. When he found them on top of any empty pizza box, he put the dark sunglasses on, then followed Conchino to his car.

The parking lot of Brent's apartment complex was mostly empty, being that it was normal business hours for the rest of the world and the working-class tenants were at their places of employment. It tickled Brent that he wasn't one of them at that moment. Technically, he was what he always wanted to be: an unemployed rock musician.

"You got any beer?" he said, watching the stoic giant lumber toward his car.

Conchino just silently shook his head, opening the driver-side door to his car, then sat inside. Brent got in the passenger seat. He was pleased to see that Conchino's Honda Accord was not impounded anymore, and also pleased to see J. D. in the back seat, sitting next to Deborah. He greeted J. D. with a fist bump and acknowledged Deborah with a nod.

"Hey, Brent!" J. D. said enthusiastically. "Glad you're with us!"

"I guess," Brent said. "What's the deal?"

"We're going to visit Rita's grave and I thought you would like to join us," Deborah said, calmly.

"Sounds depressing," Brent replied. "Do you have any beer?"

"We can get some on the way, if you want," she said. "Is that what you want?"

"Yes, that's what I want," he said, his elbow against the window, his arm propping up his weary head.

Conchino started to drive the four friends to the cemetery where Rita was buried, but not before stopping at a convenience store on the way to buy Brent a six pack of cheap beer. Deborah handed Brent a ten-dollar bill from the back seat and he ran inside the store to buy the alcohol he desired. When they arrived at the cemetery a few minutes later, Brent was already on his second beer and feeling much more jovial. Conchino parked his car near the great lawn of Memorial Cemetery, away from the other cars in the lot, all there for a memorial service for someone else. J. D. spotted the Cadillac that Reverend Jackson owned and remembered the gaudy automobile from Rita's funeral, but he didn't mention it to the others.

The sun perched high in the pale blue sky, its light and warmth baking the thick grass of the cemetery. The friends got out of Conchino's car and trudged through the hot grass. Deborah led the three men to Rita's gravesite, winding through the tombstones, mausoleums, and memorials. J. D. read the headstones out loud with the curiosity and enthusiasm of a child.

"Hen-ry Bo-dine. Born 1918. Died 1944. WWII Veteran. In the Arms of the Lord," J. D. recited. He continued with the next headstone. "James McCall. Born 1922. Died 1964. Beloved Son, Father, and Husband."

"Are you going to read them *all*?" Brent said, annoyed.

"All of these people must have lived fascinating lives," J. D. chirped.

"They're just *people*," Brent grumbled, gulping the last of his beer, crushing the can, then tossing it beside the headstone of Mr. McCall. "Dead people."

J. D. picked up the discarded beer can, put it in his pants pocket, and scurried after the others.

When Deborah arrived at Rita's grave, she lovingly patted the top of the marble marker of her dear friend.

"Good morning, sweetheart," she said, then chuckled. "I mean, good afternoon. Time just flies. Doesn't it?"

The four friends stood around Rita's grave, the sun baking their shoulders while a breeze swept across the cemetery grass. Cars could be heard in the distance, driving up and down I-35, in pursuit of unknown destinations. A butterfly fluttered out of thin air, charting a haphazard course between their bodies. Deborah marveled at the butterfly and wondered aloud if its presence had any significance.

"I know you are here with us," Deborah said, her grief overwhelming her.

J. D. respectfully nodded, then began reciting the inscription on her headstone aloud.

"Here Lies Rita Jackson. Beloved Wife of Reggie Jackson Sr. Adoring Mother. Loving Grandmother. And a Friend to All. Born—"

"You don't have to read it all," Brent scoffed, interrupting J. D. "We can read to ourselves, you know."

Irritated, Conchino jabbed Brent roughly with his elbow. He stopped complaining and rubbed his assaulted bicep. Deborah noticed the commotion between them, then smiled like a mother watching over her bickering children, more adoring than irritated. She reached into her purse and pulled out a small metal box, then sat it on top of Rita's headstone. It was one of Rita's most prized possessions: her recipe box.

"The five of us in Unit 3 were like a dysfunctional family," Deborah said to the others, stepping back from the headstone. "I know we didn't all get along sometimes, but we looked out for each other when we could."

"Yeah, right," Brent muttered sarcastically, under his breath, although everyone could hear him perfectly.

Deborah, nonetheless, continued.

"And I know I made mistakes. I'm really sorry for that. If I had known that my actions would have caused such pain for everyone, then I wouldn't have done it. All I can say is that I'm sorry and I hope that everyone can accept my apology."

She stopped, then graciously lowered her head. J. D. looked at everyone, affected by what Deborah was saying.

"I accept your apology," he said, smiling at Deborah.

She smiled back at him, then said, "Of course you do. You're a nice young man."

J. D. blushed. Brent rolled his eyes.

"So," Deborah continued. "I wanted us all to get together at Rita's grave because she loved us all. She loved working for the T-DUB. She loved baking us treats. And she loved buying our lottery tickets!"

The other three chuckled because, of course, that was true.

"And we all had a pact. If we ever won that cost-savings prize, then we would share it. And even though we unfortunately lost that, we did, however, win some lottery money. A *lot* of lottery money."

The three men raised their heads, gazing at Deborah. They were extremely curious, to say the least.

"How much is '*a lot?*'" Brent said.

"It's a lot," she said, smiling.

"Like live-your-dreams a lot?" J. D. said.

The three men moved closer to Deborah, looking for an explanation.

"Yep," she said.

She took a deep breath, then explained to them what had happened, how she had been given the metal recipe box at Rita's house after the funeral, and how she had found the lottery tickets lovingly organized inside, especially the section marked for Unit 3, the section containing the winning scratch ticket. When Conchino dropped her off at a convenience store outside of her neighborhood, the clerk inside validated all the lottery tickets for her, except for one scratch ticket. When the terminal flashed a message that she should go to the main claim center, the clerk handed the ticket back to her and said, "You have to take this one to the claim center downtown." When she asked him how much it was worth, he told her he didn't know and that the claim center would assist her.

So, the next day, she asked her neighbor Steve to drop her off at the lottery claim center downtown. When the claim specialist behind the thick glass window told her it was a million-dollar winner, she fainted. When she came to, she thought she was dreaming, but the lottery employee assured her that it was real. She just couldn't believe it.

"You're telling me that we won a *million* bucks?!" Brent said, astonished. "Are you kidding me?"

"$1,000,523 to be exact."

"Fuck yes!" Brent exclaimed, raising both hands to each of his companions for a high-five. They all appeased him with a congratulatory slap, even Deborah, who awkwardly gave him a high-five in return.

J. D. rubbed his forehead, a little confounded, then said, "I can't believe it."

"I still can't believe it," Deborah concurred. "We'll each get $200,104, more or less, when split five ways. Rita's kids should get her share, of course."

"When do we get it?" Brent said, greedily rubbing his hands together. "There's a lot I can do with that kind of cash."

"It should hit my checking account tomorrow. Then I'll write you each a check."

Brent knelt down on Rita's gravesite, smiled lovingly at the headstone, then wrapped his arms around it and hugged it.

"I love you, Rita," he said, still embracing the monument tightly. He looked up to Deborah, then said, "Are you going to quit?"

"I already did. I called Schneidermann and tendered my resignation."

"Awesome," Brent said, standing up and wiping blades of grass from his jeans.

"We all should quit. It's what Rita would have wanted," Deborah said.

"Really?" J. D. said, curiously. "You think so?"

Deborah nodded. J. D. looked up at Conchino, who had a huge grin on his face, his eyes bright with optimism and hope. It warmed J. D.'s heart knowing that, for a brief moment at least, luck was on their side, and that maybe a new future had been laid out for them from beyond the grave by their loving coworker.

"What do you think, Conchino?" J. D. said to him. "Do you think we should quit our jobs at the T-DUB?"

His stoic friend could no longer hold in his enthusiasm, smiling so broadly that it hurt his face, then he forced his pursed lips to move so he could speak.

"Most definitely."

The jaunty butterfly suddenly returned, flapping its yellow wings as it flew around J. D.'s head, then darting at Conchino, before turning up toward the sky and ascending further. It flew a meandering course up higher beyond his reach, and J. D. waved to the butterfly as it flew away, thinking it was probably off to find Rita's children and grandchildren at her house.

At that moment, it seemed possible.

36.

J. D.'s commute to work on his new bicycle—a like-new one he purchased from a desperate college student raising money for marijuana, beer, and new sneakers, who listed it on a bulletin board near the Texas Department of Unemployment and Benefits for an unbelievably low price of $200—became more tolerable for him since first moving to Austin, even though the cars and trucks he shared the road with were just as aggressive and noisy as ever. He didn't understand why the morning commuters and drivers were so angry. If they were driving to work, then shouldn't they be happy to have a job? If they were driving home from work, then shouldn't they be happy they had a home? There was so much to be thankful for, if they had a job and a home to drive to. J. D. was feeling especially grateful for having those things as well as having good friends. He ruminated about recent events and the good fortune bestowed upon him from his coworkers while he rode his bicycle to work. After Deborah told him about the lottery jackpot money they would be sharing, the only thing he could think about doing with his portion was helping his parents with their ailing business back in Brady, Texas.

Boy, will they be surprised! he thought as he pedaled his bicycle through Hyde Park—the neighborhood he called home—doing his best to stay in the bike lane.

He was still getting used to riding the new bike. Its levers and switches were in distinctly different locations on the handlebars and frame compared to his previous bicycle, but that didn't bother J. D. too much. He was pleased to have any bicycle at all—mainly because he needed transportation to get to and from work—and he hoped that whoever stole his old bicycle from outside of the police station the day he bailed Conchino out of jail was at least happy with his trusty bike and making good use of it.

I had some good times riding that bike, he thought. *Good times indeed.*

Out of the cacophony of car horns and tire screeches, one car horn honked a tune more playful than angry—a series of quick beeps instead of a sustained, furious blast. When he looked up to see who was teasing him, he saw Conchino's Honda Accord pass him, his coworker's hand waving back at him from above the car, extended out the driver-side window. It pleased him to recognize Conchino's car but it also pained him to see the backseat empty, Rita's kind face no longer watching him through the rear window as she used to do. Deborah was not in the back seat, either, having quit her job at the Texas Department of Unemployment and Benefits a couple of days before.

It will be quiet at work today, he thought, as he continued to pedal his bike.

When he arrived at work, he pulled into the underground parking garage and parked his bicycle in its usual place. Of course, he didn't see Brent's beat-up SUV, formerly parked catty-corner in a nearby spot with empty beer cans and cigarette butts haphazardly tossed underneath it. He locked up his bicycle and went upstairs to Unit 3.

Inside, he found Conchino standing at his desk, packing his personal belongings into a cardboard box: car parts, tools, audio equipment, and the like. J. D. sat his bicycle helmet on his desk, then set his lunch box inside the bottom drawer—the same routine he had performed for days on end when he arrived to work. He was a creature of habit, and the routine pleased him. He sat in his chair, watching Conchino pack the box. There were a few unemployment applications on J. D.'s desk, waiting to be entered into TAPES. Both Deborah and Rita's desks were clear of any of their personal belongings—barren work stations that used to exude love and camaraderie. On the other hand, Brent's desk was still covered with papers and binders, probably left for the new supervisor to parse through when they arrived (whenever that would be). The empty office saddened J. D.

"It's gonna be awfully quiet around here," he muttered.

Conchino didn't say anything, as usual. While he continued to pack, J. D. reached into the bottom drawer of his desk and pulled a snack from his lunch box, wrapped in plastic wrap. He unwrapped it and offered some to his friend.

"Want some brownie with pecans on top?" he said, lifting the delicious gift for Conchino to see.

Conchino stopped packing and accepted it, sitting down to enjoy it. J. D. pulled a corner off his own brownie, then set it in the bottom of the drawer for the army of sugar ants to consume, just as Rita had instructed him to do. The two friends quietly ate their treats.

When Conchino was done, he wiped his mouth with his forearm, then said, "After I'm done, I have to go to the passport office. Will you go with me? I've never applied for a passport before."

J. D. was surprised with his request, mostly because Conchino had never asked him for help in person before. Conchino seemed to J. D. to be a self-reliant type of guy—one to never ask anyone for help except that time when he needed to be bailed out of jail (his parents were out of town)—so any request of any kind for assistance was surprising, to say the least.

"Sure," J. D. said. "I'll go with you."

"Thanks," Conchino said, then he packed more of his things into his box.

J. D. turned on his computer and got ready to enter applications into TAPES. He only had a few on his desk, so he knew it wouldn't take him too long to enter them. He had grown adept at data entry, just like his coworkers in Unit 3; the repetition of his duties as well as the passing of time ensured that he would only get better and better. As he waited for his computer to boot up, he watched Conchino pack.

"Why do you need a passport?" he said.

"To go to Japan."

"Why are you—" J. D. stammered, then remember something Conchino had told everyone in Unit 3. "Oh! To help your grandfather?"

Conchino nodded.

"And that's what you're doing with your portion of the lottery money?"

Conchino continued to nod.

"That's very nice of you," J. D. said, logging into his computer while continuing to talk to his coworker. "I'd like to help my family, too. It's the right thing to do."

He soon began entering applications into TAPES. But after fifteen minutes or so, they were all entered and he didn't have any more on his desk, which was strange. There was usually a mountain of paperwork, but since Unit 3 was currently lacking in data clerks, maybe the workload had been diverted to a different unit. He turned to Conchino, who was done packing his box with his belongings.

"Ready?" he said to J. D., who returned a quizzical look.

"You want to go *now*?"

Conchino nodded.

"But we just got to work," J. D. said, confused.

"I don't work here anymore. And you don't have any more work to do anyways."

J. D. couldn't disagree with him. So, after he pondered his dilemma for a bit (should he stay or should he go?), he decided he would go with Conchino, mostly because he wanted to be helpful.

"Let me leave a note on the door, just in case anyone comes looking for us."

Conchino watched him scribble some words on a Post-it note, then J. D. grabbed all of his things like his helmet and lunch box. When they left Unit 3, J. D. stuck the note on the side of the door facing the hallway. His note said:

OUT FOR A BIT. SOMETHING IMPORTANT CAME UP. BE BACK SOON.

When they got to the car, Conchino helped J. D. disassemble part of his bicycle so it would fit in his trunk, then they drove the few miles to get to the passport office, the closest one being on the edge of campus to the University of Texas at Austin. This particular passport office mostly served students, but anyone was welcome to use their services, which made it a good choice for a short wait. Most students couldn't afford to travel internationally anyway, but Conchino could. He took a number for his place in line and sat in a plastic chair next to J. D., who was gawking at his surroundings.

"This place is cool!" J. D. said, beaming. "I'd love to see the world."

Conchino didn't say anything. He slumped in his chair with his hands in his lap.

"Are you going to eat sushi in Japan?"

Conchino raised his shoulders, as if to say, *I don't know*.

"Are you excited?"

Conchino nodded.

"Will you bring me back a ninja star?"

This question got to Conchino—right in the middle of the place deep within his body where laughs mysteriously came from—and he released a deep, guttural guffaw that startled everyone else waiting to meet the next travel assistant. J. D. smirked, happy to have entertained his friend, but not for long. His mirth soon turned to solemnity.

"I'm serious," J. D. said. "Will you bring me a ninja star? You'll be in Japan for crying out loud."

Conchino nodded, happy to appease his simple friend.

"Great! I look forward to hearing all about your trip when you get back."

Conchino extended a fist to J. D., who returned an amiable fist bump to the gentle giant. They continued to wait until Conchino's number was called.

37.

When Deborah parked her new car in front of Rita's house, she admired the leather seats and luxurious interior of her German sedan. She quickly decided to do three things with her portion of the lottery winnings, and the first thing she did was buy herself a car. The jalopy slowly dying on her driveway—a sad reminder of the poor life she would gladly be leaving behind—was unceremoniously towed away. She gave the tow truck driver a $50 tip and he dropped her off at the closest Mercedes dealership. She bought a like-new sedan that was only five years old, and proudly paid with a personal check. So, as she gathered her belongings while sitting in her fancy car in front of Rita's house, she couldn't help but feel like she was living in a dream. She wrestled with the notion that maybe she didn't deserve the good fortune that came her way, but also couldn't help but think about the hardship and struggle she had endured raising her son by herself, and all the years she lived hand to mouth from day to day. Whenever guilt crept in her mind, she quelled the cynicism by telling herself that she would spend her time in her new life being charitable and helping others, starting at that moment.

She got out of the car and approached Rita's house. Janice and her brother Reggie Jr. were sitting on the front porch, drinking beer from plastic cups, pretending they were sodas instead of alcoholic beverages. Reggie pulled over a chair for Deborah to sit on, then hugged her before she sat down.

Reggie slyly revealed what they were drinking and offered her some, but she demurred.

"I prefer wine? Do you have any?" she said.

Reggie pondered her request, then remembered a dusty bottle of red wine wedged in between two boxes of cereal in one of the kitchen cabinets.

"Want me to go look for it?" he said.

Deborah nodded. Reggie ran inside to check if it was still there. Janice smiled at Deborah, then patted her on the leg.

"I'm so glad you came by," she said. "Mama loved you so much!"

Rita's grandchildren could be heard playing inside the house. The sound of them happily playing warmed Deborah's heart.

"I loved her, too," she said, blushing. "She was like a sister to me."

"That's a fancy new ride you got there," Janice said, looking at the Mercedes sedan parked at the curb.

"Well, it's not *new*, but it's new to me. My other car was a piece of junk—literally. I needed something nice to drive."

"Word. I feel ya!" Janice said, slurping some beer from her red plastic cup. "A nice ride makes you feel good. Doesn't it?"

"Yes, it does. How are you doing? You holding up OK?"

Janice's head sank. She stared at the bubbly contents of her cup, swishing the beer in a circle, fishing in her mind for the right words.

"I knew I was going to miss my mama. I just didn't know how *hard* it was going to be. I miss her so much. She did so much for us. You know? For our family," she said, trying to hold back tears, but her eyes sprung a leak.

Deborah couldn't help but feel affected by Janice's impromptu display of emotion. She missed Rita, too, very much. She could only imagine the pain Janice was feeling. She embraced Janice warmly.

"I know she did. She loved you all very much. And that's why I'm going to help you."

The second thing Deborah decided to do after learning of the lottery winnings was put Rita's share in a trust for Rita's children and grandchildren. In doing so, she informed Rita's children that she would be the manager of the trust and meet with them regularly to discuss how she would invest it, as well as help them with their own personal finances. It was something she really wanted to do for Rita's family. And although Deborah had told the others in Unit 3 that she had quit her job, in reality, she had quietly retired from her employment with the State of Texas. And during her retirement, she would need something to do to keep her busy. And what better way to spend her time than to help her best friend's children and grandchildren? It was the thing she wanted to do most.

When Reggie came back out of the house with a cup of wine for Deborah, it startled him to see his sister in her arms, but it didn't surprise him. Janice had been especially emotional since the passing of their mother and he felt bad for his sister. He was also close to his mother, but not as close as Janice.

"Everything all right?" he said, handing the cup of wine to Deborah. She released Janice and accepted the wine.

Janice wiped her face, then said, "Yeah, yeah. I'm OK. It just happens sometimes—the crying."

"I was just telling your sister that I was going to help you all as much as I can," Deborah said, smiling. "It's the least I can do."

"Right on," he said, slurping his own beer. "Is that why you stopped by tonight?"

"Oh, no. I had something else to tell you guys. A surprise!"

"A surprise? Ah, shit! Is it bad?" Janice said. She wiped her face some more, then laughed.

"I hope not. Follow me," Deborah said, then stepped off the front porch.

Janice and Reggie followed her through the yard and to the sidewalk. They looked at each other with bewilderment. They didn't know where she was going, but assumed maybe she had something in her car. When she reached her car, she made a left and trudged up the sidewalk. They followed her. When they reached the house next door, Deborah stopped and then raised her arms triumphantly.

"Tah-dah!" she said excitedly.

Janice and Reggie stared at the ramshackle house with a "For Sale" sign in its overgrown front lawn. The house had not received love in decades and looked closer to condemnation than for habitation. Janice was confused while Reggie chuckled. Little did they know that the third thing Deborah planned to do with her portion of lottery winnings was make a huge life change, one that would affect Rita's children and grandchildren.

"Yeah, that's the haunted house we used to play in when I was a kid. It's been for sale *forever.*"

"Are you buying this house?" Janice said, confused.

"Yep!" Deborah said, a toothy grin appearing on her face.

"Why?" Janice replied. "It looks scary."

"Because I really want to help your family. I want to be a part of your family. I'm going to sell my house and remodel this one."

"Really?" Reggie said, laughing. "'Cause this house is gonna fall down!"

"It just needs a little love. I'll even take the fence down and join the yards together. The kids will have two yards to play in. And I can watch them while you work, just like your mama Rita did."

"But don't you have your own son to take care of?" Janice said.

"He's grown. He doesn't need me anymore!" Deborah said, snickering. "But you do. And this is where I want to be."

Janice's eyes welled up again and the uncontrollable crying returned. She embraced Deborah, who returned a jaunty hug, also extending an arm to embrace Reggie. The three held each other tightly, standing on the sidewalk in front of Deborah's new future home.

"Your son don't mind you moving into the hood?" Reggie said, wiping tears from his gruff facial hair.

"Nah. He's on his own now. He doesn't need me."

"Mama would be happy you doing this," Janice said, smiling through tears.

"I hope so," Deborah said.

"This calls for a toast!" Reggie said. "Let's go back to the house for more beer and wine."

Janice and Deborah agreed, so they followed Reggie back to the front porch for more adult beverages, to check on the kids inside, and to make sure the children hadn't broken anything while they were next door looking at Deborah's new house.

"I'll go in and get us more," Reggie said, taking their plastic cups with him.

"Check on the kids, too. All right?" Janice said. She and Deborah sat back down in their seats.

"All right," he said, then went inside the house, the door slamming behind him.

"Reggie's right. This neighborhood is pretty rough," Janice said, looking at Deborah. "You don't mind moving to the hood?"

Deborah chuckled, then said, "What do you mean? It's nice around here."

Janice's eyes bulged from their sockets in disbelief. She didn't agree with Deborah's assessment of the neighborhood at all.

"Sheesh, you must be *crazy*," she scoffed.

"Maybe so," Deborah said. "Maybe so."

38.

Brent looked to the horizon through the windshield of his speeding, beat-up SUV—Highway 71 loping over the rolling hills, cutting through swathes of bluebonnets and prairie-fire—then turned to his friend J. D. in the passenger seat. J. D. gazed out the passenger side window, as if in a trance. The travel game of *I Spy* that they had been playing for the previous fifteen minutes conceded to silence, mainly because they simply ran out of unique things to spot, and rather than start a different game, they just took in the beauty of the Texas Hill Country.

"Maybe I should retire my rock 'n' roll dreams and move to the country instead," Brent mused, the accent of his voice morphing into that of a crazed redneck. "I could wrangle me some doggies on a ranch!"

J. D. didn't respond to his silly pronouncement. He continued to gaze out the window.

"You OK, buddy?" Brent said.

J. D. snapped out of his trance, adjusted his posture in his seat, then said, "Sorry. I just forgot how beautiful it is out here on the way home."

Brent turned his attention back to the highway, his right hand on the wheel and his left arm propped leisurely against the driver-side window.

"It sure is purdy out here!" Brent said, continuing with his countrified accent. "I'll be hankerin' for some grub when we get to Brady."

"I know the perfect place to get some BBQ when we get home," J. D. said, perking up. "They have the *best* chopped brisket sandwiches in town."

"Yee-haw!" Brent hollered.

J. D. chuckled. There he was riding shotgun in Brent's SUV with his bicycle strapped to the roof rack and a duffle bag of clothes on the floorboard between his feet. An unexpected series of events at his new job in a new city with his new friends turned the dream of a new life upside down, and a weekend trip to his old home in Brady, Texas, certainly seemed like a good idea. He did miss his hometown and his parents. He also worried about the precarious situation their family business fell into, but he never would have imagined that he would be visiting so soon, even if it was just for a long weekend. He initially hadn't planned to go back home until at least Thanksgiving, and that was still a long way away.

"By the way, did you ever tell Schneidermann that you are going to quit?" Brent said.

"Who said I was going to quit?" J. D. said, then reached down into his bag on the floorboard and pulled out a couple of cookies. "Want one?"

He showed the cookies to Brent.

"Yeah, I want one."

J. D. handed him a cookie, keeping the other for himself. Brent folded back the plastic wrap and chomped half of it. J. D. rationed his by carefully nibbling it.

"I'll think about it some more when I get back. I still have my lease. I'm still a full-time state employee. You know?"

"Yeah. You always were the responsible one of the bunch. Aren't you?"

"Yeah," J. D. said, then chuckled, thinking about the others in Unit 3, missing Rita, Deborah, and Conchino.

A few days before, when J. D. asked Brent for a ride to Brady, Texas, he scoffed at Brent's suggestion that he just buy a new car for transportation back home. J. D. didn't want to waste his newfound fortune on something as absurd as a new car when his preferred mode of transportation was his trusty bicycle.

"Besides," J. D. told him at the time. "Your SUV is perfect for taking my bike to Brady. I'll want it to ride around town while I'm there."

Brent couldn't argue with that, or with the idea of an impromptu road trip over a long weekend to help his friend. Brent had never spent time in that part of Texas, and the thought of a weekend in the Hill Country sounded like a pleasant respite from city life. The roof rack of his SUV was perfect for transporting a bicycle, and he could finally meet J. D.'s parents. J. D. had spoken so highly of them, and their generosity with snacks was appreciated by everyone in Unit 3—Brent maybe most of all. He had nursed many hangovers with treats sent from J. D.'s parents.

Soon enough, they reached Brady, Texas. As they pulled into the tiny town after Highway 71 merged into Highway 87, the reality of its size in contrast to the city of Austin materialized before Brent's eyes. The businesses that lined both sides of Brady's main throughway were apt for their location and boggled Brent's urban sensibilities. There was a feed store, a tractor dealership, a Ford dealership that sold only pickup trucks (not even a single Mustang GT sat on the lot), a Mexican café on one side and a southern comfort food restaurant on the other side, a gun shop combined with a pawn shop, a taxidermy, and a quaint antique store. The lack of hipster music shops, clothing stores, microbreweries, and trendy bistros distressed Brent.

"This is insane!" Brent whined, as he slowed his SUV down to the local speed limit of 35 mph. "What do people *do* around here?!"

"It's different in Brady than in Austin."

"I can see that. We'll have to create our own fun, I guess. Where can I buy some beer?"

"There's a drugstore near my family's business."

"To the drugstore! Where do I go?" he said, excited at the prospect of cold beer.

"At the third light, take a left, then you'll see it in a bit on the right."

"10-4, little buddy!"

When they arrived at the drugstore, Brent parked his SUV in front, marveling at the retro building's fancy façade of red brick when he turned the engine off—its large glass window and door crowned with an old-timey shop sign of bronze letters. It was called Johnson's Drug Store, and a neon sign in the window indicated it was open. The building was originally built in the 1920s by the patriarch Ben Johnson, then remodeled in the 1950s by his son Stan Johnson, when its current style and appearance froze in time. The current owner, Ben Johnson II, was the great-grandson of the original Ben Johnson and felt no need to update its façade, even keeping the sides of concrete masonry in their original state. The inside also looked just as it did when J. D. was a child, which was pretty much the same as it did in the 1950s, except for a few hairline cracks in the plaster walls and the tile floor.

"Whoa!" Brent said. "This building is a trip."

"What do you mean?" J. D. said, curiously.

"It's like a relic, straight out of the past. Are there more buildings like this around here?"

"Tons!"

"Cool!" Brent said as he exited the SUV. He followed J. D. through the glass entrance door.

Inside, a bell tinkled as the two friends were greeted by someone out of sight from the back of the store.

"Good afternoon!" a voice could be heard saying.

"That's probably Mr. Johnson," J. D. whispered to Brent, who walked to the furthest part of the drugstore from the entrance, where a couple of coolers waited for them.

"That figures since it's called *Johnson's Drug Store*," Brent said, sarcastically.

The two coolers mostly contained sodas, juices, and milks, but the one on the left contained the sole six-pack of beer: Lone Star Beer. J. D. opened the cooler to retrieve the beer and a Coke for himself.

"That's it for beer?!" Brent gasped. "This town is killing me already."

J. D. snickered, then closed the cooler door. As they made their way to the counter to pay for their beverages, the two friends came upon a massive display of the very snacks they had enjoyed frequently back in Austin, the ones J. D.'s mother had lovingly shipped to him on a regular basis. The display of cardboard and paper contained them all: pecan pralines, Danishes with pecans on top, pecan rolls, pecan logs, cookies with pecans, mini pecan pies, and more. J. D.'s eyes lit up and, even though he had his fill of snacks on the road, he couldn't help himself. He just had to buy more. He loved these snacks that much. Brent couldn't believe it.

"It's the mother lode!" he gasped. "Is this where your mom gets them?"

"Yep," J. D. said, piling as many snacks as he could in his arms along with the six-pack of beer and soda. "The pecan farm where these are made is not too far from here."

"Really?" Brent said, noticing that J. D. could barely carry it all, so he took the beer from him. "Let me help you."

"Thanks!" J. D. said.

As he took some of the snacks from J. D., Brent's attention was caught by a moving image up on the wall. When he looked to see what it was, he discovered an old-style, thirteen-inch tube TV mounted up there. It broadcast its image silently and was tuned to a cable news channel. Images of Governor Bennett and Chairman DeMarco alternately flashed on the screen with a scroll beneath, a ribbon of red with bold white letters sliding from right to left. Brent curiously read what was on the screen but J. D. was completely disinterested.

When they reached the counter, they dumped the snacks and drinks on it.

"Are you seeing this?" Brent said, watching the TV.

"I don't care for the news," J. D. said, disinterested.

"It says DeMarco is under investigation for accepting bribes. And the ethics investigation of Governor Bennett is now on hold."

"That's nice," J. D. said, staring at the mound of pecan snacks on the counter. "Did we get enough?"

Brent chuckled at his friend. Right then, the owner of the distant voice from the back of the shop revealed himself, but it wasn't Mr. Johnson. It was someone else J. D. recognized, and his unexpected appearance in the drugstore shocked J. D.

"Well, I'll be darned!" J. D. said, his face lighting up when he saw the man. "If it isn't Daryl Scruggs!"

"J. D. Wiswall! What in tarnation are you doing here in Brady?! Did you move back?"

"No," J. D. said, blushing. "I'm just visiting, but I might just consider it."

"Well," Daryl said, folding his thin arms in front of his lab coat. "I'd have someone to go tip cows with if you did."

They both snickered, the way two young boys would if they were up to no good. Brent watched the two old friends with astonishment. Their boisterous camaraderie was in stark contrast to J. D.'s typically quiet demeanor back in Austin.

"Maybe we'll do that while I'm here."

"Ah, I'm just joshing you," Daryl said, smirking. "What are you doing back, then?"

"I came to help my folks out. They're not doing so good."

"Really?" Daryl said, confused, his mouth twisting beneath his nose as he contemplated something. "I saw your parents the other day. They said they were doing great."

"That's weird," J. D. said. "Well, keep a lid on it, then. Alrighty?"

"Alrighty, then," said Daryl, smiling again. "Call me if you want to hang out. Is this all?"

J. D. nodded and Daryl rung up the drinks and snacks. After saying their goodbyes, Brent and J. D. got back in the SUV, then proceeded a few blocks down to J. D.'s family business.

"Where do you know that guy from?" Brent said curiously while he drove. "You didn't even introduce me."

"Oh, sorry. Daryl and I went to high school together. I had no idea he was working at Johnson's Drug Store. That's crazy! I thought he moved away."

When they arrived, Brent parked in front of a building similar to the drugstore—originating in the 1920s and remodeled in the 1950s—except this one was made of limestone on the front instead of red brick. The sign above the window was not a bronze one either, but one of the vinyl tarp variety, a temporary solution strung up there after a tornado had zipped through Brady ten years before, ripping down the original metal sign, which somehow never got replaced. The name of the business on the vinyl sign was "Wiswall Bonds and Insurance." On the sidewalk out front sat a bicycle rack with a little boy's bike chained to it, secured with a combination lock, and a black and green paint job with the word "HUFFY" in white lettering on the frame. J. D.'s face lit up when he saw it: his old bike.

"It's still here!" he called out.

"What is?"

"My bike!"

"Oh."

"But it doesn't look like anyone is at the shop," J. D. mused, rubbing his chin and looking in the window. "I wonder where my parents are."

"There's a note on the door. Maybe they went somewhere."

Brent turned off the engine and they got out of the car. J. D. pulled the note off the glass door and read it aloud, a scribbled message on a Post-it note. It said:

OUT FOR A BIT. SOMETHING IMPORTANT CAME UP. BE BACK SOON.

Undeterred by the note, J. D. attempted to open the door anyway—squeezing and pushing on the handle—but it was locked.

"Darn it!" he lamented. "Oh well. They'll be back soon."

"Do you want to try to call them on their cell phones?"

J. D. laughed loudly as if the question was completely preposterous, then said, "My parents don't have cell phones. Check out my old bike, though."

J. D. stood over the old bicycle and beamed just like he had when he was in elementary school. The fact that it was rusty and weathered didn't diminish any of his enthusiasm for his childhood mode of transportation. The bike was built for a boy and much smaller than the one mounted on top of Brent's SUV.

"I had some good times on this bike! I thought maybe my parents threw it away or something."

"Looks like they didn't," Brent said, sarcastically.

"Yeah."

"What are we going to do now?" Brent said, looking around. The small-town street was deserted except for a stray cat slinking across it.

"I don't know."

Brent looked further down the street, then curiosity struck him as he spotted the building next door—a dilapidated, abandoned structure with its windows boarded up, graffiti scrawled on one side, and a "For Sale" sign out front.

What a dump! he thought, but his curiosity was piqued.

"What's that place?" he said to J. D., walking toward the building.

J. D. followed him.

"That used to be a BBQ restaurant. It closed down a long time ago after a kitchen fire. They used to serve great brisket sandwiches, and bands would play there on Friday and Saturday nights."

"Live music, huh?" Brent said, curiously. "Let's go inside."

The two friends walked over to the abandoned, old BBQ joint. Brent examined the front of the building, then attempted to open the front door. It was padlocked shut, so they walked around to the back, stepping over broken glass and pieces of plywood in the tall grass. Finding a window in the back with loose boards, Brent looked around for onlookers, pulled the boards off, and carefully climbed inside. J. D., without hesitation, climbed in after him.

Inside, wooden dining tables with the chairs stacked on top—covered in dust, cobwebs, and dead bugs—sat in suspended animation. Bats, birds, and rats had decided to make the building their home not long after it was abandoned and had littered every flat surface with their dung droppings. The musty smell of decay offended their noses. Old Texas license plates and gas station signs adorned the walls, hung there with rusty nails. In one corner, the remnants of a stage remained with a single chair on it, an old guitar case resting on the padded seat. Brent beelined to the stage and opened the guitar case. It was empty except for a yellow guitar pick.

"I bet this place used to be cool," Brent said, setting one foot on the stage and then looking around. He could imagine himself playing an acoustic set on the stage, if the BBQ joint wasn't in such disrepair.

"You should buy it and open your own club," J. D. joked, snickering. "Your band could play every week."

J. D. expected Brent to laugh as well but he didn't. A curious look appeared on his face, one with a bit of optimism.

"That's not a bad idea," he said.

"Really?!" J. D. replied. "I was just joking."

"I bet this place is dirt cheap. And who doesn't like beer, BBQ, and rock 'n' roll?"

"Are you serious?"

"Maybe," Brent said, looking around some more, redecorating the abandoned restaurant in his mind. "I could make something of this place."

"That would be awesome," J. D. said, smiling. "What would you call it?"

"I don't know. I'll think about it. What should we do now?"

"Well," J. D. said, mulling his question. "We could go for a bike ride. I could show you around."

"Where am I going to get a bike? We only brought yours from Austin."

"You can ride the one I brought from Austin and I'll ride the one in front of the shop."

"The little kid bike?!" Brent blurted, then laughed, his arms folding across his gut. "It's for a little boy."

"I don't mind. Let's go! I'll show you around."

"All right."

They carefully climbed out the back window through broken glass and nails, then walked back to the SUV. J. D. helped Brent take his bicycle down from the cargo rack. When he attempted to unlock the combination lock to release his childhood bicycle, he was surprised that not only did he remember the combination, but that it opened on the first attempt.

"Yes!" he squealed.

Brent rolled his eyes at J. D.'s small victory. J. D. maneuvered the bike away from the rack, then squatted on the seat. The frame was way too small for a man of his size, but J. D. didn't seem to care. He beamed like he was twelve years old again, one knee jutting out awkwardly as he rested his foot on the pedal.

"Ready?" he said to Brent.

"You look ridiculous. You know that?"

"I don't care. Let's go!"

"OK."

Brent mounted J. D.'s city bike and followed his friend into the street. Unlike in Austin—where there were angry car and raging truck drivers in the congested streets—there were no cars, busses, or other vehicles to avoid. They rode down the empty, country road together with a Hill Country breeze to their backs. There wasn't a soul around except for the two cycling friends; the cat had disappeared. As they rode their bikes past a few other abandoned businesses and a couple of mobile homes in overgrown lots, the asphalt street slowly morphed into a dirt and gravel road. The pale blue sky stretched above them and a vulture circled up high in the distance. Barbed wire fences arose between cactus plants, with cedar trees on either side of the dirt road, and a plume of dust trailed behind them as they pedaled away from the small town. On their right, a cattle ranch sprawled as far as they could see with a variety of cows and steers dotting the grassy property, either grazing for grass or resting in the shade of trees. On their left, an orchard of pecan trees zigged and zagged across the immense property past the barbed wire fence. J. D. raised his hand, indicating to Brent that he wanted to stop, then skidded his bike to a dusty standstill.

"This is Precious Pecan Farms," J. D. panted, trying to catch his breath. "Most of the pecan snacks sold in town are made here."

"That's fascinating," Brent joked.

"I know the family. Want to check it out?"

"Why not?"

J. D. mounted his small yet trusty bicycle and continued down the dirt road for another mile and a half or so. A series of signs on the right alerted them of the nearing proximity of a pecan shop, which announced in bold lettering: PECANS! They soon found the entrance to the property on the left with an open, metal gate. A wrought iron sign above the gate spelled out "Precious Pecan Farms." They rode through the gate and up the gravel driveway toward the farmhouse that sat at the top of the hill among a few other buildings: a barn, a storage silo, and a shop. The driveway was also lined with pecan trees, and at the base of each on the ground were blue vinyl tarps. The blue tarps seemed strange to Brent and he couldn't help but question their purpose.

"What are those blue blankets for?" he said, huffing as he pedaled his bike up the hill.

"Those are tarps for collecting the pecans. It keeps the pecans from getting wet if they lay in the grass. They'll be ruined if they get wet."

"Ah," Brent said. "You love pecans so much that you even know how to collect them."

The driveway also had signs with bold lettering and red arrows, pointing curious visitors to the pecan shop up the hill. At the top, Brent and J. D. parked their bikes in the grass in front of the shop. Brent watched two sheepdogs barking at them and worried briefly that they might run toward them to attack, but he could see they were chained to the front porch. On the door to the shop was a sign that said "Closed," adding in small letters below that that the shop was opened only on Saturdays. But when J. D. pushed on the door, it was unlocked so he just went inside, as if he was welcomed to go in anyway. Brent followed J. D. into the pecan shop, keeping a cautious eye on the barking dogs.

Inside was what Brent imagined was J. D.'s heaven. Everywhere he could see, anything that could be made from pecans was for sale. It was a plethora of all things pecan, and J. D. was smitten.

"Mmm," he purred. "I want it all!"

Brent laughed. The two had the shop to themselves and they perused the aisles of the vast variety of products. Brent wasn't aware that so many different things could be made from pecans. It was a bit overwhelming. At the end of the candy aisle,

J. D. raided a sample basket holding pieces of pecan praline. As he scarfed them down, Brent blushed from his friend's overindulgence.

"I think you have a *serious* problem," he said.

"You're probably right," J. D. replied with his mouth full.

While gobbling the samples, a large man wearing overalls and a dirty white T-shirt, with thinning gray hair and a Cheshire cat grin, entered the shop from a back door. His heavy work boots stomped across the wood floor. When he saw J. D., he stopped in his tracks, aghast with his presence in the shop.

"Well, doggonit! Who do we have *here*?!" he said, his arms spread wide, inviting J. D. to give him a hug.

"Hi, Mr. Hemphill!" J. D. said, falling into the farmer's open arms.

They embraced tightly for a moment while Brent awkwardly looked on. When they separated, Mr. Hemphill just smiled and stared at J. D., shocked with his presence. His mouth hung open wide.

"I thought you moved away to the big city for good," he said, rubbing his chin. "Are you moving back home?"

"I don't think so, Mr. Hemphill. Oh!" J. D. exclaimed, pointing to Brent. "This is my friend from Austin. His name is Brent."

Mr. Hemphill extended his hand to Brent for a shake. When Brent extended his hand in return, Mr. Hemphill commenced to crush it with his dry, calloused hand. It was the size of a boulder compared to Brent's normal-sized hand.

"Nice to make your acquaintance! A friend of J. D. Wiswall's is a friend of mine!"

"Nice to meet you as well," Brent sighed, shaking the pain from his crushed hand.

Mr. Hemphill pressed his large fists into his hips, steadying himself, then turned back to J. D.

"How are your folks?" Mr. Hemphill said, concerned. "They doing OK?"

"Not sure yet," J. D. said. "I haven't seen them. We just got into town."

"Just got into town? Then you must be hungry. How about a slice of pecan pie?" he said, grinning. "The wife made it this morning."

"We'd love some!"

J. D. looked at Brent, who was still recovering from the handshake. He nodded.

"Great! Come sit at the table in the corner by the window and I'll bring you some."

J. D. and Brent sat down at the table. Mr. Hemphill promptly brought over a pie tin with half a pie still in it, a few plates, and some forks. When he sat down, he carved a few pieces from the remaining pie half for his guests.

"I already ate half of it!" he blurted. "My wife makes a darn good pie!"

"Yes, she does," J. D. said, licking his lips. "How are you doing?"

"Oh, I'm living. But I've been having problems with my back and my hip. I got a slipped disc in my lower back and sciatica in my left hip. The pain is unbearable some days," he said, wincing just thinking about the excruciating pain. But then he noticed the two friends staring at him and not eating their pie. "You go on and eat up now, before I eat your portions!"

J. D. and Brent did what they were instructed to do, shoveling pie into their mouths.

After a few bites, J. D. said, "What are you going to do?"

"I don't know. I'm getting old. I'm thinking of selling the pecan farm."

"Selling the farm?!" J. D. exclaimed, chunks of pie flying from his mouth, his eyes open wide as if trained upon an apparition. "Why don't your kids run it?"

"They're all gone and moved away. None of them have any interest in running a nut farm. It's a *lot* of work."

"Yeah, I bet," J. D. sighed.

"A corporation expressed some interest in buying the farm but I don't want to sell my farm to no corporation. I'd only sell it to someone who wants to keep it a family farm."

Brent snickered, which irritated Mr. Hemphill, who thought it rude that Brent would laugh at his conundrum.

"What's so funny?" he said, visibly irate.

"Oh, sorry. I'm not laughing at you."

"Then, what's so funny? Do tell."

"Well, J. D. loves pecans so much. You should sell it to him."

J. D.'s mouth dropped, mostly from Brent's abrupt comment, but then from the realization that he would love to run a pecan farm, especially this particular pecan farm, one that he felt deep nostalgic pangs for. Mr. Hemphill's irritation soon turned into joviality. He couldn't imagine young J. D. buying his farm, though.

"J. D. wouldn't buy my farm," he chuckled, then turned to him. "Would you?"

J. D. froze in place, heavy in contemplation. He imagined himself wearing overalls and driving a tractor. He could see himself managing the property with the help of his parents, or even his friend Brent, if he decided to buy the old BBQ joint and open his own music venue. It certainly seemed possible to J. D. because of the good fortune that had recently come his way.

"Maybe," J. D. said sheepishly. "I don't know."

Mr. Hemphill eyed J. D. up and down with serious consideration, then said, "Well, I tell you what. If you *did* have the means to buy this farm, then you would be the first suitor I would listen to. You hear me?"

"Yes, sir," J. D. beamed.

"You boys finished?" Mr. Hemphill said, reaching for their plates.

They both nodded, pushing their plates toward their gracious host. The farmer picked up the dishes and set them behind the counter.

"I hope you don't mind. It was nice chatting with you, but I have to get back to my duties."

J. D. and Brent stood up, pushing their chairs to the table.

"We don't mind, Mr. Hemphill," J. D. said politely.

"Can I use your restroom?" Brent said.

"You can whiz 'round back," he said, pointing a thumb toward the out of doors. "J. D.?"

"Yessir?"

"Show your friend where to go. OK? And here—" He grabbed a pecan roll from the counter, then tossed it to J. D. "This is for you."

"Thanks!" J. D. said, grinning from ear to ear.

Mr. Hemphill winked at the two friends, then stomped through the shop and exited out the back.

J. D. turned to Brent, slipping the pecan roll into his pants pocket, then said, "Come with me."

Brent followed J. D. out the front of the shop and around to the back, where three holly bushes sat in the shade. J. D. unzipped the fly to his pants and urinated in the bushes. Brent gleefully followed his lead and took a whiz.

"This is awesome," Brent sighed.

"Yeah," J. D. said, zipping up his fly after he was done.

"Want to ride back to see if your parents are there?"

"Yeah."

"We can check out the old BBQ joint again, too. I think I could turn it into something cool. Come on!"

They mounted their bicycles and Brent was the first to peddle off, but J. D. didn't follow him. He stood there and watched Brent ride down the hill alone. A plume of dust rose from the back tire and floated across the pecan orchard. Brent waved at some farmhands gathering pecans from blue tarps that skirted the bottom of tall, majestic pecan trees as he barreled down the hill. As J. D. watched him, he was consumed by feelings of hope and optimism, as he surveyed the vast farmland. Visions from his childhood flooded his mind and he couldn't help but feel that he had stood in this very spot before and thought this very same thing, that maybe one day he would own this place. It seemed to him like he had done that before.

Behind him, an engine roared to life, startling him. He turned around to see Mr. Hemphill sitting on a tractor, adjusting the gear shifter so he could drive the green machine over to the silo, probably to unload the trailer full of pecans that was hitched to it. The sheepdogs barked at the rowdy machine. He watched the farmer for a brief moment, then turned to see where Brent was. He was at the bottom of the driveway, standing next to his bike and waving back at J. D. So, he mounted his bicycle—the tiny one from when he was a boy—then coasted down the driveway. He raised his arms in the air as he careened down the hill, his fingers outstretched, and the warm Hill Country breeze on his face.

It's good to be home, he thought, as he joined his friend at the bottom of the hill.

The two friends pedaled their bikes back to town, so they could get those brisket sandwiches that J. D. had been raving about the entire trip. J. D. could then tell his parents the good news about winning the money, his desire to help them with their ailing business, and maybe—just maybe—about this opportunity to buy the pecan farm from Mr. Hemphill. It seemed to him, at that moment, to be the right thing to do.

About the Author

Scott Semegran lives in Austin, Texas with his wife, four kids, two cats, and a dog. He graduated from the University of Texas at Austin with a degree in English. He is a bestselling, award-winning writer and cartoonist. He can also bend metal with his mind and run really fast, if chased by a pack of wolves. His comic strips have appeared in the following newspapers: *The Austin Student*, *The Funny Times*, *The Austin American-Statesman*, *Rocky Mountain Bullhorn*, *Seven Days*, *The University of Texas at Dallas Mercury*, and *The North Austin Bee*. Books by Scott Semegran include *To Squeeze a Prairie Dog*, *Sammie & Budgie*, *Boys*, *The Meteoric Rise of Simon Burchwood*, *The Spectacular Simon Burchwood*, *Modicum*, *Mr. Grieves*, and more.

Books by Scott Semegran

Boys is a collection of stories about three boys living in Texas: one growing up, one dreaming, and one fighting to stay alive in the face of destitution and adversity. There's second-grader William, a shy yet imaginative boy who schemes about how to get back at his school-yard bully, Randy. Then there's Sam, a 15-year-old boy who dreams of getting a 1980 Mazda RX-7 for his sixteenth birthday but has to work at a Greek restaurant to fund his dream. Finally, there's Seff, a 21-year-old on the brink of manhood, trying to survive along with his roommate, working as waiters and barely making ends meet. These three stories are told with heart, humor, and an uncompromising look at what it meant to grow up in Texas during the 1980s and 1990s.

2018 IndieReader Discovery Awards: Winner for Short Stories

"The writing is sharp and unpretentiously thoughtful, and since each of the main characters finds solace in companionship, this is an affecting literary depiction of the comforting power of friendship. Each of the stories can be read on its own, but taken together, they make a coherent, thematic whole, skillfully produced. An endearing collection that deftly captures the need for youthful fellowship." — *Kirkus Reviews*

"Verdict: With nary a dull moment, Scott Semegran's *Boys* features short stories filled with unexpected nuances that draws readers right into the heart of his well-developed characters." — *IndieReader*. 5 Stars. IR Approved.

"Semegran's work is evocative and replete with relatable, recognizable characters... who find comfort in friendship. With its descriptive flair and flashes of humor, *Boys* offers an engaging read—one short fiction fans are sure to enjoy." — *BlueInk Review*

"Raising difficult questions of morality, this slice-of-life narrative is as heartfelt as it is entertaining... *Boys* is compellingly realistic fiction. Its fantastic details, interesting construction, and humor make it worth the read." — *Foreword* Clarion Reviews. Clarion Rating: 4 out of 5.

***

From Kindle bestselling writer and cartoonist Scott Semegran, *Sammie & Budgie* is a quirky, mystical tale of a self-doubting IT nerd and his young son, who possesses the gift of foresight. The boy's special ability propels his family on a road trip to visit his ailing grandfather, a prickly man who left an indelible stamp on the father and son. The three are connected through more than genetics, their lives intertwined through dreams, imagination, and longing.

Simon works as a network administrator for a state government agency, a consolation after a promising career as a novelist flounders. He finds himself a single parent of two small children following the mysterious death of his adulterous wife. From the ashes of his failed marriage emerges a tight-knit family of three: a creative, special needs son, a hyperactive, butt-kicking daughter, and the caring, sensitive father. But when his son's special ability reveals itself, Simon struggles to keep his little family together in the face of adversity and uncertainty.

Sammie is a creative third-grader that draws adventures in his sketchbook with his imaginary friend, Budgie, a parakeet that protects him from the monsters inhabiting his dreams. Sammie is also a special needs child but is special in more ways than one. He can see the future. Sammie seemingly can predict events both mundane and catastrophic in equal measure. But when he envisions the suffering of his grandfather, the family embarks on a road trip to San Antonio with the nanny to visit the ailing patriarch.

Sammie & Budgie is an illustrated novel brought to you from the quirky mind of writer and cartoonist Scott Semegran. The novel explores the bond between a caring father and his children, one affected by his own thorny relationship with his surly father, and the connection he has with his sweet son is thicker than blood, going to the place where dreams are conceived and realized.

2018 Texas Authors Book Awards: First Place Winner for General Fiction

2018 Texas Authors Book Cover Awards: First Place Winner for Fiction

"Illustrated throughout by Semegran, this book is the author's best... An unconventional, beguiling, and endearing family tale." — *Kirkus Reviews*

"The novel's delights abound... Semegran is a gifted writer, with a wry sense of humor." — *BlueInk Review* (Starred Review)

"The writing quality is excellent and the dialogue between Simon and Sammie is immersive." — *Foreword* Clarion Reviews. Clarion Rating: 4 out of 5.

***

Other Books by Scott Semegran

The Spectacular Simon Burchwood
The Meteoric Rise of Simon Burchwood
Modicum
Mr. Grieves

For more information, go to:
https://www.scottsemegran.com/books.html

***

Find Scott Semegran Online:
https://www.scottsemegran.com
https://www.goodreads.com/scottsemegran
https://www.twitter.com/scottsemegran
https://www.facebook.com/scottsemegran.writer/
https://www.instagram.com/scott_semegran
https://www.amazon.com/author/scottsemegran
https://www.smashwords.com/profile/view/scottsemegran

Mutt Press:
https://www.muttpress.com

CPSIA information can be obtained
at www.ICGtesting.com
Printed in the USA
LVHW090556300319
612335LV00005B/429/P